My Rodeo Man

The Texas Kincaids Book 1

Bonnie Phelps

To my amazing husband for all of his support and for introducing me to the meaning of true romance! To my daughters for all their encouragement and support. To all the men and women of the rodeo world who keep the spirit of the Old West alive!

Contents

Chapter One

"Don't do it Ash," warned Lauren Royall, latching onto her friend's wrist. "That lower than pond scum, piece of cow shit, isn't worth it. Think about it. For *one* small moment of satisfaction, the jerk could take you to court and sue you for damages. Do you really want to pay for a new paint job on this hunk of junk?"

Ashley Drayton, petite, with wild, wavy, raven hair and the kind of curves women visit plastic surgeons to get scowled at her BFF. Reluctantly, she lowered the key she held like a dagger, poised to plunge into the heart of an obviously meticulously refurbished 1955 Chevy truck.

"Can you believe the nerve of that man? Told me something came up so he'd have to cancel our date tonight. Something came up all right – a ditzy blonde." Ashley vibrated with rage.

"That's why I dragged you out of there so fast before you dented *his hood ornament*, so to speak."

A gust of January wind moaning through the Texas Hill Country oak trees had the women pulling their tailored wool coats a little tighter. How odd, thought Ashley, to be standing in the parking lot of one of the oldest dance halls in the area plotting to extract revenge on yet another scourge against womankind rather than having a good time inside.

Anger hit Ashley hot and stormy. "Wouldn't it feel great to strike a blow for all the women who've been made to feel like they are worthless and unlovable?" She pumped her fist in the air. "It would do wonders for me. Besides," she said with a saucy shrug and a back flick of her booted foot, "he'd have to prove it was me. Lots of people pass through this parking lot." She tossed her head letting the breeze catch her long, dark tresses.

"While professionally I don't recommend revenge as a strategy, are you willing to accept the consequences?"

"Oh, keep your marriage and family counselor psycho-babble to yourself, Lauren," grumbled Ashley, but she tossed the keys in the air, catching them in her palm before tucking them back into her sequined clutch. While the temptation to hit the creep in *one* of the places it might hurt, she couldn't do it. Her soft heart wouldn't let her. She couldn't deliberately hurt another person the way she had been hurt most of her life.

"What is it about me that pulls all the jerks within a sixty-mile radius into my orbit? Is it a pheromone thing? Do I send out a signal that attracts only cheaters and deadbeats?"

"I thought you didn't want to hear any of my psycho-babble," Lauren said with an unladylike snort. "But since you asked, the sooner you realize there is something wrong with *them* and not *you*... *and* stop letting your mother influence your choices, the sooner you'll find that love of your life you're searching for."

Lauren turned Ashley to face her. "Repeat after me, 'I am an amazing woman, a terrific friend and lots of people love me.'" Both women shivered as another blast of cold air swept through the sea of heavy-duty pickup trucks surrounding them.

Ashley gazed into the clear, star-studded sky. "I know I've spent too many years choosing men I thought would make my mother respect me, but the men she approves of can't *all* be 'Mr. Too Wrong For Words,' can they? Some of it has to be me." She leaned against the truck she had just threatened to key and glanced up at the willowy Nordic beauty towering over her.

"You'd think I'd learned my lesson after the Bill debacle," she made air quotes when she said his name, "but no sooner do I vow to turn over a new leaf, move halfway across the country, I fall for Sam, another Mr. Jerk Face." She motioned with her thumb toward the building, "another lying, cheating, sleezeball."

Lauren chuckled as she leaned against the car and gave Ashley a friendly hip bump, which given their height difference, hit Ashley just above her waist. "You do have a fairly unique track record where men are concerned, but I know you're going to be okay. You just need to trust yourself."

"Thanks, pal," Ashley returned the friendly hip bump. "I still can't believe it. Bill – the man I agreed to marry – broke my heart, cleaned me out, and left me holding the bag. He was supposed to be the last straw. Well, I think it's time to activate my plan."

Lauren crossed her arms and sighed. "Truth time, you didn't have deep feelings for Sam. At most, your pride was hurt. But looking on the bright side, you are becoming more cautious about who you trust." Lauren hooked her arm through Ashley's, "Ash, let's be honest..."

"I hate it when you say that. It always comes right before you hand that bitter pill to me." She smiled sadly and leaned into her friend. "Go for it. I can take it."

"Put the quintessential bad boy in front of you and you see Prince Charming, a knight in black armor."

"And that's exactly why I need a way to distinguish between Prince Charming... a kind, caring, responsible man, who loves me unconditionally... and the Bad Boy... a sexy, cocky, narcissistic player who hurts me. I should have seen the signs, seen what they really were, seen they were as responsible as two-year olds, but I didn't. Obviously, I need some help."

"Sweetie, while I agree you haven't always made the best relationship choices, I don't think this system of winnowing out the wheat from the chaff is going to help you choose wisely," Lauren scuffed the dirt with her foot. "You have to work through the issues we've been talking about, before things will change."

Both women looked up when they heard the crunch of gravel under booted feet as two men walked toward them.

"Lauren?" asked Mr. Tall and Incredibly Handsome. He stepped a little closer and tipped his hat back for a better look. "It *is* you. Are you alright?" He stepped forward, clasping her arms in his hands, then almost immediately scooted back like he'd been burned and crossed his arms. "What in the world are you doing standing around in a parking lot in the middle of the night? You could be mugged, or worse. It's just not safe. What are you thinking?"

Ashley arched a brow and looked from her friend to Mr. Tall and Incredibly Handsome. This must be Lauren's on-again, off-again. The Crème Brule guy, hard on the exterior and gooey underneath.

Interesting. Ashley shifted her gaze to the mouth-watering hunk of masculinity standing next to him. Shoulders like Hercules tapered down to a narrow waist and he was tall enough she'd probably have to stand on a box to kiss those tempting lips. On the ability to make a woman want to get her hair mussed meter, he had definite potential. He looked like just the ticket to make her forget her latest 'bad choice' and ease the ache in her heart or pride or whatever it was gnawing at her.

"What we were thinking," Lauren answered, "is that my friend and I needed a quiet place to talk for a few minutes and a little bit of fresh air… and hello to you too Nate." Lauren smiled sweetly at Mr. Tall and Incredibly Handsome. Turning slightly, she addressed the other man, "Hi Zach, nice to see you again."

"Always a pleasure," Zach drawled as he gave Lauren a quick hug before extending his hand to Ashley. "I'm not going to wait around for one of these two," he nodded toward Lauren and Nate, "to remember their manners and introduce me to the prettiest gal this side of the Rio Grande."

He plucked off his hat and held it against one of the broadest chests Ashley had seen in a while. "I'm Zach Kincaid, Nate's brother, and if you ladies are not otherwise spoken for and are planning to head back in for more dancing, I would be more than happy to escort you." His voice had the smooth rasp of fine malt whiskey.

He plunked his hat back on his head of close-cropped hair, crooked both arms and offered one to each lady.

"I'm Ashley," she said stepping up to him all flirt and sass as she put her arm through his. "Count me in, cowboy." She felt the tingle all the way down to her red-painted toenails as her fingers made contact with his arm. The man was built, all male and muscle beneath his long-sleeved chambray shirt. When a tasty treat came wrapped in a cowboy hat, boots, and jeans so tight they brought images of dark corners and stolen kisses to mind, she was a goner.

"Me too," added Lauren with a little shrug and smile over her shoulder at Nate as she slipped her arm through Zach's.

Nate scowled but walked up to Lauren and switched her arm from Zach's to his.

"So, Ashley, do you have a last name?" asked Zach as they set off toward the dance hall.

"No, like Beyoncé and Madonna, I only need one." She chuckled at his puzzled expression. "Just kidding. It's Drayton. Ashley Drayton."

"Feisty little thing. Got it." He made a check mark in the air with his finger. "You don't sound like you're from around here. Where did you call home before San Antonio?

"Charleston, South Carolina. Born and raised there. And are you a Texas boy?" She walked her fingers up his arm. His eyes darkened and she got a thrill knowing she had caused the reaction. Men were so easy.

He swallowed then flashed a grin that set her heart galloping. "Through and through. The Kincaids have been in Texas for generations. My family owns a ranch just north of here. What do you do for a living?"

"I'm an accountant. I moved here to join a small firm," she answered, "and what about you?"

"My chief claim to fame is that I'm a World Champion Team Roper." He pointed to a belt buckle about the size of Rhode Island. "When I'm not riding the rodeo circuit, I help my dad run our spread," he replied.

"You compete in rodeos? Sounds dangerous, but it looks like you still have all your body parts and your teeth are either intact or you have an amazing dentist."

"Yes ma'am, I do. While team roping is not quite as tough on the body as bull and bronc riding, broken bones and pulled muscles are occupational hazards. That said, everything you see – teeth included – is all me." He spread his free arm wide and posed.

"Good to hear. I'd hate to see that very spectacular body messed up," murmured Ashley in her soft, South Carolina drawl.

Zach chuckled. "You let me know if you want to see more." He winked. "I'd be happy to oblige."

Ashley merely graced him with a sultry smile.

THE NOISE CRASHED INTO them like a wave. They had to hunch forward to absorb it as they walked through the door. Music from the live band, the stomp of the dancers' boots, and the buzz of hundreds of very loud conversations flowed around them. The little spitfire on Zach's arm seemed to soak up the energy and apparently couldn't wait to get on the dance floor. Her feet, head, hips, and shoulders were already picking up the beat. Zach watched the movement and his mouth went dry.

And that smile in the parking lot? He'd felt the earth shift beneath his feet and sweat trickle down his back. For such a tiny little thing, she packed a punch.

7

"Quite an impressive collection," Ashley paused, her manicured nail pointing to a wall filled top to bottom with images of famous and famous hopefuls.

"We've been lucky to hear some of the best in the business," said Zach. He placed his hand at the small of her back enjoying the feel of the music pulsing through her body and ushered her through the dining area and into the dance hall. The room had a stage and dance floor at one end, long trestle tables and benches in long rows at the other end and pool tables in a side alcove. The smell of beer and fried food hung in the air.

Zach stopped, feet apart, to scan the room and check out the action. He was seemingly oblivious to the many female heads swiveling his direction.

"Looking for the next notch on your bedpost, cowboy? Lots of ladies to choose from tonight. A target rich environment if I ever saw one." Ashley fluffed her hair and smiled at some man who was checking her out.

Zach glared at the man who wisely ambled off in the other direction. Couldn't the idiot see this woman was with him tonight? Zach. Didn't. Share.

"Any chance you could be one of the ladies under consideration?" His mouth quirked up in a slow, sexy grin. The way she sucked in a quick breath then looked away told him she was just as attracted to him as he was to her.

"Not on your life." She smacked her palm against his chest and gave him a shove. "I'm here to dance so let's get moving."

"Works for me... and for your information, I'm not checking out the ladies, they're checking me out. Not much I can do about that."

"Cocky are we?"

"I prefer self-assured. Here, let me help you with your coat." His breath caught in his throat as the coat slipped down her arms. The lady had curves to spare and God in his infinite wisdom had put them in all the right places. She put Dolly Parton to shame with that tiny waist and breasts that would fill even his big hands.

"I can see I'll be spending my evening beating off the competition. Talk about the lady with the red dress on and cowboy boots... mmm, mmm... Oh, Lauren, you're looking fine, too," he added as an afterthought. "We'll go check your coats. Why don't you two go grab those spots?" he nodded toward some empty spaces at one of the tables. "Can we fetch a drink for you on our way back?"

Both ladies nodded.

"What's your poison?" he queried.

"Corona," they said in unison.

"Ah, women after my own heart." Zach placed his hand over his heart and sighed contentedly.

Ashley watched the two brothers walk away. "The man should be in a designer jean commercial. That butt of his sure makes me want to buy a pair." She leaned in close to her friend and yelled, "So what about you and Nate? What's the story?"

"Not sure at the moment. Even though he doesn't think we're right for each other, in the end, he won't know what hit him," Lauren ran her tongue around her lips. "He just needs some help layering a little gray into his black and white world and I intend to put that paint brush in his hand."

9

She paused and tried to look like the thought had just occurred to her. "By the way, Zach is quite a catch. Not only is he a big rodeo star but will one day own, the Rocking K Ranch."

"I don't know, he hasn't picked the most secure way to earn a living – and rodeo and risk-taking – seem to go hand-in-hand. I'm not asking for much from a man and I'm not cutting anyone slack because they're sexy as sin. That was the old me," Ashley yelled. "New me, has a plan."

"Oh, you and your plan," Lauren yelled back. "I still don't think it's a good idea."

"What plan?" asked Zach taking a seat next to Ashley on the bench and handing her a beer.

Zach put on his poker face as she looked him up and down apparently coming to a decision. "You seem like a nice guy and my best friend is dating your brother so you might as well know the score from the beginning. I don't want any hard feelings down the line. Let's go someplace a little quieter and talk," suggested Ashley.

"Sure, grab your beer and let's head to the bar in the dining area." Zach stood up and offered his hand to Ashley. He smothered the grin dancing at his lips when he felt her hesitation before placing her hand in his.

When they reached the bar, he pulled out a stool for her, then settled on one right next to her. "So, what is this plan and what has it got to do with me?"

"First a little history so you understand where I'm coming from," she said. "To say my love life has been a disaster is putting it mildly." He noticed how she forced her shoulders to relax but her hands restlessly twisted the beer bottle back and forth. "Every man I've been seriously interested in ended up being a cheating, lying, narcissistic jerk. The last guy, my fiancé, the man who was supposed to protect me and love me forever, left me high, dry, and nearly penniless."

She shrugged, "I was stupid. I trusted him and put everything we would be sharing in our married life in both our names... condo, bank accounts, my precious little red Miata – lost it all. When he dumped me, he put a big hole in my financial security... it was a mess."

"That's harsh. I can see why you're skittish." He put a hand on her arm and tilted his head to look into her eyes.

"That's when I decided my life needed a new direction so I moved here and set up some guidelines to help me weed out the undesirables."

"I'm listening," he said.

"To start with, Mr. Right needs to have a good, steady job with great benefits. Shows he's responsible." She ticked the list off on her fingers as she talked. "Second, if there is even a hint in social media or from his friends that he's a player – he's out. Third, he needs to be involved in something that helps others. Shows he has compassion. And finally, risk-takers and gamblers are out. These seem to be the traits the men who hurt me had in common. I don't think I'm asking a lot, just an honorable man with a good job." She sat up a little straighter, if that was possible, and squared her shoulders ready to do battle.

"So where does that leave someone like me in your grand scheme?" he asked. "I'm an honorable man."

She took a dainty sip from her beer. "Friends?" she asked hopefully. "I'm sorry, but you just don't seem like a good risk and I refuse to give my heart to a jerk." She cringed and touched his arm, "Not that you're a jerk and I'm sure you're an honorable man, but I have to be careful."

"And what makes you think I'd be interested in dating you?"

She opened her mouth, closed it, then said, "Nothing. I guess. You and your brother came here without dates so I assumed you came to pick up women... and I'm a woman."

"That you are." He raised a brow and let his gaze travel over her body. "By that reasoning, should I assume you and Lauren came here to pick up men? I'm a man." He smiled as sweetly as a wolf could smile. "You didn't come with dates."

She narrowed her eyes and crossed her arms. "We came here to dance and have some fun, not hookup with random guys."

"But what if you met someone you were attracted to? What then?"

"If he asked me out, I'd probably accept but before I get serious, he's going to have to meet my basic guidelines or there *is* no relationship."

"Interesting theory," he responded, but the wheels had already started turning. Friends, huh. He'd see about that. "Want to dance?"

She held out her hand and let him lead her back into the dance hall.

The lady had moves like nobody's business. Watching her dance sent his heart rate and temperature into overdrive. Lordy, the woman made it hard to put two thoughts together.

Her hips moved in a smooth side to side motion accenting a tush that was as close to perfect as any he'd ever seen... and he'd judged quite a few in his time. His hands easily spanned that tiny waist. As they two-stepped around the floor, he twirled her and was rewarded with a better look at legs that any red-blooded man would die to have wrapped around him. When he bent her back, he basked in the feel of that silken hair against his arm and the sight of those lush breasts straining against the fabric of her dress. If the song could go on for the next hour at least, he wouldn't complain. In fact he might get down on his knees and thank his lucky stars.

He saw her glance every so often at the couple dancing nearby. If the man was looking, she'd execute a particularly seductive move. What's going on here, Zach wondered? Is she trying to make him jealous or that other guy jealous?

Near the end of the song, Zach got down on one knee and placed his hands at her waist so he could twist her side to side and feel the sway of her hips. When he rose, he pulled her so close a dime couldn't fit between them, bent her back then pulled her upright and kissed her. Her lips, so soft and tender, scorched his soul.

The set ended and the band bounded off stage for a break. Zach took her hand in his, brought it to his lips then led Ashley back to their seats. He settled himself on the bench beside her, resting his elbows on the table behind him. He used two fingers to push his Stetson further back on his head and stretched those long, muscled legs out in front of him.

Zach nudged her with his elbow. "You like that guy?"

"What guy?" Ashley asked all innocence.

"The one you were putting on a show for."

"Oh." She shook her head slowly. "No. I thought about trying to make him jealous but," she looked at him like he was the last bar of premium chocolate on the shelf, "I've since changed my mind and decided he is not worth my time. He dumped me for the skank he's dancing with and that pissed me off. I wanted to get even."

She pulled out her lipstick and smoothed the deep, red color over her lips. Zach licked his and swallowed hard.

He cleared his throat. "That says something about his intelligence right there. His loss, my gain, is the way I see it." He stood and angled his head at Nate indicating he should join him. "Well, I think it's time to refresh those drinks."

·♥·♥·❤·♥·♥·

"I SEE WHAT YOU were trying to do," Lauren hissed in Ashley's ear as soon as the men were out of earshot. "Are you really sure you want to make Jerk Face jealous? You realize Sam is so conceited he'll probably think you want him back." She paused, "You *don't* want him back, do you?"

"No." Ashley made a hex sign. "It didn't take Zach long to figure out what I was up to. He sees too much." Ashley sighed, "It's a shame he's not suitable happily-ever-after material." She clasped her hands tightly in her lap. "While too yummy for words and his kiss…" She rolled her eyes. "The tingle is still happening, but I'm determined to stick to my plan."

Lauren shook her head. "Ashley, did you ever think that maybe it was their wealth, social standing, or Ivy League education – the qualities your mother thinks are important – that made those losers you fell for the way they are? There's more to a good man than a steady job with good benefits."

"True," Ashley nodded, "so maybe I need to add, 'no narcissists need apply' to my list. There has to be some way to keep from falling for the bad boy over and over again."

Lauren glanced up. "Speak of the devil," Lauren muttered. "Don't look now but here comes Sam."

·♥·♥·❤·♥·♥·

"OH QUIT LOOKING so sour," Zach chided his brother. "You get to spend the night dancing and enjoying the company of a gorgeous woman and you look like you've eaten a whole jar of pickles. Get over yourself."

"What do you know? I don't see you settling down any time soon," groused Nate.

"I didn't say anything about settling down," said Zach, "only ditching the sour. You're making some interesting connections, big bro." He chuckled in a way that only a younger brother can at the discomfort of an older sibling. "But as far as settling down, it's only because the right woman hasn't walked into my life yet," he shrugged, "that and timing I suppose. Too busy rodeoing and ranching to have given much thought to getting serious about a woman," Zach drawled. "But as long as she loves ranching and rodeoing, I'm ready and willing to give up my bachelor ways when she does show up."

He elbowed his way to the bar. "Four Coronas, Ma'am," he held up four fingers then tipped his hat slightly to the bar maid. Zach snagged the four bottles off the counter, turned and handed two to Nate.

"The woman drives me nuts," Nate muttered. "If only she were a little more conventional."

"And by conventional, you mean was born and raised in Texas, looks like the girl next door instead of a super model, cooks dinner every night and it damn well better be meat and potatoes and if she never has to travel farther than 100 miles from home she'd be happy as a clam?"

Nate scowled. "Smartass."

Zach looked at his brother and shook his head, "Well, try and lighten up and have a little fun, bro. I don't want these ladies looking elsewhere, at least not right away."

"Looks like someone is trying to muscle in on your territory," observed Nate. Given the glower on Zach's face, he had already noticed.

Can I shoot him, Zach wondered? From the look on Ashley's face, the guy she called Jerk Face was invading her personal space and Zach didn't like it one bit. Look at him, trying that 'lean in' move, getting kissing close and pretending he just wants to talk to her. Time to let this guy know where things stand.

Zach plastered on his most devilish grin and sidled right up to Ashley. He strategically positioned himself between the interloper and the lady he had started thinking of as his.

He slipped his arm across her shoulders, "Mister, it looks like you're digging one deep hole for yourself by talking to my date." Zach nodded toward an extremely disgruntled blonde who was shooting daggers into Sam's back. "Personally, if I were you, I'd make tracks back over to the woman you're with or you might find yourself flying solo."

"Her? Women like her are a dime a dozen. If she takes off, I'll just find another." Sam tilted his head, nose in the air, eyes filled with disdain.

"Spoken like a true gentleman," Zach responded.

"You only need to be a gentleman when you're with a lady," Sam replied.

"Any woman you're with is a lady," Zach ran his hand up and down Ashley's arm.

"Yeah, well it wasn't so long ago that your date, was my date, so that makes her a..."

"Stop it right there." Zach glared like an angry bear.

Ashley grabbed Zach's hand before the two got into it and started pulling him toward the dance floor. "Let's dance." She wiggled her hips and smiled enticingly as she backed toward the thick of the action.

"I'm yours," Zach grinned, "and can't wait to get my arms around you again, but no more trying to make someone else jealous."

Ashley crossed her heart with one finger. "I promise. And thank you for rescuing me."

As she stepped into his arms, she said, "I can't imagine what I saw in him. Another indication that my scum bag detector needs some serious recalibration. I don't seem to be able to tell the good guys from the bad."

"It's easy," Zach chuckled. "Us good guys wear white hats." He tipped his head down so the brim of his white Stetson touched her forehead, then he gave her a twirl and pulled her in close as he two-stepped her backwards.

"Haven't you heard about wolves in sheep's clothing? Jerk Face could wear a white hat and he would still be lower than a snake's belly."

"You do have a point," Zach swallowed a laugh, "but for the record, my hat is white and Jerk Face is wearing a brown hat."

"Okay, until proven otherwise, I'll semi-trust you, but I'd be willing to bet that not *all* your hats are white."

"I do pull a dark one out from time-to-time." His lips touched her ear. "I don't claim to be an angel, but I believe in treating women with respect no matter what color hat I'm wearing."

She snuggled deeper into his embrace. For now it was enough to luxuriate in the feel of him until the music ended.

As they walked back to the table Zach put his arm around her waist and pulled her in tight, then kissed her on the temple. "You smell good," he whispered.

"Thank you."

"You want to get out of here?" At her suspicious expression, he quickly added, "There's a diner just down the road that serves breakfast 24 hours a day – and it's the best you'll ever taste."

"Why is everything in Texas always the biggest or the best?"

"Because it's the truth," his mouth quirked up in a way that would make even the most devout man-hater melt at his feet.

While she still wanted to keep on dancing, especially if it meant staying in his arms, she heard herself saying, "Sure, sounds good. I've never had breakfast so late at night, but remember – just friends." She paused mid-step so that he bumped into her, "Oh wait, Lauren came with me and I'll need to take her home. Maybe we could do a rain check?"

"I bet I can talk my brother into making sure Lauren gets home safe and sound," he nodded toward the dance floor and said couple locked in a tight embrace. "In fact, I doubt it will take much persuading."

Zach walked over to Nate and Lauren and after a brief discussion, rejoined Ashley.

"We're all set. Prepare yourself for a little taste of heaven"

Good thing he couldn't read her thoughts or he'd know what little slice of heaven she really hungered after. Perhaps another one of those earth-shaking kisses? Keep thinking, only friends, only friends.

Chapter Two

♥

"WHEN YOU SAID IT was just down the road, I thought you meant a few blocks, not forty miles," Ashley said as Zach helped her out of her car.

"Honey, forty miles *is* just down the road in Texas."

"Right, I forgot. *Everything* is bigger in Texas."

"Damn straight." Ashley felt his eyes following the movement of her butt as she walked past him into the diner and put an extra swing in her step. The man was Adonis in a Stetson, all six foot of him and a girl couldn't help but put on a show.

He leaned down and whispered in her ear. "My mama taught me to be a gentleman and let the lady walk in front. Little did I know my manners would give me one of the best views in Texas."

Obviously he knew that one way to a Southern woman's heart was good manners, she reflected. While his comment shoved him a little closer to the bad boy corner, she could live with that *and* being one of the best views in Texas didn't hurt.

"Welcome. Table for two?" Zach nodded at the hostess. "Follow me, please."

He saw Ashley's eyes go big when a waitress scurried by carrying a plate filled with the house specialty.

"I hope that cinnamon bun is destined for a table of ten to share," she whispered.

"No Ma'am, that there is thee pounds of mouthwatering goodness that a man will only share with someone special. Otherwise, it's all his." He gave her hand a squeeze and she felt the jolt of electricity tap dancing along her spine. "Want to share?" he leaned into her playfully.

"Friends only... remember?" she murmured when her brain started working again.

"If you say so." He smiled and nodded pleasantly at the many women they passed. She supposed he had to acknowledge them when they were eyeballing him like he was the house specialty. Hard to ignore that kind of interest.

He pulled out a chair and helped her get seated earning a few more points in the tally she didn't realize she'd been keeping. One mark for manners and one demerit for noticing the other women.

Zach placed his hat on the table as the young waitress slipped the menus in front of them. She held up the coffee pot in an unspoken question. Zach nudged his coffee cup forward which the waitress promptly filled making sure he got an eyeful of her charms. "Can I get you anything else?"

"Decaf, please," said Ashley pulling the woman's attention away from Zach. The waitress's smile as she filled Ashley's mug was as fake as the Prada purses sold on the street corners of New York.

When Zach mouthed 'decaf' and raised eyebrows, Ashley added primly, "I have to work tomorrow and regular will keep me awake."

"Did I say anything?" he asked.

She frowned, "Not out loud, but you intimated that decaf is for sissies."

"You don't have to justify yourself to me." He held up his hands in peace. "By the way, what color are those eyes of yours?" He rested is his forearms on the table and cradled his coffee in his large, strong hands.

"Violet comes closest." She gazed into his sky blues and treated him to that flirtatious look Southern women have spent centuries perfecting. Reel them in, then decide if the man should be catch and release or plopped into the cooler to keep.

"So what do you do when you aren't burning up the dance floor and driving men crazy.

"My life is basically boring and right now mostly revolves around work. Tax season kicks into high gear in another few weeks," she said. "It's not a topic for party conversation, but it does occupy a big chunk of my waking hours."

"If you don't talk about your job, what *do* you talk about at parties?"

"Growing up in my social circle, girls were trained to be the perfect Southern debutante – ask questions, look interested in what the men say, and appear to be demur. Our job was to make the single men feel like kings."

"Only the single men?"

"In the world according to my mother the whole point of an unattached, young woman attending a social function was to find a suitable husband. Married men were not part of our circle."

"What about married women? Why would they go to a social function?"

"To gossip about the women who aren't there, push their daughters at eligible men, and keep their husbands in line, or at least, discreet. There is nothing more formidable than a Southern matriarch, and husbands forget that at their peril."

"And you subscribe to the theory that you need to keep your man in line?"

"Nope." Her lips made a popping sound when she pronounced the 'p.' "If a man can't keep *himself* in line, then he's not the right man for me. I plan to marry for love, or not at all, a concept my mother cannot understand."

"Your parents didn't marry for love?"

She shrugged. "No, but not unusual in my world. Pedigree trumps feelings. Your spouse needs to come from the right family, have attended the right schools, and be wealthy."

The waitress stopped at their table, order pad poised. "What can I get for you?"

"I'll have the chicken fried steak," Zach rubbed his hands together.

"Fruit salad for me, please."

"Coming right up," the waitress said.

"Surly a little thing like you is not on a diet? What are you, about five foot two and a hundred pounds dripping wet?" Zach asked.

"A woman never discusses her weight." She graced him with a Queen Elizabeth stare but her smile softened the reprimand. "No, I'm not on a diet. That is *soo* not my style. I just don't like to eat a heavy meal this late at night."

"Glad to hear you're not one of those women who thinks she needs to live on rabbit food to attract a man," he drawled.

"No, but realistically if a woman doesn't look appealing, her chances of catching a man's interest plummet faster than the boobs of a woman over sixty."

When Zach stopped choking on his coffee, he said, "On that note, back to our conversation, if I want to learn more about you, parties are out. What about a coffee shop?" He gently nudged her foot under the table.

"Sure, this is as good a place as any. What do you want to know? My life's an open book."

"How could someone as amazing as you end up with the string of losers you've talked about?" He paused for a couple of beats, a puzzled expression on his face. "I mean, are all the guys in South Carolina crazy, or blind or both?"

"And let us not forget the guys in North Carolina where I went to college, and now we can add Texas guys to the list." She looked at him frankly. "No, I'm beginning to think it has something to do with me. I obviously have a character flaw that makes me choose lying, cheating, thieving, low-life cretins over and over again. Wash, rinse, repeat. That's me."

"Don't be so hard on yourself. In my opinion, any man who treats a woman like that ought to be horsewhipped." He reached over and took her hand rubbing his thumbs lightly over her soft skin. "Maybe you're just looking in the wrong places. Where are you finding these guys?"

"They're boys I grew up with, met at college, people who were part of my social circle – pretty typical scenarios – but if there is a loser out there, he will find me and I will fall for him."

"So where do you look now so you don't meet the same kind of guy?"

"I've thought about joining young professional groups, doing more charity work or connecting with a single's group that offers cultural activities. Those seem like good places to meet serious-minded men. No matter where I meet them, I am determined to take a closer look at their character before letting them into my heart."

"Sounds like you don't plan to meet your ideal man at the rodeo."

"Not likely. As I understand it, you only earn money if you're one of the winners, otherwise it's cash down the drain... so rodeoers don't meet the steady job requirement. They're drifting through life... while doing what they love is great, where are they going to be when they're fifty? I want someone who is responsible, who has a life plan."

"It's true, we don't get paid if we don't win. A lot of guys just get by and their day job pays the bills. But no one's job is certain anymore. We could all find ourselves on the street when we're fifty."

"True, but rodeoing is also risky so they don't meet that criteria and by reputation, the non-player clause is questionable. I'm standing firm. Rodeo men need not apply."

"Well ma'am, if you don't mind me saying, you're leaving some of the best men I know on the table." He twisted his coffee mug back and forth by the handle. "We're a very loyal, hard-working bunch of guys, committed to perfecting our craft, big on family values and our word is our bond. Sounds to me like you could do a lot worse."

"Honey, every man I ever dated promised me the sun and the moon but delivered swamp land instead, so excuse me if I want proof before I decide to trust a man."

Conversation stalled as the waitress slipped their plates in front of them.

"My goodness," Ashley's jaw dropped, "are you really planning on eating all of that?"

"Sure 'nough." The obvious pleasure on his face as he prepared to tuck into a 'Texas-sized' plate piled high with food, made her laugh.

"I don't know why you don't look like the Pillsbury Dough Boy."

"Ranching and rodeoing is hard work and tends to keep a man fit."

"I can see that."

"If you are going to keep looking at me like I'm the main course on a starving man's menu, we need to take this party someplace more intimate."

"No need." She held up her hands, palms facing him. "But, to my detriment, I do admire a good-looking man especially if he is a little bit bad," she said caressing him with her gaze.

He shifted in his seat, his jeans feeling a bit snug in the crotch.

She daintily sliced a piece of cantaloupe, and after she had chewed and swallowed, continued, "It does make sense that running a ranch would keep you in tip-top shape. My family owns a working plantation in South Carolina and there always seems to be something that needs to be fixed, animals that need tending or crops that require attention."

He sat back visibly surprised. "Really? A plantation? Like in 'Gone with the Wind'?"

She chuckled and shook her head. Her hair swung in slow motion like one of those sexy hair commercials causing all his brain activity to travel south and pool between his legs. It was all he could do to clamp down on the impulse to jump over the table and kiss her senseless.

"I guess it could be compared to Tara minus the cotton crops, slaves, mansion, and hoop skirts." Ashley waved her hand in front of her face like a fan and fluttered her lashes.

"Huh," he said, a puzzled frown creasing his forehead.

"Plantation. 'Gone with the Wind.' Remember?"

"Oh, yeah. Sorry... mind wandered."

Her look told him she knew exactly where his mind had wandered. Her smile reminded him of something sleek, sexy, and exotic stretching and purring.

"Uh, so tell me about this plantation of yours." He nervously repositioned his hat on the table. What was it about her that made him feel like he was fourteen again and still wet behind the ears where girls were concerned... not knowing what to say, how to act, what to do. He thought he was past all that.

He loved her smile and the faraway look in her eyes as she thought about how to answer. "You care about your land." He said it as a simple statement of fact.

"Yes, that's the place I've always felt most at home," she answered thoughtfully. "My brother, Michael, and I took over the day-to-day management when we were still in high school. Mostly because we loved the place, but also because no one else in the family was interested in spending more than occasional weekend there hunting and fishing. They would have sold if it became too burdensome. Practical to the core, my family."

She popped another piece of cantaloupe in her mouth and chewed saucily. He waited patiently, fascinated by the movement of her mouth.

"Luckily, Michael wanted to keep it in the family as much as I did. If I had been the only one, the family would have let it go. 'It's not a woman's place to run a working plantation,'" she singsonged a phrase she'd obviously heard a lot. "It shouldn't have made a difference. Historically women have kept the wolves at bay and homesteads working when the men were absent."

"Amen to that one," he agreed. "My mama has as much to do with running the ranch as my dad. They're quite a team."

"So you approve of a woman carrying her weight in business?"

"Darlin', I not only approve, but the woman I eventually settle down with, has to *want* to work the ranch with me."

"You say that now, but will you say that after the ink has dried on the marriage certificate?"

"Okay, sounds like a bit of a sore spot and maybe too heavy a topic for our first non-date," he folded her hand up in his. "I know you have one brother and it sounds like you're close to him. Any other siblings?"

"Smooth transition and nice dodge," she said, "but don't expect to get off so easily next time." She pulled her hands out of his. "I have two other older brothers. William Blaine Drayton IV – name's a bit pretentious but it suits Blaine to a 't' – and Jonathan. I'm the baby." She paused, "I've met Nate. Any other Kincaids roaming around?"

"Our youngest brother, Josh, rounds out the Kincaid sibling count. No girls – much to my mother's sorrow who kept hoping to have the chance to buy frilly stuff. It figures, the first grandchild, Josh's son, was a boy. I'm the middle child."

"Ah, let me guess, the famous middle child syndrome rears its ugly head?"

He narrowed his eyes, wondering if he should ask but decided to take the chance. "Explain?"

"This is what I get for hanging out with Lauren… lots of psychological theories. According to studies, middle children are over-achievers and/or class clowns in their quest to get noticed, are the family peace makers, feel less pressure to conform and are more outgoing and flexible than older and younger siblings. Any of that ring true?"

"Never thought about it, but I guess I would have to be an over achiever to get where I'm at professionally. I'd say I am more of a conformist than either of my brothers since I'm the only one who followed in my dad's and granddad's footsteps. Peacemaker in a house full of boys… not so much. Outgoing? Yeah, I like people. Sounds like the theory is partly true for me. How about you? Are you the typical, spoiled baby of the family?"

"You'd think being the only girl and the youngest to boot, that I would fit the stereotype, but sadly no, I was viewed as less valuable than the boys. '*You're too little and you're a girl, you can't do that.*' Naturally, whatever it was I couldn't do, was exactly what I wanted to do." She used her fork to chase a piece of fruit around on her plate. "I probably turned out more like a middle child fighting for attention. I didn't fit their image of what I should be, so I wasn't the most popular child in the family."

"And what did they expect you to be?"

"Perfect little lady, of course. Seen and not heard. Someone they could easily ignore but trot out to perform on cue when convention dictated children should be present."

Wow," he looked as stunned as he sounded. "Even though our upbringing was rough and tumble, we were always there for each other and knew we were loved. I can't imagine what it must have been like for you. Sounds lonely."

"Lonely?" She shrugged. "Most of my life I just felt like an ornament you hang on the tree." She quickly glanced at her watch. "Oh, my, look at the time. I've got to go."

"To repeat your words... nice dodge. I'm guessing your family dynamics is another touchy subject?"

"Sort of, but I really do need to go. I have client meetings scheduled all day tomorrow and need to get my beauty sleep."

"Well darling', given how gorgeous you are, you must get lots of sleep."

"Smooth, very smooth." She licked her finger, held it in the air and made a sizzling noise.

As he helped her into her jacket he said casually, "I'll be in town next Wednesday to finish filming a promo for one of my sponsors. Any chance you could join me for lunch? I hate eating alone." He tried a 'poor me' look hoping to make her laugh.

It worked and she chuckled. "I can't imagine you would *ever* have trouble rustling up a dining companion. Just crook your finger and half the females in the county would come running."

"You think only half would come running? I'm wounded." He placed his hand over his heart and staggered back.

"Sweetie, the other half are either too young, too old or too married." She turned and looked at him obviously considering the wisdom of accepting his invitation. He held his breath while he buttoned her coat and snugged it around her looking intently into those fascinating violet eyes.

"OK, why not? Next Wednesday for lunch." She fished into her purse and pulled out a business card. "Here's where you can pick me up."

She had a sneaking suspicion her acceptance had a lot to do with the amazing things his touch did to her insides. The simple act of buttoning her coat had most likely short-circuited her rational brain and made her feel all warm and yielding.

·♥·♥·♥·♥·♥·

THE NEXT EVENING ASHLEY plunked down on the sofa, kicked off her shoes, put her feet up on the coffee table and patted the cushion beside her. "Lauren, I want all the dirt on the Kincaid family. You've been dating Nate for a while now so spill," she said as she took a sip of wine.

Lauren settled herself on the couch and tucked her long legs under her. "Be happy to share what I know, but I also want to hear about you and Zach after your left the club last night." She tapped her cheek with her forefinger. "Let me see, where to begin?" She paused for a moment sifting through her thoughts.

"They are a long-time ranching family on both sides, very proud of their heritage. Tons of aunts, uncles and cousins, live within a 200-mile radius. You can't shake a stick in this part of Texas without hitting one of their relatives... and they love to get together. Right after we started dating, Nate took me to a family barbecue and I swear half the state of Texas was there. Family is important to them."

"Sure different from our tiny families. A couple of aunts, uncles and cousins, that's it," Ashley said.

"It was a bit overwhelming at first, but they made me feel welcome." Lauren popped a bite of cheese and cracker into her mouth. "Zach's the only one of his immediate family who stuck with the family business."

"Yeah, he told me that, but not much else other than he's the middle child. Tell me more." Ashley twisted on the sofa to face Lauren.

"Nate is a large animal veterinarian so he's at least involved in some way, but Josh, the youngest of the brothers, completely broke with tradition and is a software engineer for a company in Austin. He's also getting divorced which is unheard of."

"Since I know you're not blind, you've noticed that both Zach and Nate are *real* easy on the eyes," Lauren continued.

Ashley licked her lips. "That's the understatement of the century. And sex appeal... I'm sure there's a law somewhere against one human being packing such a punch, let alone two brothers who could easily pass for Chippendale Dancers. Zach and that 'come hither' smile of his would earn him enough in tips to live like a king."

Lauren belly-laughed until tears trickled down her cheeks. "Sorry. The image of uptight Nate wearing nothing but a Tuxedo thong and bow tie is too funny for words. Not that he wouldn't fill them out just fine but..." She started laughing again.

Once Lauren caught her breath she continued. "And as unbelievable as it may seem that so much deliciousness could be found in one family, Josh is right up there with his brothers in the eye-candy department. When the three of them are together, there is no doubt they are brothers."

Ashley laughed, "And putting lascivious thoughts in the head of every female with a heartbeat."

"You got that right," chuckled Lauren, "but based on their person-alities, I'm not sure they're from the same planet."

"How so? Ashley asked. "Nate seems fine to me."

"Oh, he's more than fine, just a little stuck in his ways, but I have plans to loosen that boy up."

"I'll bet you do." The two giggled like a couple of teenagers plotting the capture of their latest love interest.

"What I mean," Lauren continued, "is that Zach is outgoing but with a tendency to push the envelope, thus his bad boy image. Nate is a by-the-book kind of guy and can't understand why everyone doesn't follow the same internal compass he does. Josh is introverted and very shy but with a mind like a steel trap. He can solve any puzzle you throw at him. Despite their very different personalities, they would defend each other to the death."

"All in all, a really nice family and one I very much hope to become part of someday." Lauren took another sip of her wine. "So tell me about Zach. What do you think about him? Did you guys have fun after you left the club?"

"He's an interesting man. Not the right man for me, mind you, but I'd like to be his friend. Trouble is, when we were dancing, it was only him and the music, nothing else existed. When he pulled me up against him and we swayed pelvis to pelvis, his strong arms wrapped around me, foreheads touching, I could feel the steam rising and the air around us crackling." Ashley sighed and flopped back against the sofa.

Lauren smiled knowingly, "Your sigh says it all. Honey, there is no way on God's green earth a woman can be friends with a man like Zach, unless, of course, that man is gay – and I don't think our Zach falls into that category."

"Any man who can kiss the breath clean out of a woman like he does, most definitely prefers the ladies." Ashley paused, rubbed her palms together. "Remember that roller coaster ride we went on last summer?" She waited for Lauren to nod her head. "Well let me tell you, the thrill from those drops pales in comparison to Zach's kiss."

"Uh, huh." Lauren had skeptical written all over her face. "Friends? Right!"

"Don't give me that look. Zach and I *can* be just friends. While he knows how to treat a woman, I'm not convinced he cares which woman he's with. He's an equal opportunity lover."

"He may give the impression that he lives in the moment but there is a deep well of grit and determination running through that man's veins so don't let his devil-may-care attitude fool you."

Ashley held up her index finger, "Enough about Zach. Remember that hunky guy – Robert – I met at the Crystal Charity Ball last month? He called today and invited me to another charity event on Saturday. It has something to do with the college championship game and gourmet food so it should be fun. I'm going to fly to Dallas on Saturday and back home on Sunday. I have hotel reservations but who knows what could happen? He certainly meets all my Mr. Right criteria. Just saying, my plan might be working."

"It took him long enough to get back to you, but if you're happy, I'm happy," Lauren leaned over and gave her friend a squeeze.

Ashley patted Lauren's knee. "I'm going to miss our little after-work chats once I move, but I am looking forward to having my own place again." She yawned and stretched, "Well, time for bed. Busy day tomorrow and I want to make sure my desk is cleared for this weekend and my big date with Robert."

Chapter Three

♥

ASHLEY HUDDLED UNDER HER umbrella as she scurried – at least as quickly as one could in four-inch stilettos – across the golden-colored grand entry patio to Robert's front door. Gorgeous landscaping surrounded the impressive Mediterranean Villa-style home. She admired the way the stones in the middle section were arranged so several inches of well-manicured grass created a crisscross pattern. A fountain that could have graced any Italian plaza burbled merrily in the center of all this awesomeness. The front balustrades around the porch and second story balconies overflowed with colorful flowers. The mini mansion literally screamed that someone with style and taste and money, money, money lived here.

Gracefully, head high and back straight, she climbed the five steps to the door and pushed the doorbell. Ashley did a quick double-take as a pleasant, bell-toned chime played "Home, Home On The Range." Goodness she thought with a small, surprised moue. Robert Matthew Pritchard III had struck her as interesting, now she added quirky to the growing list of attributes.

Robert opened the door and stepped forward in greeting, placing an arm across her shoulders and drawing her in to the foyer. "My, my, don't you look good enough to eat," he cooed. "Love that up do with just a few curls around your face. Very elegant and very classy. I predict all the ladies will be green with envy."

"Where are my manners? Here, let me take your wrap." He folded the garment over his arm and made a twirling motion with his finger. "Darlin', let me see." He eyed her critically as she spun in a slow circle. "Your little black dress is just right for this event. Are those Christian Louboutin heels? Way to make a statement!"

"Good eye, but how did you know?"

"Two sisters who regularly con me into taking them shopping," he chuckled, "especially if I bring my credit card."

"And have those siblings counted every one of their lucky stars to have a brother like you? Mine wouldn't be caught dead taking me shopping, let alone relinquish any of their hard-earned cash."

"Sounds like they will never receive the big brother of the year award with that attitude." His perfectly whitened teeth peeked out of his perfectly proportioned smile. "Besides, I figure I'm earning good karma by being nice to my sisters."

Ashley laughed. "My brothers' lack of interest in shopping did have one benefit, I developed wicked shopping skills. I'm always on the lookout for a deal." She posed to better display her shoes. "Saw these babies at Barneys and couldn't help myself. There is at least one advantage to being petite, I don't wear the most popular size so can often snag a bargain."

Ashley spun around slowly again, taking in the details of the place Robert called home. The finest Italian marble flooring, a wide staircase curving up to the second-floor overlook, soft butternut-colored paint covering the main walls, furniture that looked custom made... the place whispered no-expense-spared. The intricate wrought iron chandelier hanging above the foyer cast a warm glow on an otherwise gloomy afternoon. A glimpse into the dining room to her left revealed a sumptuous décor in deep wood tones, plush high-backed chairs and rich Moroccan-red paint on the walls.

"Impressive," she whispered in awe. "I'm almost afraid to touch anything. Your taste is impeccable." The place was a bit ostentatious – like the man's name but also welcoming like the man himself.

"Thank you." He accepted the compliment graciously. Yes, the man with the perfectly tousled blonde hair and custom-cut suit would be a fine catch for some lucky woman. Ashley figured she was due for some luck in the man department.

"I know we will be eating a lot this evening, but I do have some refreshments prepared to tide us over. Right this way."

He walked her through the kitchen off the formal dining room and into a circular breakfast area overlooking the backyard and adjacent golf course.

"Well, if this isn't a little bit of heaven, I don't know what is," she sighed. "I love to play golf even though I'm not very good at it. I think it's being outdoors in beautiful surroundings that hooked me. That and the cute outfits."

"Golf? Something else we have in common. We'll have to play sometime."

"I'd like that. It must be wonderful sitting here with your coffee in the morning. What a view!"

"Yes, I pinch myself daily. Never in my wildest dreams did I imagine I'd be where I am today." He pinched himself and spread his arms wide as though introducing his domain to the world. "The house sits on an acre but with the golf course view, it feels much more expansive. Except for the occasional errant golf ball, it's very nearly perfect."

He picked up a Waterford wine glass. "Can I pour you a Chardonnay or Cabernet Sauvignon?"

"Chardonnay, please." He handed her the wine and a small China plate just as the oven timer dinged. "Please help yourself. I have just one more appetizer to get out of the oven."

She followed him over to the kitchen and leaned against the granite-topped island. "I have kitchen envy, you know. This is every cook's dream. I would get down on my hands and knees and scrub every inch of this house to have a set up like this. Looks like you put all this to good use." She ran her hand over the marble pastry insert then tapped one of the copper pots hanging from a circular rack above her head.

"Oh, I do," he said as he pulled a pan of baked zucchini rolls stuffed with ricotta cheese and herbs out of one of the double ovens and placed it on a cooling rack. He quickly slid a serving plate out of the cupboard and used tongs to arrange the hot morsels on it.

"That smells delightful," she said as she reached over to snag one.

He playfully held the plate above his head. "Wait until we sit down so you can truly savor the experience."

"You don't play fair," she pouted.

He put the plate on the table and pulled out a chair for her. "Good things come to those who wait." He wagged his finger at her like a metronome.

"Alright, alright," she sighed dramatically. "So what do we have here?"

"This is a zucchini cheese wrap. This plate is avocado, basil and tomato crostini and these are prosciutto wrapped cantaloupe balls," he said pointing to each with a flourish. "Just a little something light to keep us from dying of starvation before we get to the event. I've also learned it's best to be prepared since you never know how much food you will actually get at one of these things."

"Tonight's chefs will have nothing on you." She picked up one of the crostini and took a dainty bite. "So far I know you have excellent taste in home décor, you are an incredible dancer, a fabulous cook, enjoy golf and thanks to your sisters, know your shoes. Tell me more about the remarkable Mr. Pritchard."

He laughed. "Sweet cheeks, Mr. Pritchard is my father. I'm just plain ol' Robert. As far as the decorating is concerned, one of my best friends is a top interior designer and my mother insisted I take ballroom dance classes as a kid. The cooking part, I love to eat great food but get tired of always having to eat out to get it. So there you have it. My life in a nutshell. And what about you, anything changed since the Crystal Charity Ball last month?"

"I found a house and am moving in next weekend. I'm renting for now but the owner is open to a sale eventually. As much as I love Lauren," she touched his arm, "I can't wait to have my own place again. I have enough furniture to get started but will have to do some serious shopping in the near future."

She paused and snapped her fingers. "Hey, you should come furniture shopping with me. It would be so much fun and you obviously know your stuff."

"That does sound like fun. I do love to shop and would be honored to be an aide-de-camp on your little shopping expedition. Mind if I bring my design guru along? He knows all the most fabulous shops. What style are you looking for?"

"Style" she paused crinkling her forehead in thought. "I love shabby chic. I lean toward white with touches of my favorite color, lavender..."

"Like your eyes."

"What a sweet thing to say. Thank you." She rose on her tiptoes and placed a soft kiss on his cheek. "I guess my tastes favor dreamy with a touch of rustic. And yes, please do bring your friend along. If he did all this," she made a sweeping motion with her arm, "then I know I'll be in good hands." She clapped and did a little happy dance before giving him a big hug. "I am so excited!"

He glanced at his Rolex. "We'll have to leave in about 20 minutes, so I need to start cleaning up. A little more wine?"

"No, but let me help," she said as she picked up the wine glasses and carried them to the sink. "I'll dry."

·♥·♥·♥·♥·♥·

THEY WALKED INTO THE cavernous hall chatting companionably about the list of chefs, the unique food choices waiting for them and the upcoming title match between the two top college teams. Since both teams hailed from north of the Mason-Dixon line, they didn't have ties to either, and were just looking forward to a good contest.

"I love grazing so this is like Nirvana. The smells are incredible and the food looks like something out of a gourmet magazine. Mmm, mmm... Now if they were only giving away recipes." She hooked one elegant arm through his and looked right and left. "Where should we start?"

"I've heard good things about that new barbeque place and I see their station right over there." He nodded to their right and a long line of people.

Ashley grabbed his arm tightly. "OMG. Look! Look! There's Randy White." She pointed excitedly. "And there's Preston Pearson... I can't believe it. Let's go get a picture," she said dragging him over to the football celebrities in question.

"You are quite the football fan, I see," he said once the requisite digital memories were made and quickly posted to Ashley's Facebook page. "Turn you loose in a room full of football players and the so-phisticated lady becomes a scamp."

"And what kind of self-respecting Southern woman would I be if I didn't love football, especially college ball? Go Tigers!" Ashley pumped her arm in the air. "While I do tend to keep the scamp caged, she occasionally comes out to play."

Before they could reach the barbeque food station they'd originally targeted, Ashley made a sharp U-turn and detoured toward one of the dessert stations. "Oh, would you look at those brownies. Okay, we have to stop here first. Can't you just taste that chocolatey goodness?" She wiggled her arm through the crowd and snagged two plates.

"Remind me never to get between you and your dessert," Robert laughed. "You're like a kid in a candy store. Who would have thought that a tiny little thing like you would be an avid foodie?"

She sighed dramatically, "Much as I hate to exercise, this event means I'll spend a few extra hours at the gym this week," she glanced down at her program and all the restaurants represented, "but it will be *so* worth it. Now let's go check out your barbecue."

Ashley had just taken a bite of the Pecan Smoked Baby Back Ribs, when she felt an unmistakable presence enter the room. Just like a kid connecting the dots in a picture, her eyes found Zach, Nate, and what must be the third brother, Josh, standing in the entryway. Zach seemed to have a sixth sense about where to find her as well and immediately directed his steps her way. Zip, zing, zap and a ton of sizzle started in her scalp then tunneled south straight to the gut. What is it about that man that revs up her engines?

"I'll be darned," drawled Zach in his turn-your-in-sides-to-molten-lava voice after he made his way to her side. "You were just in my dreams and now here you are in the flesh. I am one lucky man." He leaned forward and let their lips brush briefly. "Hello," he said with that smile that melted her heart.

Despite the brevity – or maybe because of the brevity – her lips, her heart, and every female bit of her wanted more. Momentarily at a loss for words, something totally out of character for her, she just stared.

Zach waved a hand in front of her face. "Aren't you going to introduce me to your friend?"

Her cool mask fell back into place. "Zach, I'd like you to meet my *date* for the evening, Robert Prichard... Robert, this overly friendly fellow is Zach Kincaid."

The men shook hands. "And these are my brothers, Nate and Josh," said Zach.

"I've heard of you. Nice belt buckle," Robert observed. "Pro rodeo World Champion Team Roper three years in a row. I saw you at the last Stephenville rodeo. Those runs you made were amazing. Didn't think that steer could be caught in under 5 seconds."

"I had no idea you followed the rodeo," Ashley said to Robert.

"I'm a Texan so there's a little cowboy in all of us. He glanced across the room. "Sweetie, I see one of my clients over there and I need to go say hi. If you want to chat with your friends a little longer, that's fine by me. Just catch up with me when you're done." He looped his arm across her shoulders and gave her a quick, friendly squeeze.

"Sure, I'll be along shortly," she said with a puzzled frown.

The brothers exchanged an 'is this man crazy' look.

"Bet you're not used to having your guy leave you stranded. Frankly I'd say he is one bubble off plumb," Zach rubbed the stubble on his jaw. "Far be it from me though to look a gift horse in the mouth." He hooked his thumbs into his belt loops and rocked back on his heels. "I'd be more than happy to keep you company."

He glanced over at his brothers. "Don't you two have someplace else you need to be?"

Nate looked at Zach and shook his head. "No, I'm fine right here. Josh, you?"

"Me neither," Josh said. He stuck out his hand, looking a bit uncomfortable, but smiled shyly. "Hi, I'm Josh," he said to Ashley.

Zach scowled at his brothers, then turned his back on them to face Ashley. His brothers shrugged and wandered off to the next food station.

"You've got just a bit of sauce right here." He touched her chin with his thumb while he feathered his finger across her lip.

Everything stopped like one of those freeze frames in the movies. She couldn't form a coherent thought for the span of thirty seconds.

She gazed deeply into his eyes lost in their Topaz depths and in a room crowded with people, filled with noise – there was silence.

A man bumped Ashley as he reached for a sample on the table jolting her back into action. She dabbed at her chin with her napkin.

"Did I get it?"

"Almost... Here, let me help." Zach softly kissed the spot on her chin, then used his thumb to wipe away the trace of sauce that remained. He sucked the remnants off his thumb and smiled in that way that short-circuited her system and had fireworks exploding in her brain. Didn't wolves have blue eyes she wondered? If the smoky look he was giving her was any indication, then it would seem he wanted to devour more than the smidgen of sauce on his thumb.

"Thanks," she whispered, her usual witty repartee disappearing into the ether, but somewhere she heard the tom-tom beat... Good boy. Bad boy. Choose. Choose. Choose.

He wanted to whoop for joy at the dazed expression on her face but was afraid his expression matched hers and decided to shelve the implications of his reaction. Talk about a herd of stampeding cattle churning their way through his gut. Damn, was about all his brain could process which is why he said the most inane thing possible.

"Didn't peg you for a football fan."

"Hmmm," she murmured as she moved out of the fog. "I'm a woman of the South so why ever not?" She stepped back putting distance between them.

He stepped closer, crowding her, wanting to rattle her, maybe make her question that silly plan of hers. Like real love is something you can fit into a neat package he scoffed.

"I don't know. You strike me as a champagne and caviar woman more than a beer and pretzels fan." He snagged his hat by the crown, held it in front of him like a shield and shuffled his feet.

"Really?" She looked up at him through the veil of her thick, dark lashes. "Not very observant are you? I drank beer at the dance hall when we met. I guess there is a lot you don't know about me... Now if you will excuse me, I need to rejoin my date." She stepped around him and walked off, her posture regal and features carefully steeled into detached indifference, so different than his dance hall siren.

When Nate and Josh sidled up to Zach, Nate made pretend guns with his hands and pointed them at Zach. "The great Zach Kincaid... shot down." The brothers hooted with laughter while Zach sulked, but he couldn't stop watching her from across the room – watching her turn heads as she moved between the food stations. The woman was seduction personified in that slinky black dress and what those heels did to her legs was enough to make a man whimper. Every red-blooded male in the room was surely lusting after her – except the man she was with. Odd, he thought.

He wasn't thrilled when arm-and-arm Ashley and Robert left the event. They made a pretty picture, heads together, laughing. Was she going home with him? Would she be spending the night with him? An unfamiliar jealously rocked his steady world. He found himself looking forward to next week's lunch date when he'd have Ashley all to himself.

Chapter Four

MONDAY MORNING LAUREN FOUND Ashley standing at the kitchen counter nursing a cup of coffee. She was eating a whole wheat English muffin topped with peanut butter while she assembled her lunch.

"Have you already been out doing yoga?" Ashley asked then held up her hand to stop Lauren's response. "Wait. On second thought, I don't want to hear about your virtuousness."

"No need to feel guilty just because you didn't start your day immersing yourself in peace and tranquility." She flashed a devilish grin and poked her friend in the side. "But I don't mind donning the virtuous mantle because I did." She clasped her hands together in front of her face and bowed. "But you are ready to head off to work and I'm not, so we're even. How was your date Saturday night?"

"Robert is reeeaaally nice. I had a great time with him and the event was fabulous, so many football greats that it was impossible to meet them all. I'll show you the photos tonight of all the elbow-rubbing I got to do." She faced her friend. "You will *never* guess who else showed up."

"Nate and his brothers," Lauren stated calmly bursting Ashley's rumor-sharing bubble.

"How did you know?"

"Nate mentioned they had tickets when we talked on Friday."

"And you didn't tell me I might run into them?" Ashley fumed.

"You'd already left to meet Robert," Lauren shrugged.

"And your thumbs were broken so you couldn't text me with the news?"

"I thought you weren't the least bit interested in the comings and goings of the Kincaid clan, so didn't think it was important." She fluttered her eyes at Ashley. "Was I wrong?"

"You're right. I'm not the least bit interested in that footloose and fancy-free hombre, but I was there with Robert – who could be 'the one' – and didn't appreciate Zach horning in." With studied indifference she started placing her lunch items into her tote.

"If you say so," Lauren smiled serenely. "By the way, I asked Nate if they could help you move this weekend. All three will be showing up with pickup trucks and trailers in tow. I cancelled the moving van and crew."

"You didn't!"

"I did and I want to hear, 'thank you Lauren for saving me a lot of money that can now go toward fabulous furniture purchases' coming out of your mouth."

Ashley rolled her eyes. "Okay, thank you. Speaking of moving, Robert and his decorator are going furniture shopping with me in a few weeks to help me fill in the gaps." She touched her friend's arm. "You should see Robert's house! It's way beyond fabulous!!"

"Furniture shopping? You're taking this man you've dated twice now, furniture shopping?? I'm trying to form an image in my mind of Zach going furniture shopping with you." Lauren shook her head. "It's just not happening."

"Robert has exceptional taste." Ashley said primly then grinned, "but you're right, Zach would be a bit out of his element. Robert, on the other hand, can help turn my house into a showcase. That's one of the reasons I enjoy being with him. Shopping with Robert is like... "

"Shopping with your girlfriends," Lauren finished. "Doesn't sound like a red, hot romance to me."

"Excuse me, but lots of great relationships start out as great friendships first," Ashley closed the kitchen cabinet with a resounding *thwack*. "Sorry," she scrunched her shoulders and grimaced. "It slipped from my fingers. So what if Robert and I are friends for now? I can live with that, especially given my history with red, hot romances. I'm tired of getting burned."

"I hear you," Lauren dabbed at her face with her towel. "On another subject, are you still having lunch with Zach this week?"

"Yes, on Wednesday." Ashley picked up her lunch and briefcase. "I have to dash. See you tonight."

· ♥ · ♥ · ♥ · ♥ · ♥ ·

ZACH PULLED OPEN ONE of the glass doors and stepped into the reception area of Bartlett, Simon, and Thompson CPAs located in one of San Antonio's downtown high-rise buildings. Dark green wing chairs separated by small side tables lined the walls. Mile deep carpet the color of cinnamon covered the floor. Green plants and neatly displayed financial magazines were strategically placed around the room. Vibrant paintings of Texas landscapes in heavy frames hung on the walls. A beehive of activity took place beyond the glass wall behind the tall reception counter of polished wood that jutted out into the room in a semi-circle. He walked up to the reception counter and smiled at the young woman waiting to greet him.

"Hi, I'm here to see Ashley Drayton."

The receptionist returned his smile, then her eyes widened. "Oh my gosh, you're Zach Kincaid. I saw you win the National Championship in Las Vegas in December. You and Matt smoked the competition."

"Thank you," he said as he tipped his hat.

"I'll buzz Miss Drayton and let her know you're here. Would you like to take a seat? Can I get you some water or a soda?"

"No on both. I'm fine." He rested his forearm on the high countertop and leaned in to chat.

"She'll be right out," the receptionist said as she gazed up into the handsome face that graced so many rodeo posters.

And that's where Ashley found Zach a few minutes later engaged in conversation with the firm's sweet, young receptionist. What a flirt he is, she thought. She could almost see the young woman's heart doing the same flip-flops that Ashley's was doing at the sight of him.

He was the pied piper of women with a string of them following those sexy broad shoulders and narrow hips anywhere he wanted to lead. Most likely the nearest bedroom – that would be her choice – or not she thought hurriedly. Ashley rubbed a spot on her diaphragm to ease the knot taking up residence there, then shifted her shoulders to release the tension. Dang man, ought to have a neon 'heart-breaker' sign hanging over his head.

Zach glanced up. Did the world just tilt on its axis? He felt the urge to jump in the air and click his heels together at the sheer joy of seeing her again. This look was different than the playful woman in the red dress and cowboy boots he met last week at the dance hall. Today she was more like the elegant woman he met at Saturday's event – no less stimulating judging from his reaction, just different. She wore a severe business suit with her hair done in some sort of bun thing. Course a man could still appreciate the view of shapely legs and the way that tight skirt molded her perfect butt. Those sexy heels made him think of a different kind of business altogether. He hoped he wasn't drooling.

Ashley approached him with hand outstretched. "Hello Zach, so good to see you again," she said in a cool, cultured, all-business tone. "I hope your filming went well."

So this is how it's going to play. "I got all the right words out so my sponsor was happy and that's what counts."

Looking from the perky receptionist to Zach she asked, "Do you two know each other?"

"No, just met," Zach replied, "but it turns out, Cindy here, is one of my fans." He winked at the young woman who blushed furiously.

"I see." Ashley turned to the receptionist, "Cindy, Mr. Kincaid and I will be in a lunch meeting. I should be back in the office in about an hour." She pivoted back to Zach. "I made lunch reservations at just down the street. Shall we go?"

He raised his eyebrows, recognizing the popular eatery. "Lead the way. You look nice by the way." He paused, considering. "Very professional, aloof."

"Thank you, except for that aloof part maybe." He held the door open for her. "A woman has to dress the part if she wants to be taken

49

seriously, especially someone like me who happens to be height challenged. There's something about being 5'2" that apparently distorts a man's vision."

Zach figured the male reaction had more to do with her sexy Ferrari figure than her height but decided it would be best not to mention that.

· ♥ · ♥ · ♥ · ♥ · ♥ ·

ONCE THEY WERE SEATED, he said, "That was some shindig on Sunday. Robert seems like a good guy. Do you plan to keep seeing him?"

"Oh he is and yes I do," Ashley gracefully placed the linen napkin in her lap. "He's sweet as can be, owns one of the largest real estate firms in the Dallas area, haven't heard or read anything about him breaking hearts and he doesn't seem to gamble or is involved in extreme sports. In my book, he's very nearly perfect." She smoothed her hand along her hair ensuring no tendrils had escaped.

Conversation stalled as the waiter returned, took their order, gathered their menus, and left.

"Enough about my life. Tell me about the commercial you just taped. I've never been part of anything like that. I'd love to hear what it's like. What did you have to do?" Ashley's eyes held quiet curiosity but something else simmered beneath the surface. He could feel it.

"We'd already filmed at our ranch to show the rope – the product I'm promoting – in action with me and Matt, my partner, in the arena. Today we filmed the talking head shots against a green screen segment so that can be edited in later."

He couldn't help himself and reached across the table to capture her hand in his. Breathing slowed as he toyed with her fingers. He stared into violet eyes and she into eyes the color of robin's eggs, as the seconds ticked by.

A discrete cough pulled them back to the present. They looked up at the waiter as he slid their steaming plates in front of them. "Be careful, the plates are hot," he cautioned.

For a minute there, Zach was sure he'd been tossed into the middle of some Bogart and Bacall film scene filled with sexual tension. Gauging from Ashley's expression, she'd been there right along with him and wasn't thrilled with the detour their thoughts had taken.

Zach decided to ignore whatever that interlude had been. "Where was I? Oh, commercials. Ropes are just one of my endorsement deals. I also do commercials for animal feed nutrient enhancements, saddles, and boots." He shifted a booted foot out from under the table and into the aisle where she could see it.

"Nice boots," she murmured as she gently grasped her knife in one hand and her fork in the other precisely cutting through her Chimichanga.

"Endorsements bring in a nice chunk of change and someday, when I retire from the rodeo, will help keep the ranch on solid ground." He could see from her quizzical expression that she was probably wondering the same thing he was, why was he telling her this? Was he trying to impress her? Show her he was just as good a provider as Robert? What was wrong with him today?

"Diversifying your income stream is always a good strategy." That was lame she thought. You couldn't have asked him an intelligent question about the products he endorses? She gave herself a mental

51

head slap. "This food is amazing. I need to add some Mexican recipes to my repertoire."

"You cook?"

"Don't sound so surprised," she teased. "Yes, much to the consternation of my mother who believes only the household cook should handle food preparation. I love to cook, especially baking, but am constantly searching for new recipes to try."

"Well if you ever need a guinea pig to test recipes on, I'm your man." He smiled fondly with a faraway look in his eye. "My mama cooks up a storm and was always experimenting. Luckily for us, she had a knack for pulling things together." He took another bite of his enchilada, closing his eyes to better savor the flavors of cheese, chicken, and Pico de Gallo sauce.

"Your mother sounds like quite a woman."

"That she is." He cocked his head to the side. "I know you like to dance, cook and your mama raised you to be a lady – even if she may not have succeeded," his slow smile made her wish she had a fan, "but your rebellious streak had you running the family plantation instead. How does being an accountant fit into that picture? Seems a little strait-laced for a rebel."

"I've always had a head for numbers and solid organizational skills so accounting came naturally. It also helped keep peace in the family since accounting is an acceptable occupation until I find a respectable husband. After that, according to my mother, my job is to use my social and charitable activities to make my husband a pillar in the community."

Zach's head snapped back and his eyebrows shot up. "Why don't you tell me how you really feel about your mother's plans for your life? Is that why you want someone like Robert because he passes muster?"

"No, that's not why I'm attracted to Robert. I like him because he's different than the other men I've been involved with and I think it's time I tried something different. What's the saying, if you keep doing the same thing and expect different results, you're crazy? I'm tired of being crazy." She realigned her silverware.

"I hear you. No more crazy." He rested his forearms on the table and leaned forward. "So if you hadn't felt compelled to go into accounting, what would you have done?"

"Tough question. I've never really thought about it." She paused scrunching her forehead in thought. "Managing the plantation has always been deeply satisfying... deciding which crops and livestock are best suited to the land, how we might diversify our operation, looking for trends and new business opportunities... I suppose I might have gone that route all things being equal. I might also have enjoyed running a children's charity or a food bank... but I guess we'll never know."

"Why do you say that?" He looked puzzled. "You can always change course. In fact sometimes life doesn't give you a choice, you either change or turn to dust. I see that all the time in the rodeo. We age out when our bodies can't do what we need it to do, or there's an accident or a family crisis and then you need to find something else that makes you want to get up in the morning. While rodeo is how people know me, it's what defines me, someday I'll have to give it up."

"I think that's the most I've heard you say in one sitting." She ran her hands over the napkin in her lap smoothing out nonexistent wrinkles. "Even though my parents are a bit distant, I think they do love me in their way and I don't want to cause them pain. While my natural inclination is to raise a little hell," she smiled sweetly but mischief danced in her eyes. "I'm okay with compromise."

"I understand wanting to please your parents but I also know it's important to choose your own path... not try and be something you're not." He flashed that heart-stopping, devilish grin. "Just remember, you *are* in Texas now where the song says, 'Don't Fence Me In.' Words we live by around here."

The waiter stepped up, "Would you like me to clear your plates? Can I get you some coffee and dessert?"

"No on coffee and dessert, but thank you," Ashley said. "Just the check please."

When the waiter set the folder with the check in front of them, Zach quickly snatched it up. "I'm paying. I invited you out to lunch, remember?"

Ashley held up her hands in surrender. "Far be it from me to tread on a man's ego. Feel free... but Lauren did tell me that you and your brothers will be helping me move on Saturday so I thought lunch was the least I could do... You are still planning to help?"

The worried look on her face jangled every protective nerve in his body. "Have no fear, darlin' the cavalry will be on Lauren's doorstep bright and early Saturday." He put his hand over hers. "Don't you know that it's part of the cowboy creed. We never go back on our word. I won't let you down."

Chapter Five

♥

"So how did your lunch date go?" Lauren asked as the pair settled on the sofa for their evening chat.

"It wasn't a date," Ashley wagged her finger at her friend. "Just two acquaintances sharing conversation and a meal. When you and I go to lunch, it's not a date."

"Yeah, but I'm not one scorching hot cowboy who makes a woman think about a tumble in the hay."

Ashley rolled her eyes. "Get your mind out of the gutter. Yes, he is attractive and ruggedly handsome and fun to be with, but I'm not going down that road." She crossed her arms decisively. "He does have more layers than I expected, though."

"Given how competitive the professional rodeo circuit is, how driven someone has to be to get to the top *plus* run a successful ranch operation, it only makes sense his 'aw shucks' manner hides a complicated man."

"You're right but I was still surprised to find an intelligent, perceptive man under that Stetson when what I expected was an all macho, jump-right-in-without-looking man." Ashley shrugged. "I guess I pictured him as Rambo on a horse. Someone who takes out an army with one hand tied behind his back."

Lauren's attempt to stifle her laughter turned into a snort. "What you're saying is that you thought he would lasso you, throw you to the ground, and ravish you?"

"A girl can only dream," Ashley sighed, then slapped her forehead with her palm. "I have to stop thinking like this or I will never break the bad boy cycle. What is *wrong* with me?" she wailed.

"Nothing is wrong with you except maybe you read too many fairy tales as a kid. Most people are not all good *or* all bad but somewhere in between. Here, have some popcorn." Lauren leaned forward to pluck the bowl from the coffee table and placed it between them. "You know what I think...?"

"No but I have the feeling you are going to tell me." Ashley poked her friend in the ribs with her elbow.

Lauren put on the marriage and family counselor face she usually reserved for smart-mouthed teens, then continued. "As I was saying, you expect the bad boys you're attracted to, to behave like princes instead of the toads they really are. In reality we all have warts, some folks just have more warts than others. Someday you will fall for the guy whose warts aren't fatal. Until then, just like the rest of us, it's all trial and error."

"So maybe with Robert I've finally broken the bad boy spell?" she asked hopefully.

"Do you really feel all warm and glowy when you're with Robert? You can't wait to see him again when you're apart?" Lauren arched her brows and gave Ashley that 'tell me the truth' look.

Ashley frowned, then flopped back against the sofa cushions. "No, but maybe that will all come in time. We've only dated twice and I really do like him. He's warm and charming and we could be best friends. Isn't that a good basis for a lasting relationship?"

"Mmm, hmm," Lauren nodded her head sagely, "and how does Zach make you feel?" She held up her pinky finger. "Pinky swear?"

Ashley hooked her pinky finger with Lauren's. "Swear."

"Most likely the way Nate makes you feel. Like you've just started down the ski run and a shiver of excitement tingles all the way down to your toes. I want to jump into his arms and kiss him silly to see if the next kiss will be as mind-shattering as the last." Ashley covered her eyes with her hand. "I'm doomed." She rolled her head to the side to look at Lauren, misery etched in her delicate face. "Why can't I feel that way about someone like Robert?"

Lauren bent her head over her chamomile tea, inhaling deeply of the calming, herbal scent. "You like bad boys. They give you permission to cut loose, step out of the prim and proper role you've been forced in to."

Restless, Ashley got up from the sofa and walked over to the dining table where she started wrapping the dishes waiting to be packed. "I'm listening, but I need to keep my hands busy."

"Bad boys don't care whether or not you like them. They're a challenge. They love pushing the boundaries and give women a chance to walk on the wild side. There is a part of you that identifies with your bad boy and sets your attraction meter ticking. Let's face it Ash, you can't resist a challenge and walking on the wild side is your specialty."

"Is not."

"You and your little red Miata say otherwise – I rest my case."

"Okay, point taken. I did love the feeling I got roaring down the highway with the wind in my face, sunshine pouring in around me. My Miata spells freedom – freedom from convention, freedom to be me, freedom to explore the many roads I could take. Man, I miss that car."

"Then there is the matter of your mother pushing you into dating those guys. Granted, they were preppy bad boys instead of James Dean bad boys, but despite their polished exterior, they only cared about themselves. Personally, I don't think your mother gets it. She's as narcissistic as the men she deemed appropriate for you. *She* married a man like that and never got hurt because she doesn't care about anything other than the status your father provides. You *actually care* about other people and their feelings, so you get hurt."

Ashley placed the final dish in the box and picked up the packing tape dispenser to seal the box.

Lauren set the popcorn bowl back on the table. "Other than Robert's obvious financial stability and being the safe choice, are there any sparks? Remember, pinky swear."

Ashley eased back onto the sofa sinking into its embrace. "Sparks? Not exactly." She closed her eyes. "Since we did pinkie swear... this is embarrassing... after our date, when we said goodbye, he hugged me, kissed me on the forehead, and sent me back to my hotel, alone." Ashley grimaced, "Can't nice guys like me or am I always going to be consigned to the bargain basement bin for jerks?"

"Zach likes you."

"Great, another bad boy destined to stomp my heart under his boot. With him, I'm jumping from the frying pan into the fire cause Zach is so much hotter than any of the other men I've fallen for."

"Oh, Ashley, Ashley, Ashley," Lauren laughed. "Give the man a chance. From what I've seen, he may *look* like a bad boy, but I don't think that's who he is."

·♥·♥·♥·♥·♥·

THE DEEP RUMBLE OF powerful trucks and the clatter of trailers brought Ashley to the window. She quickly finished pulling her long, thick hair into a tidy ponytail then waltzed into the living room to let temptation, in the form of three hunky brothers, cross the threshold.

"Hi, y'all. Thanks so much for your help today, especially given today's expected rain showers."

Zach nearly tripped over his feet at the sight of her all sexy in tight black leggings and a loose-fitting sweater that barely covered her gorgeous butt. That outfit showed off everything a woman should have to drive a man to distraction and had his fingers itching to get under the hem of that sweater. What she was wearing should be illegal and probably was in twenty states. Why was she staring at him like she expected him to do something? Oh yeah, she probably expected him to say something.

"You're welcome, pretty lady. Not to worry. We brought plenty of plastic tarps. According to the weather report, the rain should be light and spotty so we should be fine." He surveyed the room. "Where do you want us to start?"

He was going to kill his brothers if either one of them made the snide remark he knew was on the tip of their tongues.

Lauren strolled into the room bearing a tray of muffins. "Hey guys, coffee is in the kitchen."

"You cook something other than that vegetarian stuff?" Nate asked.

"Yes, Mr. Meat and Potatoes man, I do, but these scrumptious morsels just happen to be one of Ashley's creations." She set the tray on the dining room table. "Someday I will get you to broaden your palette and eat a little healthier."

Zach picked up a muffin, peeled the paper wrapper and devoured half in one bite. He held the remaining half out, examining it closely. "This is amazing. What's in it?"

"They're Orange Coconut Muffins."

"Man, I could chow down on these all day. If you find the plate empty, you should probably blame me."

"Do you have any idea how much women hate hearing that a man can eat several dozen muffins a day and still look great. Life is just not fair." Ashley shuddered. "Think fingernails on a chalk board.

"You think I look great?"

"You know you do." Her inspection started at his Stetson and ended with his boots. He felt like a cell under a microscope squirming across her field of vision. "For a man that spends his days chasing cows."

His brothers cleared their throats and Zach glared at them.

"All of the boxes go and the furniture in the guest bedroom over there, plus those bar stools." Ashley slowly pivoted glancing around the room to make sure she hadn't missed anything. Nodding, "Yup, that is the sum total of my worldly possessions."

"Well this won't take long. We'll have you in your new place in no time." Zach looked at her curiously. "You travel kind of light."

"I got rid of just about everything when I left South Carolina." She crooked her finger. "Follow me and I'll show you my bedroom." She sashayed off down the hall. The woman was not making it easy to keep his mind on taking beds apart instead of putting them to a much better use.

Zach paused in the doorway inventorying the room. Boxes marked shoes covered the bed and a big stack of empty wardrobe boxes leaned against the wall. "I may have to revise my timetable just a bit." He opened the walk-in closet door. "Lady, you have a lot of clothes. Are you sure you have enough boxes?" He glanced at the shelves still loaded with shoes. "More shoes?"

"A woman cannot have too many shoes. And yes, all of that goes and yes, the clothes will fit in the boxes." She shoved the closet door shut. "I didn't say I was without sin," she snapped. "I like clothes." She counted to ten. "As soon as you clear a few things out of this room, I'll have the remaining boxes packed in a jiffy."

Zach wandered over to the bathroom and poked his head around the door. He stepped in and picked up one of what looked like a zillion jars and tubes of beauty dodads scattered across the counter. Ashley was right on his heels.

"Honey, you do know you're beautiful, right? What in the Sam Hill do you need all this for?" He motioned to the counter.

"So shoot me. I like girly products." She snatched the jar from his hand and tossed it back into the jumble. "Do you always just walk up and handle a woman's private things?" She knew as soon as the words were out of her mouth that she was traveling down a slippery slope.

Oh, there were so many things he could say here he thought.

"Wipe that smile off your face and get busy." Hands fisted on her hips, stance commanding, she tried hard but couldn't keep the gentle flirt out of her voice. "Don't you have some moving to do?"

"Yes ma'am. Gettin' to work right now." He figured a salute probably wouldn't win him any points so resisted the urge.

With the last piece of furniture stowed in the trailers or tied down in the trucks, Zach leaned against the vehicle under the umbrella Ashley carried and accepted the cup of coffee and muffin she offered.

"I thought you could use a little pick-me-up."

Yeah, he could use a pick-me-up all right but doubted she was offering what he craved. He pulled open the cab door, "Ride with me." He smiled at her indecision. "What's the matter? Afraid to be alone with me?"

"Not on your life, cowboy. I'll just go get my purse."

A few minutes later she clambered into the truck. "I'm so glad you have a running board. Sometimes getting into these things is murder on a short person."

"You climb in a lot of trucks, do you?"

"Huh?"

"Forget it."

"Nice." She ran her hands over the buttery-soft leather interior. "Looks like you have all the bells and whistles. First class all the way." Good Lord, she thought, stop running off at the mouth. Just because she'd spent the last few hours admiring the way his muscles bunched and released while he moved heavy boxes and the way his jeans molded to those powerful legs was no excuse for letting the man get under her skin.

He brushed his hands back and forth along the edges of his seat grazing her thigh in the process. "When I won the Nationals last time, this baby was part of the prize." His finger hovered over the navigation system. "Where to?"

The jolt of electricity at his light touch skimmed down her spine and lodged in her gut. Oh, my, maybe she should ride with Josh instead, someone safe, but it was too late. She quickly rattled off the address and he slipped the powerful machine into drive.

He noticed her glancing at his temperature gauge. "Are you cold? Do you want me to turn up the heat?"

"No, I was actually thinking it's a little warm." She ran a finger around the edge of her sweater pulling it away from her neck.

She gazed out the window at the passing landscape. "I love the sky here in Texas. Most days they're so bright and crisp, like a new apple." She turned back to look at him. "It's so different than the South Carolina Low Country where we see a lot of fog, rain and gray skies during the winter. So depressing. The sunshine makes me happy."

The radio blared out country music and she started bouncing and weaving in time to, 'Shotgun Rider.' "I love this song. It has such a great beat and perfect for driving. I saw Tim McGraw in concert last June in North Carolina. That man is smokin' hot."

She started belting out the chorus in a sultry, low-pitched voice."

The lyrics about waking up looking into someone's eyes would definitely put some thoughts in a man's head.

"Thanks again for helping me move." She touched his arm and smiled. "I'm sure you had better things to do with your day than lugging boxes and furniture around."

His mouth crooked up in a lopsided grin. "You always this chatty?"

"Am I bothering you? I can be quiet if you prefer."

"No, I like to hear you sing and frankly, helping you move is more fun than mending fences where I would be getting all wet and muddy right about now. I'm much happier in the company of a beautiful woman."

"And I suppose lines like that have women falling all over themselves to be with you?" Sarcasm dripped off her oh, so fake smile. She needed the sarcasm to chase away the images of him all wet and muddy. It was definitely getting hot in here.

"Ouch, prickly little thing" He stuck his finger in his mouth and sucked like he had touched a thorn. "I haven't had a shortage of women, so my lines seem to be working fine. You do know that a snooty attitude is unbecoming a lady?"

"And you know that players and heart-breakers need not apply?" Darned if she didn't wish he was sucking on her fingers instead of his own.

"You are a tough one to figure. One minute you are all bubbly and sweet as my mom's apple pie and the next you're all business and hands off. You run hot and cold. Do you do that on purpose to keep men tied in knots?"

The navigation system alerted them to their exit. "Saved by Sally," Ashley chirped.

"Who?"

"The navigation voice. That's what I call mine. Why is the voice on these gadgets always female?"

"Because women love to tell men where to go," he groused.

"Since you're doing me a favor today, I'm going to pretend I didn't hear that." She clapped her hands and bounced in her seat. "Here it is. Just pull all the way into the driveway. See how it swings behind the garage? There should be room for everyone."

"Do I look like I wouldn't have figured that out and pulled all the way in?"

"Oh, come on, I'm sorry. I'm just so excited – and before you say anything, I know I like to control things. Don't be a grouch. I promise I'll be nice."

"How nice?"

She gave him a long-suffering eye roll. "If you promise to stop hitting on me."

"What would be the fun in that, half-pint? You take the bait so well." He held up his hands in surrender when his answer was a steely glare. "Truce?"

"Sure, since flirting with every female around seems to be as natural for you as breathing, I doubt I can make you stop. But just so you know, calling me half-pint is fighting words." She made a fist under his nose then hopped out leaving the cab door open, scampering over to Nate, Lauren, and Josh as they stepped out of their trucks. Zach circled his pickup, closed the door and strode after Ashley.

"Once everything is unloaded, I have Black Bean Chili and cornbread for lunch. I don't want anyone to go away hungry."

Two hours later everyone sat cross-legged on the floor in the breakfast area off the kitchen. They'd pushed boxes together to form a make-shift table. Ashley had covered it with a cloth and placed a small vase of flowers in the middle. Quiet prevailed as they huddled over their bowls of the hearty stew.

"Woman, I have no idea why you became an accountant instead of a chef. You've got mean skills." Zach leaned back bracing himself on his arms.

"You can cook for us anytime," agreed the taciturn Nate while Josh nodded shyly.

"Nice place you've got here and that view..." Zach smiled at her as he watched her lips curve in contentment.

"The view was one of the reasons I choose this home, the wide-open spaces for a backyard had my name on it. I couldn't pass this up. That, and the complex is new, so everything is fresh and clean, it's in a nice neighborhood, not too far from work and the interior spaces are big enough so I don't feel cramped, but not so big that I have to spend all my free time cleaning."

"Not much chance you'd have to spend a lot of time cleaning with so little to clean. Kind of sparse, isn't it? I'm guessing you have plans to fill it up a bit," Zach observed.

"Oh, yes. Plans with a capital 'P.' I can hardly wait. Robert's coming next weekend to take me furniture shopping."

"A guy is taking you furniture shopping?" Nate's expression said he didn't believe his ears. "What in the world for? I guess I understand dragging a husband along so he can pay for everything, but you're just taking some guy you know furniture shopping? What kind of man is he?"

"Ah, Nate," Lauren gently laid one hand on his arm and with fingertips on his chin turned his head to face her. "He's the kind of man that doesn't feel challenged by a furniture store. Men can go shopping and actually enjoy the experience. Not all activities in life can be neatly pigeon-holed into male and female domains. Men and women both do what needs to be done." She walked her fingers up his arm and smiled as he ducked his head. "Men have tended the children and women have worked the farm and neither is worse off for the experience."

"So you'd be fine with me putting on an apron and cooking dinner every night?"

"I have no problem dividing up the household chores in any way that works best for the couple." Lauren leaned forward, propping her elbows on the boxes and resting her chin in her hands. "Nate, no matter what, I respect you and you will always be one sexy guy to me."

"As much as I enjoy listening to you two jaw at each other, here's an idea, if you two," Zach dipped his chin in the general direction of Ashley and Lauren, "don't have plans for tomorrow, we'll all be watching the playoff game at my place. Why don't you join us? We're barbecuing and hanging out, so very casual."

Ashley looked at Lauren who nodded. "I should get my house in order but who can pass up football. Green Bay against Dallas. It should be a good game. Just tell us what time and where?"

Chapter Six

♥

"It's so beautiful out here." Ashley stepped out of her BMW sedan, stopping to fill her lungs with air as crisp and clean as mountain snowpack. She opened the rear door of her car and ducked into the back seat to retrieve the food she'd brought.

Ashley watched Zach approach in his long-legged, fluid stride and felt those pesky butterflies start dancing around her stomach. His two border collies frisked around his feet then ran forward to greet their guests. Ashley ruffled the fur on their heads and scratched their ears.

"Welcome to the Rocking K ladies. Let me take that." He scooped up the baking pan and plastic container Ashley carried. "What's in here?" He lifted the foil and his eyes crossed in pleasure. "Spareribs? And cake too?"

"Yes, Hawaiian Spareribs and coconut cake. The spareribs are pre-cooked so only need to be on the grill long enough to heat and baste with the sauce."

She did a slow 360 degree pivot captivated by the wood-sided ranch house in front of her, picturesque barn to her right, corral, tree-studded rolling pastures beyond and hacienda-style, main ranch compound off to her left. "Breathtaking. I can see why you love it so much. I'd never want to leave either."

"Even though all this natural beauty is God's doing not mine, it means a lot when other people appreciate it too." He stood for a moment looking off at the horizon, a proud smile playing around his lips. "Come on inside. No sense standing out here in the cold."

She followed him up the three steps to the wide, wooden porch that formed a 'U' around the front of the house. Zach opened the front door and stepped aside so Ashley and Lauren could enter.

One look told her she was in man territory. It boasted wide oak-plank flooring, a well-used leather chesterfield sofa ringed with overstuffed pillows, a padded circular ottoman covered in black and white cowhide just begging for booted feet to rest on it and a high, vaulted log ceiling. Wagon wheel chandeliers hung from suspended beams, a 70" flat-screen television dominated one of the flat hewn log walls and a pool table and old-fashioned bar – the kind you needed to belly up to – occupied one entire corner of the room. A huge stone fireplace crackled merrily filling the room with warmth. Multiple conversations swirled around her.

"Here, let me introduce you around. This is my mama, Gloria June. My dad, Jack. You know Nate and Josh. One of the little guys tearing the place up is Josh's son, Chad. These are two of my cousins, Wayne and Brad and Brad's wife, Marie." The cousin group nodded or wiggled their fingers as Zach pointed them out. "This is Matt, my partner, and his wife, Heather."

Zach's mom uncurled with the grace of a matriarchal tigress and stalked over to Ashley and Lauren. The next thing they knew, Gloria

June had one arm around each of them, locking them in a rib-busting hug.

"So glad you two ladies could join us. I always feel out-numbered at these shindigs by all the men folk," she purred in her husky contralto. "Zach, quit gawking and go put those things in the kitchen. Father, how is that grill coming?" she said to the man whose good looks declared he was responsible for siring this clan.

"Don't know, but I guess I better go check." He got up from the leather recliner with a good-natured grunt and wink for his favorite lady.

"Yes, I guess you better," but the attractive blonde paired the statement with a warm smile.

"Come on men, let's make sure we get the food on the table before the game starts."

"Ladies, let's get the fixings put together." Ashley, Lauren, Heather, and Marie dutifully followed her lithe form into the kitchen.

Ashley gasped in delight when she spied a kitchen designed for some serious cooking. A massive Wolfe range was tucked into a rock-wall alcove, double ovens, amber-colored concrete countertops and enough space for ten people to work comfortably side-by-side rounded out the room. She ran her hand over the distressed hickory bar countertop that surrounded the sink and long working counters.

"I might have to marry your son just to get my hands on this kitchen," Ashley said.

"There are worse reasons to marry a good man," Gloria June said as she laughed and slapped her thigh. "I like your style."

"Does Zach actually use this kitchen?"

"Only if you count opening the fridge to get a beer or pull out a steak for the grill." Again, her laughter filled the room sparkling like a pure mountain stream. "When that boy want's real food, he comes on over to the main house."

She paused and pulled fresh vegetables and other salad fixings out of the fridge and handed them to Ashley and Lauren.

"I assume you two know what to do with these?" Noticing their expressions, "Sorry, didn't mean to offend. In this day and age, you never know who only knows how to open a box or grab something ready-made."

"True enough. Apology accepted." Ashley removed a Henckels slicing knife from the wooden stand. "Top of the line. Since I doubt Zach had anything to do with putting this kitchen together, let me say that I like *your* style."

"Girl, you and I are going to get along just fine. So what brought you to Texas?"

"A fresh start. My life needed a redo and Texas felt right, plus Lauren lives here."

Gloria June slipped the bowl of torn lettuce over to Lauren who efficiently dumped the vegetables she and Ashley had chopped on top of the greens. "If you don't mind my asking, what demon chased you out here? People don't pick up and leave if they're happy where they are."

Ashley pushed a strand of her long, dark hair away from her face and let the invisible string her ballet teacher always talked about pull her head toward the ceiling. "I'm not running as much as clearing the cobwebs out of my brain." She stopped to sprinkle some toasted coconut across the cake she had brought. "I wanted to put some distance between me and the pressure to be who I'm not. I want to find my own voice."

"Good girl." Gloria June put up her hand in a high five and the two smacked palms.

Marie scurried in from outside. "I'm going to start carrying the food to the table. The menfolk are pulling the meat off the barbeque as we speak... Ashley, your spareribs look heavenly."

The group gathered around the table laden with food, joined hands and said grace before filling their plates.

· ♥ · ♥ · ♥ · ♥ · ♥ ·

"Ref, what are you thinking?" Jack yelled at the television. "That was a catch! That was a touchdown. Are you blind?"

The rest of the men leapt to their feet adding their rumbling voices to the chorus of protests. Popcorn and pretzels from overturned bowls did the Mexican Jumping Bean samba across the coffee tables.

Ashley jumped up in outrage. "We've been robbed."

Lauren and Gloria June exchanged a 'they've let the looney out of the bin again' look and reached forward to start collecting the nearest dirty plates and glasses.

Ashley and Zach flopped down on the sofa together. Zach snaked his arm across her shoulders and tilted his beer bottle toward her. "Here's to next year," he said as Ashley clinked her bottle against his, took a sip and burrowed into his warmth.

"Clean-up will go a lot faster if everyone gets up off their butts and pitches in." Gloria June's tone had everyone up and snatching the nearest bowls and plates.

"Ever my darlin' wife. Your wish is our command." Jack patted her cheek affectionately. "Josh, that son of yours looks like he needs to get outside and run off some of that energy." He ruffled his grandson's dark brown curls. "Help me put the grill back in order and Chad can practice his roping." The men snagged their jackets and hats off hooks by the back door while Gloria June wrestled a wiggly Chad into his jacket.

Forty-five minutes later, dishes washed and dried and crumbs dusted up, the place was spic and span.

"Where does all this stuff go?" Zach asked.

Ashley ducked her head to hide her grin at the look mother gave son. "I swear, I don't know why I went to the bother of refurbishing this place for such an unappreciative son."

"You did it because you love all this decorating stuff," Zach groused as he hugged her. "But I do appreciate everything you do and the place does look real nice." The smile that could melt glaciers, could also melt his mother's heart.

"Such a sweet talker... but don't think I'm going to cut you any slack." She playfully slapped his arm. "That pile goes back over to the main house. Nate, Lauren, you two can cart that back for me, and Nate... that doesn't mean leaving it on the kitchen counter for me to put away. Zach, the rest goes into those cupboards. Don't give me those puppy-dog eyes. Figure it out. I'm going to see what your father and Josh are up to then head home." She gave each son a peck on the cheek, gave the girls a swift hug and strode out the door, shrugging into her jacket as she went.

"Wow, your mama doesn't take any prisoners, does she?" Ashley staggered back a bit with her hand to her chest.

"That she doesn't," Zach agreed. "Hand me the dishes, I'll put them away since I doubt you could reach without a step stool." She scowled. He laughed.

"I'm glad you're enjoying yourself, but just you remember, while dynamite comes in a small package, it packs a powerful punch."

As she handed him the last platter, he asked, "Do you have time for the ten-cent tour before you leave?"

"I thought you would never ask. Lead the way, cowboy." He took her delicate hand in his and led her through the great room. She paused to look at a painting on the wall. It was of Zach's house and barn surrounded by a field of brilliant blue flowers. "This is breathtaking."

"It's my favorite time of year so I had this made from a photo I took. The flowers start popping out around April. You'll have to come back and see them." He tugged gently on her hand and walked over to the entry where he plucked her coat off the rack and helped her into it.

Zach turned her to face him, pulling the jacket fronts together and her tight against his chest. Nerve endings all over her body came to attention, craving the kiss she was sure would come. He lowered his head slowly, giving her time to pull away. Pulling away was not an option. She wanted those full lips on hers and fueling visions of moonlight and bare skin against bare skin.

"You could spend the night so we can share more than a chaste kiss." Hope and need honeyed his voice.

"In your dreams," she sighed pushing him away. The man had no idea how unchaste his kisses were. "Friends. We're going for friends here, remember?" At least she hoped she could keep her traitorous heart from making him more important than he should be... but his kisses were addictive.

"Right, friends but I can guarantee you'll be in my dreams tonight – friends or no friends." He opened the door and motioned her on to the porch then offered his hand.

She hesitated not wanting him to think they could ever be a 'they'. The hurt look on his face made the decision for her. She put her hand in his and they walked across the broad gravel drive to the barn with the dogs trotting at their heels.

"I remember you saying you liked to ride so let's start with the barn." Zach easily slid the big barn door to one side and they stepped inside. Horses nickered softly in greeting and thrust their heads over the half doors of their stalls.

Ashley approached a sweet Bay whose ears pricked forward in anticipation and held her hand out to be sniffed by the animal's peach-fuzz muzzle. With the horse's sign of acceptance, she patted its neck.

Zach pulled a bag of sliced apples from his pocket and handed Ashley one. "I always have treats for the kids," he smiled sheepishly. A huge, Buckskin stallion nickered and gently kicked the stall door. "Ah, my boy is demanding attention." Zach moved over to the stall across the aisle, offering an apple slice then throwing his arms around the horse and patting its neck. "Buck, you big baby. Jealous that someone else is getting a little attention?"

Ashley snaked her arms around his waist, snuggling into his back and resting her face between his broad shoulders. "I can understand not wanting to share."

He turned, cupping her chin in his hand. "You can, can you? I thought you didn't like my type. Something about friends only?" Zach's lips had just claimed hers when Lauren and Nate entered the barn, hand-in-hand, shoulder-to-shoulder, heads together, laughing at some shared joke.

"If we're interrupting something, too bad," drawled Nate. Lauren punched him in the arm. "Ow! What was that for?" he said as his reserved mask slipped back into place.

"For being a really annoying big brother," Lauren chided, "and for turning back into that superhero who sees the world in this is right and that's wrong terms... leave them alone."

"What's wrong with him?" Nate drew back in shock. "He's my hero. How can anyone possibly question an American icon?"

"Nothing's wrong with your hero. He is a fine, upstanding citizen, but he can be a bit stuffy at times. A little more laughter and love in his life would be good for his soul. That's all."

Nate grunted, but recaptured Lauren's hand and gave it a squeeze.

Forehead to forehead, Ashley could feel Zach's smile against her lips. "I was just giving Ashley a tour of the property."

"Really? What property were you planning to show her, real estate or personal?" Nate smirked but used his hand to protect his shoulder from Lauren's wrath.

"Funny," Zach countered. "Ashley wanted to see the horses, but we were just getting ready to move on." Zach held up his finger to stop his brother. "Don't go there. Lauren, I don't think you've had a chance to see the place. Why don't you two join us?"

"Love to. When I was here for the barbeque last summer, I only saw the back patio and pool area and am curious to see the ranch part." She angled her head toward Nate who put his arm around her waist.

Before they moved on, Ashley whispered, "I like your kind just fine, as the sad history of my love life proves, but maybe friends with benefits is possible?"

"You two planning on joining us anytime this century?" Nate called over his shoulder.

Zack took Ashley's hand and led her down the wide aisle toward the opposite end of the building. "We've got twenty stalls in the main barn. That gives us enough space so folks can bring their own horses to the roping clinics Matt and I run. The stalls all have exterior access to individual paddocks." He gestured to a big carousel-like contraption as they passed. "Here's our indoor hot walker and next to it is our wash area. We have another hot walker and washing area outside... Tack room," he angled his head to the left so he didn't have to let go of her hand.

"The rubber padding on the floor is a nice touch. You treat your horses like royalty." Ashley observed.

"They *are* royalty." Zack stopped and lifted his hat so he could run his free hand through his hair. "This belt buckle, and all the others in my collection, belong equally to my horse." His lopsided smile made the breath catch in her throat. "Lucky for me, my horses aren't into wearing belts."

She glanced down at his belt buckle and couldn't stop her gaze from traveling just a little lower and visualizing what lay a little farther down. "Yes, lucky you," she whispered softly.

The steamy gaze Zack leveled at her telegraphed his desire to get lucky in other ways, loud and clear.

"Getting hot in here," Ashley fanned her face with her free hand.

"Sure 'nough," he agreed. "It looks like we're not the only ones."

She followed his gaze. Lauren, propped up against a stall wall, was enjoying a deep kiss from Nate until one of the horses knocked Nate's hat off. As he stopped to retrieve it, she took a few steps, glanced down with a 'got cha' smile then held out her hand to him.

"And over here," Zach said loudly, "is our veterinarian treatment room. Nate, you want to give Lauren a private tour." His expression was pure brother get even. "Ashley and I can finish up the tour without you."

Ashley stopped, turned, and held up her finger. "Uh, I don't think so, but it was a nice try. Come on you two love birds, no more dawdling. What's out this door?"

"Our training arenas, foaling barn, equipment barn, large pastures, and hay storage units." He pushed the heavy door open and they stepped back out into the cold winter air.

"I had no idea your operation was so extensive. You can't see this from the drive in." Ashley took in an array of fenced arenas, several smaller barns, hot walker, holding pens, and pastures that went on as far as her eye could see in the twilight. The main arena off to her right was ringed with bleachers, some sort of chute contraptions, and lights on poles. "This is serious business."

"That it is." Ashley heard the pride in his voice. "Besides the team roping clinics and endorsement deals, I also breed cutting horses. It takes a lot of cash to keep a ranch this size in the black, and as you said, diversity is the name of the game."

Ashley glanced up at the darkening sky. "I guess Lauren and I had better hit the road. It's been a lovely day. I had a great time." She looked up at him, "Do you know how blessed you are to have such a tight-knit, loving family?" Wistfulness tinged her words.

"As a matter of fact I do. I'm glad you enjoyed yourself. I'm leaving town for the next few weeks for the National Western Stock Show and Rodeo in Denver but will be back in time to get ready for the annual Kincaid family rodeo. I'd be obliged if you and Lauren could join us for the weekend. It will give you a good taste of what an old-fashioned rodeo is like."

"I can't speak for Lauren... though I suspect she'd be tickled pink... but you can count me in."

Zach turned her into his arms and kissed her. "I'm going to miss you."

After that kiss she knew that she would miss him too.

Chapter Seven

"OH, SWEETHEART, YOUR PLACE is fabulous," enthused Robert. "Don't you think, Stephen?"

"We're going to have fun with this," agreed Stephen. "The arched doorways, the light, the room height, these soft buckskin walls... there's so much potential here. You said Shabby Chic, right?"

"That's the style I want with bits of rustic thrown in. Ever since I first walked into the Cottage Chic store in Charlotte, I fell in love with the look. And the sumptuousness of Bella Notte and Rachel Ashwell linens," Ashley's face dissolved into coveting wistfulness, "well they are to die for, but were a bit out of my price range in college."

Stephen slapped a high-five with his new favorite client. "I hear you, girlfriend. I think our goal for today should be to find a sofa, loveseat or two upholstered chairs, coffee table, end tables and lamps and dining set."

"You are ambitious." Ashley ran a hand across her brow. "Do you really think we can find all those pieces today?"

Robert threw an arm around Ashley's shoulders and looked down at her conspiratorially. "Trust me, he can and will find all those pieces today… and some that aren't on the list, but make sure you have on comfortable walking shoes." He stepped away and stuck out his Nike clad foot. "I'd prefer my boots with this outfit," he added posing to show off his tight-fitting, long-sleeved black polo, snug designer jeans and leather bomber jacket, "but I'd rather be able to still walk at the end of the day."

Ashley eyed the high-heeled, calf-length boots in her hand. "Good point. I think I'll trade style for comfort today as well." She headed for the stairs.

"Get a move on it, woman. Time's a wasting." Stephen clapped his hands then double fist-pumped in front of him for emphasis.

The two men, huddled over Robert's smart phone, looked up as Ashley descended the stairs. "You two look cozy. What are you up to?" She could almost see the stars in Robert's eyes.

"My dealer emailed me that they just got in a 2014 Lamborghini Aventador with only nine thousand miles on it. Man, I lust after that car and I would look so hot cruising around in that."

"You would look hot driving a minivan," Stephen lightly punched Robert in the shoulder, "but toodling around town in a $400,000 vehicle might make people think they are paying you too much in commissions."

"You've got a point, but a car like that… a man can dream."

Ashley paused and shook her head to clear the image of the two of them standing so intimately together, then shrugged it off. "Boys and their toys. Okay, stop drooling over the car and let's hit the road."

·♥·♥·♥·♥·♥·

FIVE HOURS LATER, FOOT-SORE and exhausted – at least Robert and Ashley were while Stephen bounced with the energy of a man on a mission – the trio relaxed over a sandwich and iced tea, refueling for the next round.

"Stephen, I declare, if there is an eighth wonder of the world, you are it." Ashley held the cool glass up to her cheek for a minute. "I wish I could hold this against my aching feet."

"I told you he was the devil incarnate when it comes to shopping." Robert sat back and sighed. "Be grateful that he is giving us a few minutes reprieve."

"Oh, I am grateful for so much more than that. Anyone who can walk into an overgrown flea market and hone in like a guided missile on the exact perfect piece for me, know how it fits in the perfect arrangement and find the perfect accessories to make it work... well, you have my undying love." She leaned over and hugged Stephen. "You are the best! I bow down at your feet. You are just like Lady Violet in Downton Abbey. You know exactly what to do to make everything right."

"I love that show!" exclaimed Stephen. "I am heartbroken that the season is coming to an end in a few weeks."

"I love that show too!" Robert leaned in and touched Stephen's arm. "We'll all have to get together at my house and watch the season finale in my screening room." His glance included Ashley in the invitation. "Until you've seen Downton Abbey on the big screen, you just haven't gotten the full experience."

"I'll bring the finger sandwiches and homemade scones. Oh and I found a great deli that carries clotted cream that's almost as good as what I had in England."

"All right then, it's a date," Robert confirmed.

"That's going to be so much fun... Robert, you're the best." Ashley turned to Stephen. "So, where to next?"

"We have the living room under control except for an area rug, so I suggest we concentrate on the dining room or breakfast nook or maybe both. We just *have* to get you off those bar stools. I know a great shop about twenty miles from here. I'm thinking a distressed-wood plank table and white cane-back chairs," he touched his temple with his forefinger as the vision played out in his head, "maybe some floral cushions and if we can find it, a small crystal chandelier to replace the dreary fixture that's there now. I saw the perfect one in Dallas, so if we don't find something you like, I'll pick that one up for you."

"You do know I am only renting that place?"

He shooed away the thought like an errant fly. "It's no big deal to swap out lights. We can put the old one back up when you leave."

"I also saw this marvelous eggplant-colored desk in Dallas. I'll take a picture and send it to you. If you like it, I'll get that for you too. It will really tie the living room together with your office. Maybe a white, antique-finished credenza for files?"

"Stephen, thank you, thank you." Ashley hopped up, grabbed Stephen in a choke hold and showered his cheek with kisses. "You have lifted a huge weight off my shoulders. It would have taken me months to pick out the right pieces and numerous trips back to shops to return what didn't work. I can't wait to see it in my house."

Ashley had just finished washing her face and changing into comfy sweats when Taylor Swifts', "*Blank Space*," 'you look like my next mistake' lyrics trilled on her phone. She snatched her cell like a lifeline, sliding her trembling finger across the screen to answer it as she belly-flopped onto her bed.

"Hi there." Even she could hear her voice lower an octave as it whispered across the air waves to nestle in Zach's ear.

"Hi yourself," he growled in response. "It's only been a few days since I saw you, but I can't tell you how much I miss you."

"Sure you can, sugar," she said as she rolled over, stretched like a cat and reclined back against the satiny softness of her comforter and abundance of pillows. A faint hint of lavender from the sachet she used to scent her linens teased her nostrils. "You tell me how much you miss me and then I'll tell you."

She could hear the background noise and knew he was in a public place. In her mind's eye Ashley could see him glancing furtively left and right to see who might be within earshot. "What's the matter, cowboy? Afraid someone will hear you getting all mushy?"

"No, I'm afraid of getting arrested if I tell you just what I would like to be doing to you right now." His voice dropped to a smooth murmur that reminded her of silk against skin. "You're lying naked on that frilly bed of yours, sunlight slanting low through your windows spotlighting every one of your luscious curves and I'm standing in the doorway drinking it all in."

"You do have some imagination, but I like what I'm hearing. Please continue." Her limbs felt like warm, liquid honey as she sank deeper into the fullness of her bed and the tantalizing picture he painted.

The crowd noise became muffled so she assumed he'd found a more private spot to carry on their conversation. "I walk over, stretch out beside you, then kiss the dickens out of those sweet lips of yours. If I close my eyes, I can taste those chocolate covered strawberries that you like so much on your breath and I can smell the flowery perfume you wear." His sigh reverberated with need and the tension of a taut rubber band. "Next, I'll slip my hand up under that sheer piece of nothing you're wearing and caress and kiss those perfect breasts of yours. Heaven, baby, heaven." He moaned.

Her body responded as though he actually were beside her, doing all those marvelous things to her body. Her breath came in shallow gulps as she felt the heat build and swirl until she might spontaneously combust. "You've done this phone sex thing before, have you?"

"Never like this. What I've wanted from other women was a ripple in a pond. You're a tsunami." She heard an alarm dinging on his phone. "Oh shoot. It's time for my appointment in the Sports Medicine trailer." She heard the smile in his voice. "We'll have to continue this conversation later. I'll call you tonight when I get back to my rig."

"Wait. One. Minute. Why do you have an appointment with Sports Medicine? Are you hurt?" Talk about a mood killer jettisoning her from all hot and bothered to nurturer in the blink of an eye.

"During our last run, the steer cut unexpectedly as I dallied and it jerked my arm. It's probably just a sprain. On the bright side, I do still have both my thumbs. Luckily, despite our bum draw, our time was good enough to put us in the semi-finals, so I've got a day to rest it."

"You're hurt and you're still competing? And what's this about thumbs? Are you crazy?"

"Not crazy, just determined. Rodeoing with a few aches and pains is part of the business and more than a few headers have gotten their thumbs caught between their rope and their saddle horn. It's an occupational hazard, but not too common." She heard the background noise increase in volume and knew he was moving. "I'm touched you're worried about me. So what are you doing for the rest of the evening?"

"Lauren's stopping by for dinner and girl talk."

"Before we hang up, please tell me you're wearing something skimpy and sexy to keep me going?"

Ashley looked down at her sweats, "I think you'd better keep that imagination of yours fired up since it's so much better than the reality."

"Well if you aren't wearing something sexy, then at least tell this poor starving man who has to eat his own cooking tonight, what you're having for dinner."

"You are such a goof," she chuckled. "Enjoy your evening and take care of yourself."

·♥·♥·♥·♥·♥·

ASHLEY SLIPPED THE ENCHILADA casserole and corn bread out of the oven as Lauren walked through the back door. "Perfect timing. Just put the salad on the table. Wine too? You must have been reading my mind." Ashley set the hot dish on a trivet and slid into her seat.

"Don't tell me, let me guess. That silly grin on your face has something to do with a certain cowboy?" Lauren scooped a serving of casserole onto her plate.

"Silly? I am never silly." Ashley wanted to look stern but came closer to wriggling like a puppy. "But yes, Zach called. He and Matt did well in the first round and are advancing. He misses me, of course, and wishes I were there."

She paused and poured wine in each of their glasses. "He called from the Sports Medicine trailer where they were working on his arm." Her brows pinched and forehead crinkled in worry. "He'd sprained a muscle when the steer twisted unexpectedly as he dallied... don't ask me what that means, I have no idea, but I gather it jerked his arm hard. He joked that he still had his thumb. Apparently that's some sort of rodeo, gallows humor."

"And you're sticking to the story that Zach is just a friend?" Lauren's look said she thought a snowball would fare better on a Phoenix sidewalk in July than Ashley would being *just friends* with Zach.

"He *is* just a friend!" Ashley protested. "And I like talking to my friends, as you well know, and sometimes I worry about them. I don't like it when my friends get hurt. I'll be on pins and needles until he calls tonight with an update."

"Like I said, that's your story and you're sticking to it." Lauren scooped salad onto her plate and stirred Ashley's homemade balsamic dressing before ladling it onto her greens. "How was your shopping trip with Robert? I love your dining set. It's so you. Can't wait to see the rest of the place."

"I swear, Stephen is an interior design god and Robert, what a trooper, not one complaint all day. In fact, he had a lot of good ideas. As exhausting as it was, I can honestly say I had a wonderful time." She cocked her head to the side in thought. "And you're right, shopping with Robert is like shopping with my girlfriends." She smiled remembering. "A lot of joking around – dishing everyone and everything. Those two are hilarious."

"So not much like being with Zach?"

Ashley tapped her fingernail against the table as she mulled over her feelings. "Hmmm. Zach is fun and we have a great time together." A soft smiled tugged at the corners of her lips. "But I don't think he would have been nearly as patient as Robert. I probably would have seen the back end of his horse as he hightailed it out of there after the first hour or so."

"Lots of guys would be right on his heels, so I wouldn't hold that against him."

"I don't. I'm not exactly the picture of patience in a hardware store so I understand. The thing is... Robert is the kind of man I need, no... *want*, in my life, so Zach's furniture shopping preferences are of no concern to me." Ashley leaned forward and put her hand on her friend's arm, "Did I tell you, Robert watches 'Downton Abbey' religiously? He invited Stephen and me over for an old-fashioned English afternoon tea party to watch the season finale. Can't you just picture the three of us all prim and proper and high society?"

·♥·♥·♥·♥·♥·

"THANKS FOR SQUEEZING ME in today," Zach said over his shoulder as Nate watched him lead a Roan gelding in a slow circle around the corral. "Paddy seemed a little gimpy after our last practice run today."

"Good thing you called. He is favoring his right foreleg a little. Bring him inside and I'll examine him."

Once inside the barn, Nate knelt down and ran his hands up and down the horse's leg. "There's slight swelling so I think I can make a good diagnosis with an ultrasound. Take Paddy into the vet room and I'll go get the ultrasound unit out of my truck."

After the exam, Nate stood, dusted off his hands and looked at his brother. "Paddy has a suspensory ligament injury. You know the drill. Three to four months of paddock rest and then gradually start up his training regimen." Nate turned to pack up his equipment. "Have you given any more thought to retiring him?"

"Some. I'm also giving some thought to cutting back a bit myself."

Nate's head whipped around. "What? Why? Are you okay?"

"I'm fine. With Dad slowing down, I just need to spend more time at the ranch."

"Funny, I thought it might have something to do with Ashley. She's made it clear what she thinks about rodeo men. Are you caving?"

"No, I'm not caving, but I am reevaluating what I want. There are a lot of factors playing into my decision. Ranch responsibilities, our team roping clinic is taking off which means devoting more time to that, and Matt and Heather are planning to add to their brood so he's thinking about cutting way back next year to spend more time with his family. That means I'd have to find another heeler to partner with. Lots happening right now."

"Yeah, all that could give a man pause."

"All my life, it's been rodeo – junior level, high school, college, and now pro. I live, eat, breathe, and sleep rodeo. It's defined who I am and how people know me for so long. Maybe taking a year off will let me know if there's more to me."

Nate shut his medical case and faced his brother. "Didn't expect deep today, but here's my take. You could easily stay competitive for another six to eight years. If taking a year off now, helps you figure out next steps, why not? Self-discovery can be a bitch, but it's not a bad thing to do."

"Says the man who keeps his emotions on a tight rein."

Nate folded his arms across his chest. "I'm not the one making a big life decision."

"Right." Zach made a growly sound in his throat. "I've been so focused on rodeo, with everything else being secondary, it's scary to think about the 'after.'" He shrugged. "Maybe I'm tired of the grind and ready to settle down a bit. I know I've got this cocky, ladies' man reputation, but you know that's not me. It just might be time to change who people think I am, take the shine off and be an ordinary guy."

"If you need any help tarnishing that image of yours, just let me know. I'd be glad to help." Nate grinned.

"Thanks, bro. It's such a good feeling when family's got your back." Zach grabbed the lead and started walking the horse back to its stall. Nate fell into step beside him.

What's the story with you and Lauren?" Zach asked. "You looked pretty chummy before I left."

"Still are for the moment, until she decides I need an attitude adjustment again. I mean, what's wrong with me? I'm honest, hard-working, trustworthy, an upstanding citizen. Why does she think she needs to change me?"

"I don't know. It's what women do. You are the perfect boy scout. What did she call you?" Zach scrunched his brows then snapped his fingers. "I remember now, that World War II superhero. She really does know you."

Zach swung open a stall door, let the horse step inside before unclipping the lead rope and latching the door.

Nate started up the conversation where they left off. "I idolized him as a kid."

"That explains a lot."

Nate scowled at his brother. "And what's with all the rabbit food she tries to get me to eat," he shuddered and made a face, "and that blended green glop she wants me to drink. Yuk."

"I agree with you on that one," Zach commiserated. "But her heart's in the right place. She only wants what's best for you."

"I know and she is one of the kindest, most generous people I've ever met. She's smart, she's funny, she's down earth but sometimes just too new-agey for my taste. I'm not into energy therapy and such."

"Hey, she doesn't read crystals and tarot cards and she does eat meat, so it's not all bad. Loosen up a little."

"She says that a lot too, 'loosen up.' Maybe she's right. I don't know." He removed his hat and scrubbed his hand through his hair.

"Look, I'm going to call Ashley and see if she wants to go dancing tomorrow night. Why don't you and Lauren join us?"

"We'll see. The Davidson's prize mare is ready to foal so my plans are tentative... as usual. I'll check with Lauren though."

·❤·❤·❤·❤·❤·

ZACH KNOCKED AND COULD hear the tapping of heels across the wood floor. The door opened with such force the backwash almost pulled him inside, but two small fists latched onto his jacket and dragged him into the room. Ashley launched herself into his arms and the force spun them both around.

"I'm so glad you're back." He set her down and she stepped back to examine him closely. "And all in one piece I see. I'm glad it's just you and me tonight. You can tell me all about Denver and what you're doing to get ready for your family rodeo this weekend. Let me know if there is anything I can do to help your mom out. Do you like what I've done with the place?" While she chattered away, she plucked her jacket and evening purse off the back of the sofa.

"Whoa, woman. Slow down. You're like a mini twister coming down off the plains and turning a man every which direction." He shook his head to clear it. "Let me see. I'm glad that you're glad I'm back. I gave Mom your email address and she'll be in touch about a few food items she's hoping you can bring. Now stand back and let me look at you."

Ashley stepped back and held her arms out at her sides. "Well?"

"God did manage to pack a lot of perfection into one tiny, little package. Mmm, mmm... Are you sure we need to go out tonight? You did say something about being glad to have me all to yourself."

"Not on your life, buster. I didn't get all dressed up to stay home, but I did make an apple pie for later when you drop me off."

He liked the sound of that. It meant she wanted him to stay for a while. He wondered how long he could talk her into. Just the thought of waking up next to her all warm and sleep tousled from an amazing night of sex made him go weak in the knees. He whistled a happy tune as he followed her out the door.

·❤·❤·❤·❤·❤·

ZACH COULDN'T KEEP HIS eyes off the sway of her hips as she shuffled along in time to the music as they made their way to the dance floor. Lord have mercy on his soul, but every one of her jiggly women's bits was designed to catch a man's attention. He didn't like the looks other men were giving her, and from the hard-eyed stares they were getting from their ladies, neither did their partners. Ashley seemed oblivious, at least he hoped she wasn't trying to egg the other men on.

It wouldn't bother him at all if they cut their evening short and headed back to her place now. But then again, as she wiggled her hips into him this wasn't bad either. Her playfulness was infectious and so much more appealing than that business persona she wore like a dark cloud so much of the time she was in public.

"You want to get out of here?" Desire flowed through his voice like molten lava, searing and urgent.

She smiled up at him, calculation in her gaze. "Tell you what, let's play a game of pool. You win, we'll go home right after the game. I win, and we stay and dance for another hour. Deal?"

He hooked his thumbs in his belt loops. "Little lady, I cut my teeth playing pool. I accept your challenge."

"So you say," she said as she traced his lips with her finger. Her breast casually bumped against his arm as she turned away.

It was then he realized he was in way over his head.

When they got to the pool table, she neatly racked up the balls and then tested several cues for weight, balance and length before settling on one she liked. She pulled an elastic thing out of her purse and tied back her hair.

"Let me guess, you've done this before?"

"Three older brothers who all thought they were God's gift to the pool-playing universe. It became my mission to prove them wrong."

Her saccharin smile jolted every single one of his competitive genes into high gear. No way was this tiny, little thing going to beat him.

"Do you want to break, or should I?" She batted her eyes in challenge.

"You go ahead." He bit back a groan as she placed that delectable bottom of hers against his family jewels and pushed him back. If he was going to keep his head in the game, he better position himself on the other side of the table. Once there, he discovered he got an eyeful of what seemed like miles and miles of cleavage that she made sure were displayed to advantage. Ashley took a deep breath and shifted her shoulders showcasing her breasts cushiony softness as she lined up her shot. He felt need slam into his gut. Maybe two could play at this game.

Zach put the wolf in his smile and hunger in his eyes as he softly caressed the satiny wooden edge of the table. Slowly the tip of his tongue traced his full lips. His fingers encircled his cue and gently traveled up and down the shaft. The tip of her cue skittered across the felt and her shot went wide.

She glared up at him and then arched like a satisfied cat. "I guess it's your turn." He had the feeling that payback was going to be a bitch, but he'd just have to man up and take it.

He positioned his cue to take his shot. Ashley traced the edge of her top from one delectable mound, down into the valley between her breasts and then up along her other creamy orb. She ran her hands down her sides pulling her shirt tight across her ample chest before settling them on her tiny waist. Zach drew back his cue, ready to let it fly, and she put her hands under her breasts and shifted. His cue dug into the felt and he didn't even hit the ball.

"Sorry, my girls just needed a little adjustment." She shrugged.

"That was dirty pool, no pun intended," he ground out.

"My turn." She bent at the waist, balanced the cue on the edge of the table and waggled her hips.

Zach stepped up behind her, the 'V' of his legs against her butt leaving no doubt what he would rather be doing and placed his hands on her hips. He reached for his beer. "'Scuse me sweetheart. Just need to get around you."

"I'm okay calling this a draw if you are," she whispered drawing in the breath of the drowning.

He raised his finger in the air. "Check please."

Chapter Eight

♥

HER HAND TREMBLED AS she tried to fit the key into the lock. Zach's lips nibbled the nape of her neck. His arms circled her waist. One hand helped steady her hand and the key slipped into place. The knob turned. The door opened. They stepped inside. He turned her in his arms so she faced him. Feather-light kisses dusted her forehead, lingered at her temple and slowly slid down her cheek like sweet tears of happiness before settling on her mouth like a ravishing tiger.

She wasn't sure what it was about his kiss that was so different than any she'd had before. His mouth, his touch, reached into someplace deep and secret within her. That place that searched for knowing. For connection. For understanding on a primal level. No other man had found this place because no other man had looked.

Zach unwrapped her like a precious gift. Methodically unbuttoning her jacket, slipping it down her arms, letting it fall to the floor. Gentle hands glided up her arms. His touch had each nerve ending begging for more. Lips met, sighs mingled, hearts beating in time to a rhythm older than time, two souls wanted... more, so much more.

His hands cupped her face, threaded into her hair, deepening the kiss. Her busy fingers unbuttoned his jacket so her arms could circle his waist. She pulled him tighter already feeling the need to be one with him – hot, moist, and ready. His jacket had joined hers on the floor. Somehow both his shirt and her top found their way into the pile. His belt buckle hung loose, making an impression on her soft belly.

Zach pulled his face back so he could look into her eyes. "I want to make love to you," he murmured, "but it's up to you. I'll leave now if that's what you want."

"No, I want you to stay." She held his face between her hands then let her palms trail over his solid chest and along his ripped abdominals.

"Then I suggest we do this right and head upstairs."

She stood on tip toes pulling his face down to meet hers and melted into his kiss. "Upstairs works for me."

He wrapped his arms tightly around her, swinging her around, before letting her slide down his body until her feet touched the first step, all without breaking the kiss. Ashley gloried in the contact – hip to hip, the bulge in his jeans nudging her stomach, strong arms holding her, hands kneading her back, his silky hair fisted in her fingers, heat coursing through their bodies. Euphoric, ancient, and feeling more right than anything she had experienced with any other man.

Zach leaned gently into her, urging her to start moving up the stairs. When they'd almost reached the top, her heel hit a step and she tumbled backwards, landing on her butt, Zach's length stretched out against her, ravishing her senses.

She toed off her heels. He unfastened her bra. She unzipped his pants. He unzipped her skirt. Together they kissed, touched and wriggled their way to the top of the stairs. He stood, scooping her into his arms, glancing at each door off the hallway.

"This one," she indicated to her left while trailing kisses along his neck. She could feel his pulse beating against her ribs.

He shouldered his way through the door, let her slide slowly down his body until her feet touched the floor, then flung the comforter and pillows aside to expose the sheets. Her skirt slithered off her hips and pooled at her feet leaving her covered in nothing but a bit of Victoria's Secret black lace panties.

She smiled and put her hands on his shoulders as he sat down heavily on the bed. The look of wonder in his eyes told her that giving herself to him was right. He reached up slowly to caress her breast then brought his mouth to her nipple, teasing it with his tongue. She arched forward, accepting his adulation. He sat back and lifted his leg to remove his boot. She stalled his movement with a touch to his thigh.

"No, let me." She knelt down while her hands traced down his chiseled chest, along his thighs, down his calves and then up under the hem of his right jean leg, He groaned, feathering his calloused fingers across her cheeks and into the mass of curls tumbling about her face. She pulled off first the right boot and then the left.

"You do realize that you are woefully overdressed?"

Zach couldn't have said a word if he wanted to. He stood and quickly shrugged out of his jeans, his briefs following them as he kicked them off to the side and folded her into his arms, stooping to kiss her with a passion he didn't know he possessed, new, unnerving but right. He hooked his thumbs into her panties, kissing his way down her luscious body as he knelt to remove them.

She shuddered against him and they fell into bed.

Later, much later, her body evaporated into his arms. "I must admit, this friends with benefits business does have its advantages but now it's time for you to go."

"Are you sure? I could stay and we could go for round three." He ran his nose along her neck and kissed her in that sweet spot just below her ear.

Ashley shivered with want and smoothed her palm across his chest. "Tempting, but I have to work tomorrow and didn't you say something about your dad wanting to meet you first thing in the morning at the arena to get ready for the rodeo this weekend?"

"You're right." He rolled away from her and sat on the edge of the bed.

She had to admit, he did have one fine body. She ran her hand down his back feeling his spine beneath her greedy fingers.

"You keep that up and I won't be able to make my legs take me away from you." He looked around. "I don't suppose you know where my clothes ended up?"

"Sorry, can't say that watching where our clothes landed was uppermost in my mind, but I am going to enjoy watching you look for them." She put her hands behind her head and relaxed against the pillow.

He scooped up his briefs and jeans, shrugged into them and then sat on the bed beside her. Zach tenderly brushed the hair away from her face. "You're getting under my skin and I'm not quite sure what to think about that, but I'm hoping you'll give us a chance to see where this goes."

Ashley sat up, her hair falling across her breasts. "Zach, I can't promise you anything more than friendship right now." She softly brushed her lips against his. "Now, scoot. I'll see you on Saturday."

·♥·♥·♥·♥·♥·

LAUREN PULLED HER HONDA CRV into the driveway and honked. Ashley flounced jauntily down the walkway and hopped into the car, a big grin plastered on her face.

"My aren't *we* all perky and bright at 6:30 in the morning."

"Sarcasm doesn't suit you. Here, have some coffee." Ashley thrust a large, car-mug at Lauren. "Personally, I'm excited to see my first rodeo."

Lauren backed out of the driveway and set off for the highway leading north. "Don't suppose your excitement has anything to do with a very tall and very handsome cowboy?"

"Maybe a little." Ashley blushed and started fiddling with her coffee mug.

"OMG, you did it!" Lauren screeched.

Ashley waved her fingers toward the front of the car. "Keep your eyes on the road. I'd like to live another day. To answer your question, yes, we did have sex – mind-blowing, heart-pounding sex. He is one talented man." She fanned her face with her hand and exhaled slowly. "But I made it clear, we are just friends."

Lauren snorted. "You just keep on telling yourself that fairytale." She glanced over at her friend. "Ash, be honest, how many men have you had sex with and not fallen head-over-heels in love with?"

"There is always a first time for everything," a hint of testiness in Ashley's voice.

"Other than the fact he earns part of his livelihood from the rodeo, what else makes him unsuitable?"

"Have not yet confirmed or denied his player status and while ranching is a noble pursuit, the economic reality is that it's an unstable source of income. I'm tired of users taking advantage of me. I want a solid, dependable man I can count on to carry his share of the load."

"That's not what made the other guys you dated so wrong for you. Sure, they were players and risk-takers, but they were mostly self-centered, uncaring, entitled jerks. I don't think that describes Zach at all."

"I know and money isn't everything but being able to take care of yourself does indicate a certain level of maturity. For now I'm happy with what we have and plan to keep my options open. Robert is still a potential happily-ever-after candidate and with tax season in full swing, I don't have the time or energy to devote to building a serious relationship."

Ashley's phone dinged. She pulled it out and scanned the email. "Speaking of tax season, looks like I have some work to do now." Her fingers quickly tapped out a response then she reached into the bag at her feet and grabbed her laptop. "So much for enjoying the scenery this morning."

ZACH ADJUSTED THE GIRTH, settled the stirrup back into position and glanced across his horse's withers to see what the wave of appreciative murmurs was all about. His horse could have stomped on his foot and he wouldn't have felt a thing. Ashley and Lauren were strutting across the clearing and heading for the stands pretending not to notice that every man in the place was tracking their progress. Talk about being hit in the solar plexus and having all the air knocked out of you. Ashley was quicksand, sucking him in and he was beginning to think he didn't want out.

Tight jeans, her ebony mane bouncing as she walked, cowboy hat perched on her head and boots on her feet made it near impossible for a red-blooded man to look away. She must have sensed him watching because she casually looked his direction, smiled like sin with a come-hither look, turned on her heel and strolled on over. Felt like his heart would burst out of his chest like some cartoon character and the quicksand sucked a little harder.

"Don't you just look good enough to eat," she ran her hand over his muscled biceps.

"Right back at cha," he grinned. "You do know that you have every man wishing he could haul you off to his own personal cave?"

She shrugged and waved her hand in the air. "I'm not interested so let them dream." Good thing he couldn't read her mind or he'd know how hard it was to shake the memory of those strong arms around her just a few days ago – cowboy or not – holding her tight, the mingling of sweat-slick skin. For someone who was so not right for her emotionally, physically he had no equal.

She flipped back her hair and surveyed her surroundings. "This is what a rodeo is like?"

"Sort of." Zach gathered his horse's reins and started leading it to the staging area. Ashley fell into step beside him. He took her hand in his. "We hold some of the same events as the circuit rodeos but on a much smaller scale and we have a lot of events for the kids. My great grandfather started hosting rodeos for the neighboring ranch hands and it became a family tradition. It's more a time for everyone to get together and socialize than it is for fierce competition." He stopped in front of his family.

A pert, young woman rushed up and threw her arms around Zach. "Good luck. I'll be rooting for you."

Zach hugged her back and planted a kiss on her cheek. "Thanks, sweetheart. I'll take all the good vibes I can get." He turned her out of his arms, patted her butt and gave her a friendly shove.

His smile faded when he saw Ashley's thunderous expression. He stepped in front of her and put his hands on her shoulders. She twisted away.

"Ash, that doesn't mean anything. It's me being friendly, nothing else."

She looked up at him, distrust in her eyes and he felt like a ton of bricks just landed on his head. He hadn't thought how something so innocent in his mind would look to Ashley. He'd have to be more careful of her feelings.

"I've known that woman all my life. She's more like a sister and definitely not a lover."

"Been there and heard that." Ashley still held herself rigid.

"We're about to kick off the festivities so I have to go. Kiss me for luck?"

She nodded.

He bent to kiss her letting his lips linger on hers. "See you later."

Again, she nodded. "I see Lauren waving. I'd better go join her."

Ashley pivoted and walked briskly toward the stands, bottling the traitorous sigh that wanted to escape like the fizz in a shaken soda can. Why couldn't she stay away from him? There were plenty of other fish in the sea – albeit boring fish – who would make much safer relationship fodder.

Before she could settle herself into her seat, the crowd rose as a formation of riders raced around the arena. The stars and stripes attached to long poles held by the riders, whipped in the wind. Abruptly the riders stopped in the middle of the arena and whirled around to face the crowd. Everyone wearing a hat removed it and placed it over their hearts while the 'Star Spangled Banner' blared over the loudspeakers. Many sang along proudly and loudly.

After the National Anthem ended, Zach's father dismounted and took the microphone from the man who had walked out to meet him. He fiddled with the on switch, said "testing, testing" to confirm the volume was adjusted and cleared his throat. "Would you all please join me in reciting the Pledge of Allegiance?"

As "justice for all" faded into silence, Jack settled his hat back on his head.

"Thank y'all for coming out here today. We hope you stay for the weekend and stick around for the barbeque and dance this evening. We look forward to another great year of rodeoing." He paused until the 'whopping' subsided. "Let's send up a big round of applause for all our contestants and get this show started." The place erupted in boot stomping, clapping, and deafening cheers. He handed the microphone back, remounted his horse and led the group out of the arena at full gallop.

Ashley tugged on Lauren's arm to get her to lean down so she could talk to her. "These Kincaids surely do know how to make an entrance. I mean *Wow*. Don't Zach and Nate look yummy sitting up there on their horses, in those crisp, white shirts, flags flying? All this," she gazed around the arena, "really gets to you." She patted her chest and took a deep breath. "Very powerful."

Lauren nodded. "Yeah, there is something about the rodeo that chokes you up."

The rest of the morning flew by in a blur of adrenalin-packed action, the smell of dust, hay and animals in the air and lots of hooting and hollering from the crowd. Ashley admired the skill, grit, and determination of the adult competitors, though Zach and Matt were obviously far superior to the other team roping pairs. They staggered her with their speed and precision, working as one unit roping the steer in record time. She held her breath as they charged after the steer in flawless sync.

The kids riding the sheep were adorable. Watching Zach help the younger ones practice their roping skills weakened her resolve. He was so patient and gentle and it was clear the kids had a case of hero-worship. Old friends met, chatted and caught up with each other's lives. Ranching is isolated work so neighbors make the most of every opportunity to be together.

Just after the team roping event, a sultry red head planted her well-rounded behind next to Ashley. "That Zach sure is something, ain't he?" She elbowed Ashley in the ribs, "And I don't mean just in the arena if you get my drift. Ah, the things he can do to a woman's body." She put every bit of drama she could into that sigh.

"And you are sharing this information with a perfect stranger, why?" Ashley brows rose as she looked at the woman askance.

"Because he is one hot hunk and I want everyone to know that I know him, and he knows me – just so we understand each other." The woman's dislike hit Ashley like a wave.

"Ah, I see." Ashley said slowly. "You want to warn away any perceived competition and stake your claim. Message received and not to worry. Zach and I are just friends. I'm not in the market for a relationship with a cowboy." Ashley kept her tone light but felt her blood pressure spike. One more indication the man was a player and couldn't be trusted.

Like a homing Pidgeon, Ashley gaze zeroed in on Zach who had his arm looped around a pouty blonde, sharing a way-too-friendly laugh with the curvaceous vixen.

Ashley didn't like the jealous feeling snaking its way through her system, spreading its venom. She didn't like the redhead who hinted at intimacies with Zach. She didn't like the blonde he had his arm around. Most of all she didn't like feeling this way about one more man destined to break her heart.

Ashley nodded in Zach's direction. "Looks to me like you're warning off the wrong party." Miss Sultry and Steamy got up in a huff and stomped off.

Lauren and Ashley looked at each other and burst out laughing. "Nothing like a little comic relief to put things in perspective." Ashley slapped Lauren on the knee and stood up. "I don't know about you, but I feel the need to shake it off. Good luck to her trying to tie that cowboy down. Ready for lunch?"

"I am. I see Nate over by the Taco Truck. Let's go."

The pair set their course for the food service area. As they passed the corner of the barn an arm snagged Ashley around the waist and hauled her in to a deeply muscled, very masculine chest. Ashley squeaked in protest and Lauren turned in surprise, but seeing that Zach was the perpetrator, she waggled her fingers and continued on to her target.

"I have been dying to get you alone all day, ever since you strutted that gorgeous body across the barnyard this morning. I've missed you." He lowered his mouth to kiss her, but she held him off with her hand.

"Really? Not according to a sultry red head who sat next to me a little while ago. She let it be known that you two have been getting it on and you are off the market." She put her finger to his lips when he started to protest. "Course the fact that you had your hands all over a blonde, proved her wrong. You didn't look very lonely to me."

"What redhead? What blonde? I don't recall having – or wanting – my hands on anyone but you lately."

"What's the matter, Zach? Too many women, too little time? Conquests too numerous for your little brain to catalogue? I would think even you would remember whose ear you whispered in just fifteen minutes ago."

"Even if there were lots of conquests – which there are not – I'm a one-woman-at-a-time man and right now, you're it. Get used to having me around." He paused to scratch his head. "Wait a minute, blonde, wearing a blue plaid shirt, fifteen minutes ago?"

"Sounds about right."

"That's one of my cousins... The redhead? I have no idea who that could be, but if she said she's my girl, she's lying."

"I hate to sound like a broken record, but I've heard *that* line before, however, I'll give you the benefit of the doubt since she seemed to be trying to warn people off." Ashley stabbed him in the chest with her finger. "Let's get one thing straight, buster, do not trifle with my affections."

"Can I kiss you now?" he asked his lips touching hers. He felt her smile and deepened the kiss.

When he pulled away, he asked, "Are you enjoying the rodeo so far?"

"It's not at all what I expected and I wish I could stay for tomorrow but this is tax season and there is no rest for the weary accountant."

"You are staying for the barbecue and dance though?"

"Barbecue, yes and part of the dance." She patted his face. "Don't worry, I doubt you'll be lonely, what with all those cousins and such. I'm sure there is a line of women just itching to get their claws into you, one redhead for sure."

"Darlin', when you are related to half the state of Texas, lonely isn't a problem but for now, those women had better set their sights elsewhere. I'm not interested."

"That sounds like more than friends," her voice trailed off, not sure she wanted to ask the question.

"What I feel for you is uncharted territory for me." He smoothed her cheeks with his thumb. "I don't know what this is, but I know I don't want it to stop."

"For now," she breathed.

He slid his hands into her back pockets, pulled her hips into his thighs and bent down until his lips whispered against hers. "Now? Definitely. A month, a year? Possibly. Forever? Beats the hell out of me, but I'm hoping you'll stick around until we figure it out. I've never had a woman in my blood like you."

His kiss tingled its way down to her toes, made her feminine parts want, and set a firestorm loose in her belly. He might be Mr. Wrong, Wrong, Wrong but anything that felt this right had to be explored. Didn't it? When nothing more than a touch, heck, one of his smoldering glances, made her think things she knew her proper mother would tell her a woman shouldn't think, she felt she was floundering. Her foggy brain chanted maybe, just maybe, she could risk her heart again while her rational self, shouted – run!

The catcalls and 'get a room' comments had them jumping apart like teenagers caught in the backseat by Dad. His flush and heart-stopping grin tightened the noose around her heart, stopping her in her tracks quicker than one of the steers he roped. Yes, maybe, friends with benefits *would* work.

Chapter Nine

♥

"GIRLFRIEND, YOU ARE ABOUT ready to crawl out of your panties, you're so antsy. I know you're anxious to see your man, but you might want to let off the gas pedal or you'll end up seeing that *other* man."

Ashley looked at her friend. "First, there is no *your* man to be rushing to. Second, *what other* man?"

"You know, the one who wears a uniform, dark glasses, and has a shiny red light on the top of his car."

"You are such a comedian." Ashley softened the sarcasm with a tight smile.

"And don't give me that 'there is no *your* man' line. I know why you've been moping around the last few weeks and it has nothing to do with that 'I'm overworked and tired' baloney you've been trying to feed me. Face it, you miss him," Lauren winked, "or at least those hot kisses of his."

Ashley opened her mouth to protest but snapped it shut.

"What no witty repartee?" Lauren quipped. "We've been BFFs since diapers. Did you think I wouldn't notice how you snatch your phone every time it pings and how disappointed you are when it's not Zach? You don't get nearly as excited when Robert calls."

"All right already." Ashley huffed out a long breath. "So I enjoy Zach's company. So sue me." She smacked her hand against the steering wheel and wailed, "Why can't I fall for guys like Robert or Zach's brothers? Good, solid guys with dependable sources of income that aren't off rodeoing from February through September."

"Because you are who you are. Despite how unrelentingly your mother tried to stifle you, you haven't bought in to her status-is-everything shtick. Personally, I think that's a very healthy attitude."

"Are you trying to tell me that *I'm not* the perfect daughter who never gives her parents a moment's worry?"

Lauren gave her a long-suffering look. "Remember who you're talking to... your primary partner in crime? I've been party to more than one of your stunts. Wasn't it your idea to take the sailboat out on the bay when we were 12 and how about that time you decided we should break into your brothers' stash of fireworks and put on a show?"

"Enough. I will admit that I had a harebrained idea or two, but most of the time I have tried to be a person my mother can be proud of."

"Therein lies the problem. Your mother is not going to approve of a cowboy – despite all his success – even if he turns out to be the right man for you." Lauren patted Ashley's arm. "While I know us Southern gals aim to please our mamas, I think it's time to buck tradition."

Ashley sighed, "Will the guilt ever go away because I can't please her?"

"Sweet pea, mother and daughter relationships keep family counselors like me in business." She turned to look back at the road. "Not to change the subject but didn't Zach bring you dinner the other night when you were stuck at the office? Sounds like something a man who cares about you would do."

A soft smile flitted across Ashley's lips. "That *was* sweet. We haven't seen much of each other lately thanks to our crazy schedules. He said, and I quote, 'darlin', without you, it was like dark clouds were chasing me around. I needed my sunshine back. I had to see you, touch you, kiss you.'" Ashley sighed. "The heart of a true romantic beats in that model-perfect chest."

"Oh look, there's the rodeo ground's entrance."

Ashley maneuvered into the right-hand turn lane. "Zach said to meet them at the Cowboy Church service. I can't believe this is what we're supposed to wear." She glanced down at her jean-clad legs, cotton shirt and boots. "My mother would be mortified if she could see me now."

"Ash, your mother would be mortified if she knew you weren't wearing your pearls every day."

AT THE SIGHT OF Zach waiting for her at the entrance to the Auction Barn, where the church service was held, her steps stuttered and her heart beat faster than a country two-step. The man looked like he should grace the cover of the cowboy version of GQ. With sun-kissed, light brown hair all golden and warm, eyes that put the blue Texas sky to shame and a body pounded to perfection by hours in the practice arena and the rugged demands of ranch life – my, oh my, he is gorgeous.

"They are more refreshing than a tall glass of sweet tea on a hot summer day," Lauren leaned down and whispered in Ashley's ear.

"If anyone is taking nominations for the best-looking men in the universe, those two will be at the top of my list." Ashley sighed through a wistful smile.

As soon as Zach spotted her, his grin told her he'd been counting the minutes until she arrived. He took his time looking her up and down, then winked slow and sexy. He stepped forward and dropped a chaste kiss on her cheek. When he nuzzled her neck just below her ear he let her know in no uncertain terms, he wanted to do a whole lot more later.

"Glad you could join us. You just haven't had the full rodeo experience until you've attended a Cowboy Church service." He took her hand in his and raised it to his lips as they walked into the area set up for the service.

"I had no idea there would be so many people," Ashley said as she took in the nearly filled auction room. Folks clapped and sang along to the live music provided by the group onstage. It was almost impossible to keep her feet still in this atmosphere of joy and celebration. People sure took their religion to heart in this part of the country.

"Mom and Dad saved seats for us." He put his hand on her back to guide her. Zach shook hands with people he knew – which seemed like every other person – as they made their way through the crowd. His Mom, Dad and assorted Kincaid entourage were seated in the first row of the theater seating. The area in front of them, usually reserved for parading the livestock around, was filled with folding chairs. The preacher and other speakers stood to the side of the raised platform waiting for the band to finish its last song.

"Welcome everyone in the name of our Lord, Jesus Christ. We're so glad you chose to worship with us this fine morning. Let us pray."

Ashley could hardly believe that an hour could pass so quickly. When the service ended, everyone was asked to stay for refreshments in the fellowship area. She'd been mesmerized by the stories of the three rodeoers who shared how Christ had worked in their lives, the down-home humor and humility of the preacher and the solid faith of the men and women who lived this rodeo life. The experience put the whole rodeo culture in a different light.

Zach held her hand as he walked her outside. Lauren and Nate waved as they headed off toward some other building. Gloria June and Jack were quickly absorbed into a group standing in the coffee line.

"I wish I could stick around but team roping finals are up soon so Matt and I need to get ready." He brushed a gentle kiss on her cheek and squeezed her shoulder. "Why don't you hang out here with Heather and the kids? Here is your ticket," he said as he fished it out of his pocket. "You'll be sitting with our group and I'll join you as soon as my event is over." He pulled her up tightly against his chest and let his lips tease hers in a way that didn't raise too many eyebrows but clearly staked his claim. She took her time to admire that lanky stride, jean-clad butt, and broad back as he strode away.

Heather grinned at Ashley while she patted the back of her youngest who had fallen asleep in her arms. "You'll get used to the schedule after a while and having to fend for yourself. Not that Matt wouldn't move heaven and earth to make sure I was safe and knew I was loved but rodeoing is their job."

"Was it hard for you to adjust to this lifestyle, especially now that you have children?"

"It helps to come from a rodeo family. My dad was a bulldogger." She chuckled at Ashley's puzzled expression. "You'll also pick up the lingo after a while. A bulldogger is a steer wrangler, the guy who chases after a steer, jumps off his horse, and then wrestles the steer to the ground."

Heather exchanged pleasantries with a passing group who gave Ashley a speculative look. Noting Ashley's discomfort, Heather said, "I'm beginning to sound like I'm stuck in a loop, but that's something else you'll eventually accept. The rodeo is one big family and everyone knows everybody else's business. They're wondering if you plan on staying in Zach's life, which would make you part of the family."

"Right now, we're friends. Down the road, I don't know. I didn't think he was the right man for me, but I'm rethinking my stand. There's more to Zach than good looks and charm." Ashley shrugged.

"Back to your original question, how do I manage? Not always easily, but always knowing I'm part of a team helps. I have Matt's back and he has mine." She shifted the toddler in her arms then touched the head of the giggling child playing keep away with another child around her legs.

"We travel with Matt as much as we can, especially now when the boys are little. Matt Jr. is in hog heaven when he's around all the cowboys, but the older the boys get, the harder it will be to pull them away from home. Over the last few years Matt and Zach have focused on more regional rodeos so they could be home during the week as much as possible and still hit the big pot rodeos. Now that I'm pregnant again," she paused and smiled shyly.

"Congratulations," exclaimed Ashley. "How exciting for you," she said squeezing her arm. "When are you due?"

"October, which is why Matt is thinking about taking next year off so he can be with us."

"That will be quite a lifestyle shift." Ashley put her hand on the head of the child who had grabbed her around her knees and smiled down at him. "Will you be able to handle having Matt under your feet all the time?"

"I'm looking forward to it. But with the team roping clinics, their sponsorship obligations plus our ranch, my guess is he won't be around as much as I'd like."

Ashley shifted from foot-to-foot. "Do you mind if I ask you something?"

"Spit it out girl. It's obvious that something is gnawing at you."

"Did you ever worry about other women?"

"No, Matt is solid as a rock... I know countless wives have uttered these same words and had to eat them later, but with Matt it's true. Yes, there are Buckle Bunnies whose goal is to hook up with any cowboy they can, but while popular culture paints rodeo men as players, that's not who most of them are."

"So if Matt takes the year off, what does that mean for Zach's rodeo schedule?"

"He will either find another heeler to partner with or he may decide to ease up a bit." She smiled as Gloria June approached with a plate of cookies and two cups of coffee.

"You two look like you have your hands full so here's a little something to tide you over until lunch." She handed the plate of cookies and one coffee to Ashley and the other coffee to Heather. "How about I steal this little guy so you can enjoy your snack."

"You are a doll," Heather gushed as she passed the sleepy toddler over to Zach's mom.

"What do you think of the rodeo so far?" Gloria June asked Ashley.

"I haven't had a chance to see much yet but walking over here from the parking lot, I'm a little overwhelmed by how big it is."

"We'll make sure Zach shows you around after his event. The San Antonio Rodeo is quite the deal. Experiencing it through the eyes of someone who loves it, is a treat." She paused a beat. "You two looked deep in conversation. Anything juicy?"

"Sorry, no gossip." Heather chuckled. "We were just speculating about what Zach will do if Matt decides to take next year off. Any thoughts?"

"Can't say that I would be sorry to see my son around more, particularly since Jack is slowing down and could use the help. But a big part of Zach's life has always been the rodeo." Gloria June's expression turned thoughtful. "I remember when Jack retired. He was a bear of a man to live with for a while, but he eventually settled into a new routine. He loves this ranch, especially turning out the best cutting horses in the business. That's been his saving grace, but once a rodeo man, always a rodeo man. It's in their blood so they find ways to stay involved."

"How did you manage when Jack was off rodeoing?" Ashley asked.

"Much like Heather. Traveled as a family when we could and when we couldn't because the boys needed to be home, I herded boys and cattle and wrangled horses." She shrugged. "It takes a strong woman to be a rodeo wife, but that's exactly what our men want, a partner who can walk side-by-side with them along life's path." She circled Ashley's shoulders with her free arm and bent her head so their hat brims brushed. "It's been a wonderful life and I wouldn't change a thing."

· ♥ · ♥ · ♥ · ♥ · ♥ ·

ASHLEY THREW HERSELF INTO Zach's arms and kissed him soundly. "Congratulations on your win." She hopped back. "Let me see that new buckle."

He held it out to her. She pretended to sag under the weight. "That's heavy. I'm surprised it doesn't pull your pants down, not that I would object." She raised her eyebrows and vamped for his benefit.

"Well I declare, Zach Kincaid. I do believe you are blushing," she teased.

Zach grabbed her hand and pulled her along. "See y'all later. I'm going to show Ashley the sights." He whipped her around the corner away from prying eyes, snugged her tightly against his chest and settled his lips possessively on hers.

Once her brain shifted into gear again she queried with all the innocence she could muster, "And what sights would those be? I've already seen the Cowboy Boot Camp. Something behind the barn or in your trailer maybe?" She pushed him to arms-length. "Speaking of which, I never have seen the inside of that palace on wheels you haul horses around in."

"Tempting. The image of you sprawled naked in my bed in my long-haul trailer definitely makes my jeans fit funny, but sadly that rig is back at the ranch. Would you settle for barbeque instead?"

"Well, if I must." She breathed a drama queen sigh. "Why in the world do you have to have the most kissable lips? You wreak havoc on my will power."

He pulled her hand to his mouth and kissed it as they moved off to the food booth area. "It's nice to see you laughing and happy. When I brought dinner to your office the other night you were tense and all-business. At the dance hall, you're different. More like this. It's almost as though you are two different people – one with me and people you trust and then everyone else."

"I guess I only let the real me out when I'm around people I know accept me for who I am."

"I'm honored. So maybe I'm not such a bad guy?"

"Jury's still out, but there might be hope for you." She nibbled on her lip, hesitating, then blurted out. "Is this the official start of rodeo season?"

"Pretty much. Life gets real busy between now and September. Why?"

"Just wondering if seeing each other is even a possibility. A woman can't sit around and wait. We've got plans to make, places to be, schedules to keep. Did I mention Robert is taking me to a black-tie charity event in Dallas next weekend?"

"Is that the one supporting AIDS?"

"Yes... it is. I'm surprised you know about it."

He shrugged indifferently. "I'm a charitable guy. Just because I'm a cowboy doesn't mean I'm stupid or prejudiced." His pointed gaze told her he knew what she had been thinking.

Ashley had the grace to blush. "Ooops." She put her hand to her mouth. "With the super conservative, macho image cowboys have I assumed you didn't support causes like that."

"If by conservative you mean most cowboys believe in God, country, family and doing right by their fellow man, then yes, you've pegged us right." He two-fingered his hat farther back on his forehead. "But we also believe in live and let live. Besides I'm a sucker for a good fashion show." He smiled that slow smile that turned her insides to mush.

"Are you pulling my leg?" She returned his smile and slowly shook her head. "You are a man of many facets, Mr. Kincaid." She grabbed his shirt front, tugged his face down to her level and planted her lips on his with a resounding smack. Without question she could get used to the way this man made her feel.

"So still seeing that Robert guy, huh?"

"Yes. He's fun and would win my mother's stamp of approval. Besides, how many men would invite me to a "Downton Abbey" season finale tea party?"

"A what?"

"Exactly."

"On that note, I think I should quit while I'm still in your good graces. Let's go grab some grub, check out the exhibits and then watch us some rodeo."

· ❥ · ❥ · ❤ · ❥ · ❥ ·

ASHLEY TWISTED THIS WAY and that in front of the full-length mirror in Robert's guest room where she had come to transform into a butterfly for the evening. Her hair was piled in curls on top of her head, a few wisps framing her face. The metallic fabric caught the light, shimmering like a silver northern light. The floor-length strapless gown used sheer fabric between the bodice and neckline to hold everything in place so the back could plunge to just shy of scandalous. The bias cut of the dress clung to every curve. If this get up didn't make Robert sit up and take notice, nothing would. She placed her hands under her breasts. Yup, showed off the girls just fine and the slit from hem to mid-thigh would draw attention to her legs. Her stilettoes on steroids gave her petite frame some added height.

She had a hotel room reserved for the night but was hoping she wouldn't need it. He *had* kissed her on the lips the last time they'd been together. Even though the kiss had been about as passionate as kissing her brother, it was a start. Ashley turned at a slight tap on the door.

"Come in," she said striking a pose she hoped would start the sparks flying.

Robert stepped into the room and eyed her appreciatively. Unfortunately, it lacked the hunger she'd been going for.

"Well I can see that I will be the envy of every straight man there tonight and maybe even a few of the gay guys. You look marvelous." He took both her hands in his and held them out to her sides. "We will be the Belles of the ball."

She tamped down on the disappointment that felt like a lump of coal in her chest. "You look mighty fine this evening as well. That silver Tux is bound to generate buzz, and we match." She felt like she was back in second grade being a 'twinsie' with her best friend. Double darn and no sparks. Maybe they were only meant to be friends.

She giggled. "I feel like a movie star. I wish we had a photographer here to take our picture as we walk down the stairs."

· ♥ · ♥ · ♥ · ♥ · ♥ ·

ZACH STOPPED DEAD IN his tracks as he watched Ashley and Robert enter the room. Even from this distance, he could see her dress hugged her like a race car taking dead man's curve. As Robert helped her remove her wrap, the air *whooshed* out of his lungs like he'd landed wrong after being bucked off a bull. She was breathtaking, spectacular and any similar adjectives he could think of, that is, once his brain synapsis stopped sending all data south of his belt buckle. She turned toward Robert, accepting the flute of champagne he handed her and Zach saw the back of her dress – or the lack of one. Her whole tantalizing, touchable back, clear past her waist, was exposed for every guy in the place to gawk at. Why in the world wasn't that idiot man covering her with his jacket?

When Robert put his hand on her lower back to usher her forward, Zach saw red. All he wanted to do was punch the man's lights out. He didn't want any other man touching that exquisite back. Once they reached the table Zach extended his hand to Robert then leaned in to give Ashley a kiss meant to brand her to him. He loved the soft feel of her skin under his palms as he gently grasped her arms. In truth, all he wanted to do was haul her off someplace private and savor the way their bodies fit so perfectly together.

"Don't you two look fine." His slow perusal of Ashley brought a tinge of color to her neck and cheeks. "And as we say in Texas, Ashley, that dress shows off more curves than a barrel of snakes."

"Aren't you just full of surprises. Why didn't you tell me you were planning to be here?" she asked.

He shrugged. "I didn't think about it until you mentioned it at the rodeo. I checked with Robert to see if he had an extra ticket. Turns out he did, so here I am."

She schooled her features from surprise to sophisticated but she couldn't help giving him the once over. "You don't look bad yourself," she said. He was sad to see her slip back into that cool, elegant, untouchable mode.

"Glad you could join us, Kincaid," Robert said. "Why don't you sit here on the other side of Ashley where you'll have a better view of the show?" Stephen joined them and Robert turned to greet him with a manly hug and backslap. Ashley walked over and offered an air kiss to each cheek. Three other couples soon followed to fill the table.

Zach leaned in to whisper in her ear. "That's what he thinks I want to watch? The show? When I have the most beautiful woman in the place sitting next to me? Sorry, but that man is overdrawn at the memory bank." He shook his head. "Shall I make a list of the things I would like to watch you do?"

The woman next to Robert peeked around him and addressed Ashley. "Didn't I hear that you're from Charleston? Do you happen to know Amber Beaufort? She and I were sorority sisters in college."

"You're kidding!" Ashley's face scrunched up in what Zach considered one of the most adorable smiles in the universe. "Why yes, I do know her." Ashley reached out for the woman's hand. "Amber and I went to school together until tenth grade when her family moved away. Plus we were all part of Miss Madeline's Cotillion classes."

"What a small world," she exclaimed. "I'm Sarah, by the way." They squeezed hands. "Cotillion? I had no idea people still did that."

"Oh, yes." Ashley raised her eyebrows and solemnly nodded her head for effect. "Every proper, young Charleston lady went to Miss Madeline's school. We spent *many* thrill-packed hours walking around the room with binders on our heads... I can still hear Miss Madeline say," she mimicked the soft, cultured tones of her instructor, 'Do not saw your food. You are not a lumber jack... When entering or exiting a room, always face the people in the room with a smile on your face... Never put more than one-third of an eating utensil in your mouth.'" Back straight, finishing school smile in place she set her drink on the table and daintily dabbed her mouth with her napkin.

"I had no idea that etiquette rules were so detailed, but I thought a Cotillion was a dance?" Sarah asked.

"It is a dance but also a formal meal. In the South a Cotillion is still the social event of the year where debutantes are presented to society. Young ladies are expected to demonstrate their manners are such that a gentleman can take her to meet the Queen if necessary."

"It sounds like my education was sorely lacking but I guess it doesn't matter since it's highly unlikely I will ever have occasion to rub elbows with nobility." Sarah turned away to respond to a question from another guest.

Zach nudged Ashley with his shoulder. "I don't suppose there is video available of Miss Madeline's classes?"

"Sadly, there is, unless I can find my mother's stash. Then, it's history."

The waiters arrived, placing their dinner in front of them. The lights lowered and the fashion show and entertainment started as soon as the last guest was served.

Once the lights came back up, Robert looked at his phone, slipped it back in his pocket, then turned to her. "Sweetheart, I hate to do this but something has come up at work that I need to take care of right away. I'll have to leave. I'll be happy to order a cab for you and arrange to have it pick you up whenever you are ready."

"I'm sorry you have to miss the rest of the evening, but I'll be fine. I can take care of myself." She made a shooing motion with her hands. "I'm sure you dropped enough at the silent auction tables to have fulfilled your philanthropic duties. Now please, go manage whatever crisis needs your personal attention."

"I can make sure that Ashley gets back to her hotel safely," Zach offered.

"That would be great." Robert slapped Zach on the back. "That is if it's alright with Ashley." He looked hopeful.

"Sure, Zach can give me a ride if that makes you feel better."

"Thanks for being such a good sport." He bent down and absentmindedly grazed her cheek with his lips. The others at the table wandered off leaving Zach and Ashley alone.

Zach watched Robert leave and noticed Stephen was not too far behind. Coincidence? He shrugged then slid his gaze back to Ashley. Was that hunger in her eyes? He feathered his fingertips down her spine and felt her shiver under his touch. He softly nibbled his way from the base of her neck to her earlobe and asked, "I don't suppose I can talk you into exiting this shindig and holding our own private party someplace else?"

"I thought you'd never ask. Let's get out of here."

Chapter Ten

♥

THE VALET BROUGHT ZACH's rented Mercedes around and hopped out. Zach slipped the young man a tip as he handed over the key and jogged away.

Ashley wondered what the heck she was doing. She should have accepted Robert's offer of a cab, done the safe thing and returned to her hotel room – alone. Yet here she was with Mr. Bound to Break Her Heart and judging by the hunger in Zach's eyes, would *not* be spending the night – alone. She knew deep down she was okay with the way this evening was turning out – more than okay.

Zach took her hand and helped her into the car placing his palm against her bare back.

She felt the jangles of heat wriggle down her spine, pool in her stomach and kick anticipation to the front of the line. Watching him walk around the car – tall, confident, more handsome than desire was like waiting for a taste of her great aunt Hettie's Punch Bowl Cake. You longed for that tantalizing, creamy richness as it cured in the refrigerator. Your tongue could taste it long before you put that first bite in your mouth. Teasing. Tempting. Torture. That's what Zach made her feel.

He slipped into the plush leather seat, cast that soul-searing, lop-sided grin at her and asked, "Where to?"

"I'm staying at the airport Hyatt Regency."

"That sure simplifies things." The heat in his eyes took her breath away.

A puzzled frown settled on her face. "I don't understand. What's complicated about dropping me off at my hotel?"

"Because I'm hoping I'm not just dropping you off. If we were staying at different hotels, it'd be too easy for you to slip away. But since I'm staying there too, I'll have to walk you to your room." He hesitated, griped the steering wheel and looked straight ahead.

"I'll be honest here. I've been dreaming about the night we spent together and I want you like I've never wanted another woman. I'm not used to begging for companionship but I'm ready to beg if that's what it takes to be with you again." He looked at her, his expression solemn and held up one finger. "Before you grind me under your heel with a scathing remark – no, it's not just sex, although that was pretty spectacular. I like you. I like spending time with you. I want to get to know you better. There, I've said my peace." He pushed the starter button, the car purred to life, and he eased it into the line of traffic.

"Oh." Her mouth formed an 'O' and her brows reached for the sky. "Nothing like putting a little pressure on a girl. If I don't invite you back to my room, I'll be mashing your heart under my size five foot?"

He reached over and patted her knee, glancing quickly at her then back at the road. He spoke slowly. "I've never pressured a woman into doing anything so rest easy there. What you decide is up to you. If you send me packing, can't say I won't be disappointed, but I'll know you don't feel the same way about me as I feel about you."

She reached forward, turned on the radio, selected a country station and settled back to get lost in the music. Zach seemed just fine with that arrangement. He pulled into the hotel parking structure, parked in the first spot he found, and turned off the ignition. Neither spoke or moved. Quiet settled on them like a warm Texas evening, but one tinged with the charged atmosphere of a distant storm.

Zach leaned over, cradled her chin in his hand, turning her to face him then kissed her long, intoxicatingly and deeply. Her hands sidled along his jaw, through his close-cropped hair to cup the back of his head.

When they slowly pulled apart, she opened her clutch, retrieved her room keycard and held it out to him. "Room 912."

They walked to the lobby entrance hand-in-hand. She, smiling shyly. He, smiling like he'd won the lottery. He punched the up button on the elevator, slung his arm across her shoulders and tucked her closely against his side. She slid her arm around his waist, enjoying the feel of his hard body and knowing from experience how magnificent it was.

After they stepped inside the elevator, he faced her, wrapped both arms around her and nibbled his way from earlobe to the soft spot on her neck below her chin. She threw her head back to give him better access.

The doors opened as he leaned back to gaze into her eyes. An older couple stepped in as they stepped out.

"Young love," the woman murmured as she smiled at her husband who squeezed her hand.

Zach watched the doors swish shut. "I want to be like that someday. Like my parents, grandparents, aunts and uncles. Still in love into old age." He glanced at the sign on the wall indicating which way the room numbers ran and headed down the corridor to his left. When they got to her room, he held the keycard poised over the lock and looked down at her. "Are you sure?"

"Yes, I'm sure."

He unlocked the door and hit the light switch as he moved into the room. Ashley snagged the "Do Not Disturb' sign and slipped it on the outside door handle before closing the door and setting the inside lock. When she turned, she spotted him on the sofa. He'd turned on one of the table lamps creating a soft glow in the room and shed his tuxedo jacket, tie, and shoes.

He patted the seat beside him. "Wanna neck?" his voice smooth, seductive, playful, promising untold delights.

"Interesting. I thought you'd head straight to the bedroom and be naked and ready to go by the time I got there." She walked slowly toward him, swaying her hips, trailing the fingertips of one hand along a credenza while the fingertips of her other hand traced the plunging neckline of her gown.

"Unless you have someplace else you need to be, I'm in no rush. In fact, I'm looking forward to taking my time so I can explore your luscious body in great detail... every curve, every inch, every bit of you from top to bottom... thoughtfully, very thoroughly and very, very thankfully. " He grabbed her hand and pulled her across his lap.

"Hmmm, I like the way your mind works. Idolize the woman. Good strategy." She moved her fingers to the top button of his shirt.

"This dress doesn't leave much to the imagination so I think you need to be just as generous."

He smothered her dainty hands in his large, work-roughened hand. "Not so fast, missy. I said I was starting at the top and slowly, extremely slowly, working my way down to those dainty toes of yours." The husky timbre of his voice had her curling said toes in anticipation. His fingertips traced her hairline along her forehead and temple with a feather-light touch that made her close her eyes and want to purr.

"Even though I think your hair looks real nice." He cupped his hand to his ear. "What's that? It's telling me it wants to be set free." He started pulling out the hair pins. With each section that tumbled wildly around her face and down her back, he used his fingertips to massage that part of her scalp in unhurried, circular motions. When all her hair was free of its constraints, he covered her head with his hands, kneading her scalp and letting his fingers transport her.

Ashley moaned in pleasure. "You have no idea how good that feels."

Zach chuckled softly. "From the look on your face, I'm pretty certain I do."

She sighed. "Where did you learn to do this? Kama Sutra for the scalp?"

He threw back his head and laughed, a deep rumbling belly laugh. "You aren't going to like my answer."

She swiveled around on his lap, placed her hands on his chest, looked him in the eye, and scowled. "Okay. Out with it."

"When I undo the braids from my horse's mane and massage his neck, he kinda reacts the same way."

Her mouth dropped open and her eyes went round, then she collapsed against his chest in laughter. "Well, I guess if my main competition is a horse, then please, keep doing what you're doing."

Zach picked up where he left off but began using his lips and teeth to pleasure her ear. She melted into him as every bone in her body turned to liquid, languid soppiness.

Her lips caressed the hollow at the base of his throat. Her fingers slipped the top five buttons of his shirt free, then she smoothed her palm over the hard planes of his chest, raining soft kisses along the path her hand followed.

He started at the juncture of her shoulder and neck used the tip of his tongue to trace a line along her neck to her chin then back again as his fingers made quick work of the button on her gown at the nape of her neck. With no back to her gown, the bodice pooled softly at her waist.

She felt his smile against her shoulder as his exquisite lips moved along the top of her breasts. She swirled her tongue around his nipple, pleased by his sharp intake of breath and the pulsing of his desire against her thigh.

Looking into her eyes, he weighed her voluptuous breasts in his hands before lowering his head to suckle one, then the other, swirling his tongue around each nipple, delightfully and deliberately. Sparks pulsed low in her abdomen and her feminine core throbbed with contractions in preparation for their joining. He eased her off his lap, standing her in front of him. Her dress slipped to the floor. She braced her hands on his broad shoulders as he ran his hands down her ribcage, hips, and upper thighs, kissing the spot where her garter belt hooked her nylons. "Sexy," he murmured.

Kneeling in front of her, with his nose against her silky underwear, he nuzzled the tender nub at the apex of her legs. She felt her knees turn watery with pleasure, but Zach's strong hands kept her from falling. She could feel the hot, wet slickness pooling there and knew that he could too. He trailed a line of kisses to her belly button while his hands teased her nipples into taut pebbles, then nibbled and nipped his way back down her inner thigh to the top of the garter belt fastening.

Smoothly he unhooked one of the nylons, circled her leg with his hands and rolled it down, making sure his tongue and lips gave the back of her knee the attention it deserved before finishing the task and removing her shoe. He repeated the process on her other leg.

Zach stood, cradling her face and neck in his hands, mouths melding, tongues dueling, breathe coming in quick gasps, hearts beating in tandem. "I think it's time to move to the bedroom," he whispered in a voice that promised wild passion.

"Yes, please, yes, now," she whispered in response her fingers digging into his back.

He scooped her up in his arms and strode swiftly toward the bedroom.

· ♥ · ♥ · ♥ · ♥ · ♥ ·

As was her habit, she woke with the sun, sated from an amazing night of the hottest sex a woman could have. Zach's lovemaking had filled her dreams for the past month since the first time they had practiced bed Olympics. Last night proved the first time had not been a fluke. The man had serious talent. He'd made her feel things she didn't know she could feel and found erogenous zones she didn't know she possessed. Her head was still spinning, but in a good way – no make that a marvelous way. Cautiously she rolled to her side to face him, careful not to wake him.

She wanted a few minutes to drink him in. Relaxed in sleep he was still all male. Dark stubble framed his strong jaw and full lips. The temptation to kiss those lips until he woke up and made passionate love to her again was powerful... but she resisted. His broad chest, lightly dusted with hair, rose and fell with each breath. Tan, muscular arms and work-roughened hands embraced the pillow. She ached for the feel of those arms around her and those hands taking her to untold heights again. His six-pack abs and flat belly peeked out from under the sheet. She was tempted to lift that sheet and inspect at leisure the pretty phenomenal pleasure-making equipment she knew it hid. She bit back a moan of desire.

His lips quirked up in a sleepy, seductive grin, eyes still half shuttered.

She ran her palm over his hair then scratched his scalp lightly with her nails. "You're awake."

"Have been for a while but I could feel you watching me so thought I'd let you look your fill."

That smile and voice, scratchy from sleep, completed the wake-up call to her girly parts.

"What time is your flight back?" he asked.

"Not until 1:00. You?"

"9:30, so I'll need to get a move on it pretty soon. As soon as I get back to the ranch, Matt and I have to load the horses and equipment and drive to Houston. Gonna be a long day."

He noted the fleeting look of disappointment that flitted across her face. He traced his finger from her chin down through the valley between her breasts. "If you're willing, there's still time for a little up close and personal before I have to get ready."

She wriggled into his arms as nightie and briefs went flying and bodies remembered what had made last night so perfect.

Later, while Zach was in the shower, Ashley ordered room service. She had no idea how one person could eat a three-egg omelet, toast, hash browns, sausage, and a side of pancakes but that's what the man wanted so that's what he was going to get.

He wandered into the room, towel slung low around his narrow hips as he rubbed his hair with a second towel. He paused, "Stop looking at me like that or we're both going to miss our planes."

She held up her hand. "I'm going. Breakfast is on the way so I'll get in the shower now." She wiggled her hips as she strolled into the bedroom.

He looked down at the towel that was starting to tent in front of him and growled, "Get in there and lock the door or I'll have one very pissed off Matt on my hands plus blow our chance at a win in Houston."

When she came back into the room, Zach was dressed and seated at the small, round dining table tucking into his food with relish. Ashley slid into her chair, poured a steaming cup of coffee and sighed as she took her first sip.

"Is that all you're going to eat?" Zach pointed at the small box of raisin bran and bowl of fruit with his fork. "A bird would starve on that diet."

She looked at him like he must be denser than granite. "Only if that bird is a buzzard." She opened the cereal box and poured its contents into the bowl, then added the low-fat milk. "So what's your favorite food?"

He scrunched his brow in thought. "Two months ago, I would have said my mama's fried chicken but your black bean chili has knocked it out of first place. What about you?"

"Hard to pick just one." She paused, taking a mental inventory. "Garden grown tomatoes fresh off the vine and warmed by the sun. Just slice that delicious sweetness and pop it right in your mouth. Then there is Aunt Hazel's Peppermint Stick ice cream." She made a to-die-for face. "Hand churned, of course. I'd crank and crank for what seemed like forever then Hazel would unlatch the lid and hand me the dipper. I can still hear the crunch of ice against the steel container and wooden bucket." She closed her eyes remembering. "That creamy goodness on a hot, sultry summer afternoon just cannot be beat."

"Oh, man. I may have to switch my favorites." He reached over and traced his finger down the back of her hand.

"Next question. What's your favorite movie?" she asked

"Now it's my turn to be conflicted. If I have to pick one, I'd say, 'My Heroes Have Always Been Cowboys.' Not only does it show how hard rodeo folks work and the fierce competition involved, but it shows what rodeoing can do to family relationships. It's probably the main reason I've made it a point to keep a balance between family responsibilities and doing what I need to do to stay in the top tier of team ropers." He took a deep breath. "After that, action movies. I like stories about guys with a strong sense of doing what's right. John

Wayne was my hero when I was young. So let me guess, 'Gone With the Wind' is your all-time favorite?"

"Close. It is *one* of my favorites. Top honors go to '*Sweet Home Alabama*.' I love Reese Witherspoon. You can't take the Southern out of a girl no matter how hard you try... And if you want to see me all weepy, pull out an old copy of '*An Affair to Remember*.' It gets me every time." She fanned her hand in front of her eyes and exhaled. "I get emotional just thinking about it."

"That '*Sweet Home Alabama*' was pretty good."

"You've seen it?"

He hung his head. "Don't tell anyone, but my mama sometimes corrals my dad and me into watching chick flicks with her, so I've seen quite a few." He shrugged. "I like a lot of her choices. Does that make me less of a man in your eyes?" His molten grin sent an electric jolt clear down to her toes.

"Sweetheart, you could show up in a pink tutu and no one would question your masculinity."

"Ah, shucks, ma'am." He leaned his forearm on the table. "Last question because I have to leave soon. Favorite place in the world?"

"Easy one. Sitting astride Pocahontas and riding along the plantation trails in the early morning. Trees dripping with Spanish Moss, sun breaking through the low-lying clouds dusting the sky with pinks and purples and oranges, the bayous a mirror image of the sky, the frogs finishing up their nightly serenade. I hear the occasional fish jump out of the water and splash back down. Peaceful... calm... perfect." She inhaled deeply and hitched her shoulders up to her ears in complete contentment. "Where do you go?"

"Like you, an easy one. I have this favorite place along one of the streams on the ranch. There is no place on this sweet earth quite like it. A little bit of sand beach ringed with huge old cypress trees, cattle grazing in the meadow, the hills off in the distance. And in the spring... the bluebonnets, nature's show, will take your breath away. Some of my best memories are from time spent there. I still ride out there with a picnic lunch whenever I can."

He glanced at his watch. "I know I said last question, but I have to ask, 'Pocahontas'?"

"I was nine when I got my first 'big girl' horse and that was the year Disney released that movie. I fell in love with it and naturally had to name my horse after it."

"Cute. I'll bet you were adorable back then," he chuckled.

"I'm not adorable now?" Accusation filled her voice.

"No, now you're spectacular."

The smile that lit up her face made his heart pound in his chest. He'd like to keep pleasing her for a very long time, like maybe forever. She made him feel things he never felt before. Sure, he liked women and enjoyed their company, but Ashley was different.

"In that case, you're forgiven."

He stood up, stepped toward her, pulled her into his arms and kissed her like there was no tomorrow. When it was time to take a breath, he settled his forehead against hers. "Man, I don't want to leave but I've got to go. I'll call you tonight when we get to Houston and every day after that. Be near your computer at night so we can Skype. I want to see you even if I can't touch you."

She nodded. No words would come.

He walked to the door, scooped up his duffle bag, turned for one last look, then strode out of the room.

.•♥•♥•♥•♥•♥•

LAUREN PULLED UP TO the curb at the airport, waved to Ashley and popped the back hatch. Once Ashley was seated, Lauren leaned across the console and gave her friend a hug. "Welcome back, can't wait to hear all about your adventure," she said then moved smoothly into the departing traffic.

Ashley settled back in the seat and closed her eyes.

"Tired?" asked Lauren

"Mmm, hmm. Didn't get a lot of sleep last night."

"Robert finally came through?" Lauren's brows shot up in surprise and she turned to look at Ashley. "I didn't think he had it in him. Guess I miscalculated."

Ashley glanced over and offered up an 'I've got a secret' grin. "I'll share all the details, well, *almost* all the details when we get to my place.

"Dang, girl. You are such a tease. What's the speed limit here?"

Fifteen minutes later, Lauren skidded to a stop in Ashley's driveway, hustled around to help Ashley get her bags out of the back and followed her into the living room. Ashley laid her garment bag across the back of the sofa, set her carryon on the floor then linked arms with Lauren. "Come on, I'll spill my guts over tea and cookies."

She turned on the burner under the tea kettle and fished two mugs out of the cupboard. "Robert was his usual charming and witty self, but no moves were made. In fact, he left halfway through the evening on business." She filled the tea infuser with loose tea as she talked.

"The cad," Lauren huffed. "That sounds way too much like something your father would do." Lauren shuddered. "If that dress didn't get that man's motor running, he is a lost cause. What did you do?"

Ashley poured boiling water into the teapot, slipped the tea infuser into the pot, and let it steep.

"Actually, the weekend turned out so much better than I had planned. Zach showed up at the event and Robert basically threw us together. He seated us next to each other and then was thrilled when Zach volunteered to drive me to my hotel when Robert had to leave early."

"Unbelievable," exclaimed Lauren. "I'd say it's high time you wrote Robert off your list."

"Maybe, maybe not. He did call my hotel this morning and apologized profusely. Make-up flowers should be on my doorstep within the hour... and if I know Robert, no expense will be spared. Might be a chance to parlay his guilt into something more than friendship. " She shrugged. "Who knows?"

"Do you really want something more with Robert?" Lauren reached across the counter and grasped Ashley's hand. "Is *he* your heart's desire?"

"What my heart desires and what my head says makes sense are having a little trouble agreeing right now. This time though, I'm going to let my head, not my heart, take the lead."

"So what *did* happen last night?"

"Zach happened."

The song *Bad Blood* by Taylor Swift blared out of Ashley's phone just as the doorbell rang. Ashley groaned. "My mother's calling. Lauren, would you mind getting the door?"

Lauren nodded and squeezed Ashley's arm before she walked out of the room.

"Hello mother. How are you?... I'm fine, thank you, just busy at work, what with tax season in full swing..." She rolled her eyes heavenward. "Yes, I know life would be much simpler if I settled down with a suitable man and assumed my social responsibilities and I will when the right man comes along..."

Lauren shuffled in carrying what had to be the biggest arrangement of yellow roses Ashley had ever seen. She sucked in a breath then reached out to finger one of the delicate blooms. Lauren carefully set the huge crystal vase on the counter.

"No, nothing's wrong. I went to a charity function last night and the gentleman I was with just had a huge bouquet of roses delivered. They're lovely. I wish you could see them..." Ashley plastered on a resigned smile. "He owns one of the largest real estate firms in Dallas, graduated from Brown University, and his parents are from prominent Dallas families... I'm sure you will have the chance to meet him when you and father are out here in May... Yes, I have made reservations for you at the Omni. It's a five-star hotel," she hurried to add.

Lauren refilled their cups with tea, pushed one in front of Ashley and settled herself onto a stool along the kitchen island. Ashley smiled weakly and circled her neck to release the tension building there.

"That *is* interesting news. I hope Bill doesn't treat his new fiancé the way he treated me... I'm sure she's a lovely girl, but I wouldn't wish Bill on any woman regardless of who his family is... Yes, let's change the subject. How are Blaine and Jonathan?... I know I have three brothers. I talk to Michael all the time so didn't need to ask... Yes, I have already congratulated him on getting a spread in *Southern Living Magazine* on his garden designs..."

The doorbell rang again, and Lauren went to answer it.

"Wow, Blaine was named one of the top forty under forty Businessmen in South Carolina and Jonathan will be running the campaign of one of the gubernatorial candidates. Very impressive... I will be sure to sit down and write them each a note of congratulations for tomorrow's mail."

Lauren walked into the kitchen arm-and-arm with Zach's mom. "Look who I found on your doorstep."

"Mom, company just stopped by, so I need to go. I'll call you next weekend. Love you." She hit the 'end call' button.

"Oh, sweetheart, you didn't need to interrupt your call with your mama on my account. I would have been happy to wait."

"Not a problem. We were just finishing up, or at least mother had finished letting me know what a disappointment I am." Ashley closed her eyes and forced her muscles to relax. "Sorry, Mother tends to bring out the worst in me. I apologize for dumping on you." She took a step forward and hugged Zach's mom. "I'm always glad to see you. Can I get you a cup of tea?"

"I would love some tea." Gloria June said, her gaze considering and tinged with sadness.

Ashley pulled a cup from the cupboard and filled it with the fragrant brew. She set it down in front of Gloria June and slid the cream pitcher and sugar bowl within easy reach.

"What brings you to town?" Ashley asked.

"Zach asked me to bring this to you." She placed a brown-paper wrapped, flat package on the counter. "Since this is Sunday, I thought it might be easier to catch you today than during the week." She smiled like a mother who knew something was going on between her son and this lovely young woman. "Besides, I think he'll ask if you got it when he calls you this evening."

"Really?" In awe, she ran her fingers along one edge. "A picture?"

Lauren batted Ashley on the arm. "Open it for goodness sakes."

Ashley stood it upright and gently started lifting the tape and removing the paper. As the wrapping fell away, she gasped. "This is beautiful. Texas Bluebonnets with his home in the background." She turned to Gloria June who along with Lauren were pressed against her back to look at the painting. "I can't accept this. It's much too precious and I know it's one of his favorites." She swiped a tear from her eye.

Gloria June put her hand on Ashley's shoulder. "He wants you to have it. He said you fell in love with the ranch and had never seen Bluebonnets. It will look real nice with your furniture. So come on, let's pick out a place to hang it." She nudged Ashley into action.

They tried a few different spots and finally decided on a place in the living room where she could see it from the kitchen or when she was sitting on the sofa.

"Well, I have to be going. I want to get back to the ranch before dark." She smothered Ashley in an embrace then held her back at arm's length. "Zach has never done anything like this for a woman. Being the duffus male of the species that he is, he probably hasn't told you yet, but you're very special to him. Remember this painting when he acts like he doesn't care. He does, but like most men, he has no idea how much he cares or that he actually needs to tell you."

"Thank you. You are one special lady." Ashley said and wrapped her arms around her to return the hug.

"Look, I need to scoot too," said Lauren. "We'll talk in a few days. I want to hear the rest of your story."

Ashley closed the front door behind them and walked over for another look at the painting. Let's see, impressive but impersonal flowers from Robert and a very thoughtful and personal painting from Zach. She sighed. Blast, Zach was really racking up the 'atta boy' points. He'd texted to ask if she'd be free at 5:30 to Skype. She realized she couldn't wait to hear his voice and see his face again.

Chapter Eleven

ASHLEY FLUFFED THE SOFA pillows before easing into their softness. Settling back she set her laptop on her legs and fired up her Skype connection. She'd already checked her makeup but wasn't quite happy with her hair yet. She was pinning it away from her face when the familiar bubbling sound announced the call and started prickles of anticipation racing along her fingers. She clicked the video button.

Zach's handsome face appeared on the screen. "Hi beautiful. How was your flight?"

"Uneventful. You look beat. How are you holding up?"

Zach dragged his hand down his face. "Tired. We got in around 2:30, unloaded the horses got them settled, then made a few practice runs to loosen up. Now we're fixing dinner and plan to turn in early after we do a final check on horses and equipment." She could hear the clank of pots and pans in the background.

"Is Matt making that racket?"

"Yeah. He's got cooking duty today and I've got clean-up. Tomorrow we switch."

"You two can cook?"

"Not really. Heather and my mom usually send us with stuff we only need to heat, or we grill something and we're both pretty good at nuking frozen food." He paused a moment. "Did my mom see you today?"

"Yes, and I can't tell you how much I love the painting. Thank you." She threw him a kiss. "I'm sitting here looking at it now." She twirled some hair around her finger. "Um, if you don't mind my asking, why? I know it's one of your favorites."

"I hope it reminds you of me, maybe miss me a little." He lowered his voice to keep from being overheard and leaned closer to the computer screen. "There's something about you that makes me think of a field of wildflowers in the spring so I wanted you to have it."

She put her hand over her heart and made an 'I'm so touched' face as she dabbed at moist eyes. "What a sweet thing to say. I want you to know I will treasure it, always. I can't wait to see the Bluebonnets in bloom. It must be spectacular."

He brought his voice back up to a normal volume. "People come from all over the world to see them. The Bluebonnets and Texas Paintbrush start blooming in the next few weeks. Then the fields will be a carpet of blue and red. You'll have to come out and see them."

"I'd love that. From now until the end of April my life is consumed by tax returns, but I can probably squeeze in at least a partial day. What's your schedule like?"

"We plan to drive home on Wednesday so Matt can be with his family and I can check on a mare that's about to foal. Then depending upon how we do... and I expect we'll advance... we'll drive back to Houston on Monday and most likely be there through the end of the competition a week later. After that, we're home for ten days and then traveling most of April."

"Dinners ready. Come get it while it's hot," Matt hollered.

"Sounds like I need to go. I miss you." They both put their hands to the screen and touched palms. "I'll call again tomorrow. Any chance we can get together when I'm home next week, even just for a little while in the evening?"

"I'm pretty swamped but I still have to eat. How about dinner Friday night, my place?"

"See you then."

·♥·♥·♥·♥·♥·

ASHLEY STOOD AT THE stove stirring the spaghetti sauce, absent-mindedly humming along to the happy dance in her head. It had been five days, nine hours and fifteen minutes since Zach had walked out of that Dallas hotel room, but who was counting? He would be knocking on her door in about thirty minutes. Thirty minutes too long. She reached over to the plate of meatballs on the counter to start adding them to the sauce and caught sight of Robert's flowers. There they were sitting on the breakfast nook table off the kitchen, a glaring reminder of the other man in her life.

Her hand stalled mid stir. Why was it that she only thought about Robert when she glanced at the flowers he'd sent a few days ago? Would she think of him at all when those lovely blooms were tossed in the compost bin? And then there was Zach, the man who consumed way too many of her waking moments. Sky blue eyes, magnificently kissable lips, hands that could gentle a horse or set her on fire. She set the lid on the skillet and turned the flame down to simmer.

Sitting at the breakfast nook table, leg curled under her, fingering the fading blooms in Robert's flower arrangement, she only wished she could turn her growing feelings for Zach to simmer as easily. Zach's nightly calls and string of text messages throughout the day kept a smile on her lips, a spring in her step and sunshine in her heart. Robert, she feared, would never be more than a dear friend. She'd given him a chance, but so far sizzle had failed to make an appearance.

In the search for her perfect mate, would she need to give up on the idea of finding deep and abiding love and settle for something less? Could a man be a bad boy on the outside and a kind and gentle soul on the inside? Could Zach be that man? Her rich, bad boys had proven income level didn't make a true Prince Charming. What did she really want? What was important?

The knock at her door sent excitement slamming into her center. *He's here* shouted that annoying voice in her head. She unfolded herself from the chair and scurried to answer the need tightening her chest.

There he stood, all six mouthwatering feet of him, leaning against her door frame and a six-ways-to-sexy grin that never failed to make her wilt like flowers in a drought. She grabbed him with both hands and yanked him inside. He kicked the door closed with his heel.

Strong arms pulled her tight against his muscular chest, full lips fitted themselves effortlessly to hers. Her mouth opened to let their tongues dance. Heaven. Home. Hallelujah. Her renegade emotional brain overpowered her rational brain, shoved it down the basement stairs and tossed the key in the river. Emotional brain could stay lip-locked in this man's potent embrace forever. Rational brain whispered... broken heart, broken promises, broken trust.

His hands traveled up to her shoulders and slowly put enough space between them so he could gaze deeply into her violet eyes now darkened with desire. "I've missed you," he said simply.

She ran her hand down his freshly shaved cheek, relishing the fine-sandpaper feel under her palm as she breathed in the familiar fresh air scent of him. "I've missed you too."

Stepping back, she added, "Your new foal is adorable, bless its little heart. All wobbly legs, big eyes and determination. Thank you for sending me the video of his first few minutes."

"You're welcome. I like sharing what happens in my life with you." He shrugged out of his jacket and laid it across the back of the sofa then set his hat on top of it. "You'll have to come out to the ranch and see him after I get back from Houston. He's already a corker and should be real frisky in a few more weeks." He blazed a disarming smile at her. "Of course, I wouldn't fight it if you can find a few days in your schedule to join me in Houston. Keep me from being lonesome? Matt can sleep elsewhere."

"I'm sure Matt would just love being tossed out in the cold, and you, lonesome... puleeze. Buckle Bunnies line up from here to the state line hoping to get their man-eating claws into you."

"True. I can't help it if I am devilishly handsome."

Ashley socked him in the arm.

He rubbed the spot she hit. "But I only have eyes for you, sweetheart." Zach beamed like he'd said something profound.

"Sure, as long as I am within eyesight. After that..." she shrugged.

Zach's sigh was tinged with a hint of exasperation. "I know I've told you this before but apparently it hasn't penetrated that lovely head of yours yet. I'm a one-woman-at-a-time kind of guy and right now, you're my woman."

He smoothed his fingers across her furrowed brow, wiping away the creases. He wished he could do the same to the hesitation he saw in her eyes. Damn it. He wasn't one of those assholes who had treated her badly in the past. He didn't make false promises. But what promises had he made? None, came the incriminating answer. What promises did he want to make? Silence and confusion echoed in his brain.

"Are you hungry? Dinner will be ready in a few minutes. I just have to boil the spaghetti noodles and brown the garlic bread. Come on." She took his hand and led him into the kitchen.

He stopped in the arched doorway to the kitchen, closed his eyes, and inhaled deeply. "Smells amazing."

When she lifted the lid off the skillet and released the full impact of the fragrant, spicy aroma he said, "Be still my beating heart." He dropped to one knee. "Marry me so I can eat like this for the rest of my natural born days."

Ashley scowled. "Marriage proposals are no joking matter." She added the noodles to the boiling water with trembling hands.

"You're right. Sorry, didn't mean to get your hopes up." Why in the world had he said that? Jeez, time for a huge, mental head slap, but a snarky, little voice whispering in the back of his mind made him wonder if he had been joking about that marriage proposal.

"No problem. No hopes gotten up here. Friends with benefits, remember." She bent to slide a zucchini casserole out of the oven to be replaced by the pan of garlic bread and hoped the bitterness she felt hadn't come through in her voice. Given the thunder clouds hovering over him, it probably had.

She placed the hot casserole dish in a cork lined basket. "Would you mind carrying this to the dining table?" He took the container by the wooden handles, flinching slightly when their hands brushed. This was going to be one long evening she thought. Her expectations flattened like an old tire... it still had air but wasn't going anywhere fast.

Ashley flicked off the oven, pulled out the garlic bread and gingerly transferred it to a waiting napkin-lined bowl. She stuck a knuckle into her mouth that had touched the hot pan.

"That's what happens when you play with fire." His eyes dark and hooded, he took the bread bowl from her.

"You'd think I'd learn after all these years that fire burns." She turned her back to him and began ladling the sauce and meatballs into another bowl. "Why don't you take that to the table and have a seat. I'll be right in with the rest of our meal." His rigid back told her all she needed to know about his mood. She braced her hands on the counter and took a deep breath then willed her muscles to relax, summoning the calm and sophisticated Ashley. Time to crawl back into her protective shell.

After setting the bowls on the table, she took her seat. "Would you like to say the blessing or should I?"

"You go ahead."

"Thank you, Lord, for the food we are about to partake and the chance for friends to share each other's lives. Amen."

They each glanced up and, "I'm sorry," came out of two mouths simultaneously.

Zach looked down at his plate and then back up at her confusion creasing his forehead. Ashley slipped her hand across the table and touched his hand. He figured he needed to say something but had no idea what.

"I'm sorry. I'm being an ass. I apologize." He scrubbed his hair with both hands, then picked up the bowl and ladled sauce over his noodles before passing the bowl back to her. "In addition to not knowing what this is," he swished the hand holding the fork back and forth between them, "I'm worried about my dad. He just seems off. Can't put my finger on it but he's not himself."

"And here I've made your evening even more stressful. I'm sorry. I hate this time of year at work. Everyone wants everything done yesterday. Maybe we're both just a little distracted and stressed and ready to snap at the first person who looks at us cross-eyed. So what is your dad doing that seems off?" Best to move away from the topic of 'whatever this' was between them.

"He hasn't had his usual stamina. He's talked a little about his stomach bothering him. My mom has been badgering him to go to the doctor, but he's a stubborn old coot." He shook his head but his lips quirked up at the edge. "If he doesn't snap out of it soon, my mom will hogtie him and drag him to the doctor."

"I have a clear picture in my mind." Ashley chuckled. "Your dad doesn't stand a chance."

"I don't think any man stands a chance against a determined woman." Wariness crept into his voice on soft, slippered feet.

"So in all your adult life, your mom's the only determined woman you've run up against? That's why you're still footloose and fancy free, women at your beck and call?"

"Excuse me while I pull my size 12 boots out of my mouth." He did have the grace to look a little sheepish but a frown chased it away. "You've got me. There have been women who have tried to make me commit to more than I've been ready to give. They were the wrong women or it was the wrong time or both." He leveled a penetrating gaze at her. "So what? That doesn't mean I'll never settle down. Most of my adult life has been focused on building my career. There hasn't been time for distractions." He shoved a forkful of spaghetti into his mouth.

"Women and commitment are distractions?" She raised her brows, her face a mask of cool indifference. "How enlightened of you."

"My mama didn't raise no dumb cowboy. I'm not walking into that minefield." He pushed the last of his zucchini around on his plate. She sat there silently waiting. "I want the whole shebang someday. Wife, kids, trials and tribulations, and every bit of love we can cram into all those other moments, but I don't have a timetable. My life isn't all worked out."

"Fair enough." She sipped her tea, letting the sugary sweetness float around on her tongue. "I saw Heather in town the other day. We met for lunch when she was making a feed store run. Poor thing was definitely green around the gills. She's thrilled to have Matt home for a few days."

"He feels the same way. Couldn't wait to get home. I get the feeling he's chomping at the bit for this season to be in the books so he can be with his family fulltime."

"Have you decided what you're going to do yet?"

"Not yet. Still weighing my options. Rodeoing has been my life since the first time I swung a rope at a hay bale at the ripe, old age of four. It's brought me fame. It's brought me fortune. It's made the ranch secure."

"Dreams are hard to let go of and maybe it's not your time to stop dreaming yet."

"It's more than a dream. It's in my blood. For so long it's been every breath I took, but I can see through Matt that other things – family – can make you want something else, something more."

"I understand. When I had to leave the plantation, it was like tearing out a piece of my heart. I knew I would never be allowed to run the place so I finally had to move on. Wasn't easy. I mourned the loss of my dream," she rose and started collecting the dirty dishes, "but the choice was marry well, take up my place in society and produce offspring... or try and figure out what direction *I* want my life to take."

He touched her hand, rose and kissed her softly on the cheek. "Let me help."

Sadness shadowed the tentative smile she offered. "Thank you." Together they quietly carried the dishes into the kitchen. In silence Ashley rinsed the dishes and loaded them into the dishwasher. Zach placed the leftovers in containers and stacked them in the refrigerator. Ashley filled the sink with hot, sudsy water and washed the pots and pans.

Zach slid his arms around her waist and nuzzled her neck. "What's wrong with us? I've been counting the seconds until I could hold you in my arms again, smell your hair, talk to you in person... I feel like I've had the wind knocked out of me and I don't know how to get back up."

"Would you like some pie? It's apple, your favorite?"

He stepped away from her and shoved his hands in his pockets. "Sure."

Ashley pulled two plates out of the cupboard and filled them with pie. "Whipped cream?"

"Sure."

She spooned fluffy dollops of freshly whipped cream onto each slice. "Coffee?"

"Sure." He accepted the two plates she handed him. She poured the coffee and they walked slowly back into the dining room.

Once they were seated, Zach leaned his forearms on the table and looked at Ashley. "Are we going to talk about this?"

"Zach, I like you a lot, probably too much for my own good, but I have to face facts. We are not going to be more than friends." Her smile didn't reach her eyes and it looked like she was near tears. "We both want different things right now. We're at different places in our lives. Maybe if we'd been different people and the timing had been different..."

"I'm not ready to kick what we feel for each other to the curb. Maybe I'm not who you think you want and maybe I'm not ready to settle down yet, but I know what I'm feeling for you is more than friendship. I would like to give us a chance to see if we can work out this timing thing."

"I do want to keep seeing you. I want to stay in your life. Every friendship or relationship or whatever this is has its ups and downs... and if this turns out to be more... well, one step at a time."

"What exactly are we arguing about?" Zach asked. "I feel like I'm shuffling around in the dark and about to trip over a chair and land flat on my face."

"Honestly, I have no idea. Can we just chalk it up to a misalignment of the stars?" She smoothed nonexistent wrinkles out of the table-cloth. "Friends, good friends, friends who will stick together through thick and thin, always find a way to get past disagreements. Can we just put this evening behind us?"

"I'm going to have to head out." He took her hand and walked her into the living room where he shrugged into his jacket and put his hat on his head.

Zach gently tugged her into his arms and poured everything he didn't understand he wanted into the kiss. Ashley returned the favor. Both were breathless when they stepped apart. "I'll call you every night."

"I'll hold you to that, cowboy." One more kiss and he was gone. She locked the door then leaned against it. Whether he was right for her or not, she was falling for that man.

·♥ · ♥ · ♥ · ♥ · ♥ ·

ZACH LED HIS HORSE out of his stall and joined Matt outside the trailer. Matt was adjusting his stirrups in preparation for their first practice run of the day. Zach flipped the saddle blanket over his horse's withers then settled it back so it didn't rub the horse's hair the wrong way. He heaved the saddle into place, carefully cinching it. The two men worked efficiently in companionable silence. They unhitched their horses, swung smoothly into their saddles with practiced grace and set off at a walk toward the practice arena.

"It sure was nice to be home with the family for a few days," Matt said as he uncoiled his rope, "but Heather is already counting the days until I get back. How's your dad?"

"Grumping and grousing that mom's making him go to the doctor next week, but he just hasn't been himself so I'm glad she's insisting."

Matt's smile commiserated with all men everywhere. "Sounds like my dad. Do you think we'll be the same someday? Our wives fussing at us to take care of ourselves and us resisting every step of the way?"

Zach looped his rope in preparation for their run and chuckled. "The way Heather has you watching your cholesterol, I'd say your someday is now. Ready?"

"Yup."

Zach nodded at the chute tender. The gate clanked open and the steer bolted out with Zach in hot pursuit. Within seconds, Zach had lassoed the steer his loop dropping neatly over its horns and turned it to the left. Matt's rope sailed gracefully, securely entrapping the steer's hind feet. The pair made another ten runs then moved out of the arena so another team could warm up.

"Hey, Zach, can I talk to you for a minute?" asked Jake Wyatt, a heeler for another pair of ropers.

"Sure," he nodded. "Matt, I'll catch up with you in a few." Matt trotted off toward the hot walker to cool his horse down and Zach dismounted. "What's up, Jake?"

"I hear you might be looking for a new heeler." He fell into step beside Zach as he walked his horse away from the arena.

"Matt is taking a year off, but I haven't decided yet what I'm going to do."

"Well, if you do decide to keep rodeoing and need a new partner, let me know. I'd like to be considered." Jake stopped walking and so did Zach. "But I'm looking for a partner who's shooting to make it to Nationals."

"Understood. Thanks for letting me know. You're a top tier heeler and I'm honored you might want to partner with me. I'll let you know as soon as I've made up my mind." The two shook hands.

Well that put a new twist on his options. Now if he could only sort out what he wanted. He'd assumed that without his partner, he'd sit the next season out and had already started picturing the year in his mind. This offer meant he was going to have to reevaluate. Zach mounted his horse and set a leisurely pace for their rig.

Matt continued to groom his horse as Zach dismounted and tethered his horse to the trailer.

"So what did Jake want?" Matt asked as he switched the body brush for a mane and tail comb and began work on his horse's mane.

"He heard you were taking a year off and wondered if I was looking for a new partner." Zach grunted as he lifted the saddle off his horse and set it on the portable rack, then flicked off the saddle blanket and set it on a shelf below the saddle.

"News travels fast." Matt picked up the horse's tail and started working the tangles out of it. "What'd ya tell him?"

"That I wasn't sure." Zach placed a halter on his horse and removed his bridle then stopped to lean his forearms on the horse's back and look over at Matt who had also paused for a minute.

"I know between ranch work, our team roping clinics, starting a herd of Corriente cattle and sponsorship appearances, I'd stay busy." He tilted his head up, closed his eyes and let the warm Texas sun wash the tension away. "But rodeoing... I'm just not sure I can give it up yet. I know I can't do this forever... reactions slow and the new kids take over... but am I at the top of my game yet? Is it time to step back from the thing I've loved most in the world for almost twenty-six years? How are you able to step away, even if it's only for a year?"

"Because while I love rodeoing, I guess there are other things in life I love more. My wife and kids are everything." Matt swiped his arm across his forehead to mop up the sweat trickling from under his hat. "The kids are growing so fast and I'm beginning to regret what I'm missing. I'm not saying that I won't go back to rodeoing at some level, but I do know I'm never going to aim for Nationals again." He looked squarely at his partner and best friend. "Zach, you and I have logged enough miles to have gone to the moon and back several times over. I'm ready to stay closer to home and see more of my family. That's what I want. Only you can decide what you want."

Matt carefully placed his grooming equipment in its caddy, un-hitched his horse and led him into his stall. Zach went back to grooming his horse so he could start preparing for the semi-final rounds coming up in a few hours. He had a lot to think about once this rodeo was over, but until then, his mind had to stay focused on the event. He also realized he really wanted to talk to Ashley as soon as possible after he returned from Houston.

·♥·♥·♥·♥·♥·

ZACH HAD BEEN SO pensive the last few times they'd talked and he hadn't texted as much as usual. He obviously had something on his mind and their relationship had been more tenuous since their infamous dinner. Ashley really wanted to see him and clear the air, which was why she had taken a Friday off during tax season and was heading to the ranch to see him. Her car was in the shop for routine maintenance and she'd rented a Miata for old time's sake.

It felt like she'd recovered a piece of her body that had been lopped off years ago – that fun, carefree, hair-blowing-in-the-wind person who was usually overshadowed by the I-desperately-want-my-mother's-approval persona most people saw. Naturally, her mother had disapproved of the little red Miata Ashley had purchased fresh out of college and preferred the BMW Sedan her parents had gifted her at graduation. The Miata was Ashley – a dash of spice, high energy, passionate and ready to embrace whatever life had in store. The BMW was the alter ego her mother cultivated – reserved, polished, concerned about public perception, and who tucked emotional displays into a dark corner. Thank heavens for small favors, her mother had the grace to refrain from gloating when Ashley lost her beloved Miata in the 'Bill' debacle.

Ashley drew in a deep breath of the fresh country air tinged with sage and mesquite. Today was too beautiful to dwell on the negative. Today she could trot out that little bit crazy Ashley and shove carefully controlled Ashley back in her corner. Zach and his family accepted her the way she was. She worried her bottom lip with her teeth. Hopefully the tension between her and Zach was a passing desert squall... thunderclouds, wind, rain, gone... washing the dust out of the air and leaving the landscape ready for new growth. He'd sounded happy that she was coming out to the ranch. She figured that was a good sign.

She turned on her blinker, eased into the turnout then punched the accelerator, spewing a cloud of gravel in her wake. She slowed as she neared the compound, parked, and wandered over to watch Zach and his brothers play what seemed to be some form of basketball unique to the Kincaid clan. It involved a lot of bumping, elbowing, stomping on feet, and general mayhem.

"Lemonade?" Gloria June handed Ashley a tall, sweaty glass of the sweet drink topped with a sprig of mint.

"Thanks. I must admit this is the first time I've seen basketball played in boots and Stetsons." She took a sip. "Fresh squeezed?"

"Naturally."

"Are there any rules to this game?"

Gloria June chuckled and slapped Ashley on the back. "Mostly get the ball in the basket any way you can and don't kill each other or your mama will have your hide."

Nate plowed into Zach, shoulder to solar plexus, forcing him back a step and dislodging the ball. Josh did a quick grab, pivot, and ball in the basket.

"Hey, that was mine," hollered Nate.

"Doesn't look like it from where I'm standing," Josh needled. So the shy, retiring, socially uncomfortable brother, had his caveman moments Ashley thought.

"Good thing those boys all went different directions in life or I'm sure I would have attend at least one of their funerals by now. They are too competitive for their own good." Gloria June shook her head but smiled fondly.

"Lucky you, having to keep four alpha males in line. I'd be willing to bet you've got some stories to tell." Ashley took another sip of her lemonade waiting for Gloria June to continue.

Nate caught the ball on the inbound. Zach elbowed Nate in the ribs, twisted the ball out of his hands and launched it through the hoop. Jeans riding low on his hips, muscles that bunched and flowed like molten lava, a sheen of sweat slicking that work-chiseled body and rock-hard abs angling down to a magnificent... made her hot just thinking about what was tucked into those jeans.

"I think that makes twenty, gentlemen." Zach's arms shot up in victory. "Winner and champion yet again." Nate stomped on Zach's foot. "Hey! Sore loser." Zach punched Nate in the shoulder starting a free-for-all of pushing and shoving.

Gloria June rolled her eyes. "Stories, for sure. Three rambunctious boys and one stubborn as a mule husband on a ranch where injury lurked behind every rock, life was never dull. Top that with boys who kept trying to outdo each other and I should write a book."

She paused and looked over at Ashley. "Zach, though, he's a special case. He was gonna win or die trying. He would practice till he mastered whatever skill he needed to succeed in the task he set for himself, then proceed to obliterate the competition. He was never mean, but the boy did not like losing. I think that's why he's a little worried about what happens after he quits rodeoing, if he'll lose focus."

"Do you think that could happen? He'll turn into a man without a country so to speak?"

"No, while Zach thrives on the competition, he's more well-rounded than he thinks. When he quits rodeoing, he'll become the best rancher, stock breeder, mentor... just like his dad did. He'll transition just fine." She patted Ashley's arm. "All right you boys, now stop that tussling. Don't y'all have something else you need to be doing? Zach, I believe there are some fence posts with your name on them. Nate, don't you have some livestock to vaccinate? Josh, those stalls aren't going to muck themselves. Don't want you to get too high and mighty with that techy stuff and forget your roots now."

All three came to attention responding, "Yes, ma'am." They grabbed nearby towels, swiped at their faces and underarms and slipped on their t-shirts. Dutifully, they carted the dirty towels to the ranch laundry room. Nate walked over to his veterinary truck, reached in, and grabbed a case that he slung over his shoulder and strode off to a nearby pasture while Josh disappeared into the barn.

Zach sauntered up looking as cocky and self-assured as the blue jays in the trees screeching their superiority to the world. He stopped in front of her, put a large hand on each shoulder, bent down and gave her a quick, noisy kiss on the lips.

"I sure have missed you," he said gazing deeply into her eyes then grinned and pulled on her ponytail.

And the sun shone a little brighter, the flowers smelled a little sweeter, and her world settled back into the right orbit. She figured the goofy grin on her face would make him think he could have his way with her whenever he wanted – and bless his little heart, he'd be right.

He pulled her into him for a hug then looked over at his mom. "I was thinking I'd take Ashley out for a picnic and then get to work on those fences, if it's alright with you? I know how dad likes us all to be at the dinner table."

"I think we can let you skip the family meal just this once. I figured those fancy salads and cheeses and breads were yours so I put them in a cooler in your truck. You two go have a good time."

Zach leaned over and kissed his mom on the cheek. "You're the best." He grabbed Ashley's hand and walked her over to his truck, opened the passenger side door then lifted her onto the seat. His lips claimed hers in a serious kiss, teasing them apart so their tongues could play slip and slide. She wrapped her legs around his waist, dug her fingers into his hair and pulled him closer. Ashley felt the heat radiate down her neck, across her chest as it coursed its way down to her feminine core.

He pulled back, encasing her head between his hands and nuzzling her neck with his nose. "As much as I'd like to pretend the rest of the world doesn't exist, I suppose we'd best be on our way before I do something I'd prefer my family didn't see." He slid her legs into the truck, pulled the seatbelt across her lap, and snapped it into place.

After he climbed into the driver's seat, he said, "I'm going to take you to one of my favorite places in all the world for a starter and when we get back, I'll show you the colt. Little guy is growing like a weed." Putting one hand on the steering wheel, he reached for the starter button with the other but paused mid-way. He leaned back in the seat and tilted his head to look at her under the brim of his hat.

"Look, I'm not sure what happened the other night and if it was a fight, I don't even remember what it was about. Can we get back to where we were?"

"No." When he started to say something, she put her hand on his arm. "I'm hoping we can get to a better place than where we were. I think we're both trying to figure out what this attraction is between us, where it's going and what exactly we want to do about it. I'm putting my plan on hold for a while and am going to trust that you'll be honest with me. No promises, no expectations, no pressure to turn this into something if it isn't there. I enjoy being with you and would like to take it one day at a time."

Zach leaned over the center compartment and kissed her tenderly on the lips, gently cupping her face in his hands. "One day at a time," he whispered before he started the truck and pulled away from the compound.

Chapter Twelve

THEY RODE IN COMPANIONABLE silence, enjoying the warm, spring day as they bumped along the rutted ranch road. The terrain was so different from the South Carolina Low Country she grew up with. Texas was vast and rugged with air that made you want to gulp in great lungful's and a landscape painted with a broad palette of colors. South Carolina was a lush, green monotone and heavy, moisture-laden skies that wrapped you in a sultry cocoon. Ashley realized Texas was home.

"Where are you taking me, South America? Your ranch feels like it goes on forever." She twisted in her seat to face him.

"It does seem so, especially when we have to move cattle or repair fencing. With a little over a hundred thousand acres, it keeps me and my wranglers busy." He put his hand over hers on the central armrest and held it. "And as to where I am taking you, it's that favorite place I told you about. It's my thinking place. The place I go to recharge and let any cares I have flow away with the river."

"So this isn't the famous swimming hole?"

"Heck no, everybody knows where that is. This is *my* place. Each of us has a spot with a great big, invisible, no trespassing sign attached to it. We respect each other's privacy when we're in our special places."

"How much longer?"

"Just a few more minutes."

Zach spread that grin a little wider. "See the river." He pointed off to the right. "My hideaway is in that grove of trees."

He pulled the truck to a stop a minute later, leaned over and laid one lingering, toe-curling kiss on her. "Ready?"

"As I'll ever be."

He walked around to help her out then opened the door to the extended cab to snag the cooler and a blanket. Hand-in-hand they walked along a well-worn path through the trees. It opened to a small, secluded beach that skirted the river for about ten yards. It was a quiet bend, ringed by cypress and willow trees, where the water ponded up. About 100 yards away water splashed over a short drop. Just as he described it, she saw fields of wildflowers and cattle grazing against the backdrop of distant hills.

Ashley paused to take it all in. Zach watched her appreciate his place and waited patiently for her reaction, giving her time to absorb this place he treasured.

"Zach, I don't even have words for how special this is. Thank you for sharing it with me." She rose on tiptoe and kissed him softly on the mouth.

"You're the first person outside of family I've ever brought here." He smiled down at her and raised her hand to his lips. "Don't look so shocked. I don't know why I've never brought anyone else here before. Maybe it's because I'm coming here this time to simply enjoy the place and not work something out. Maybe I just wanted you to see it." He lifted a shoulder and set the cooler on the sand.

Ashley spread out the blanket and started unpacking the food, opening containers, adding serving pieces, then handed Zach a plate and utensils. After they'd filled their plates, they sat down on the blanket, Zach cross-legged and Ashley with hers tucked under her. They ate in a tenuous silence then placed everything back in the cooler. They both sat back down, side-by-side, not wanting the moment to end.

"I can see why you like coming here. The peace wipes the slate in my mind clean. It's a good spot to put things in perspective." She closed her eyes felt the gentle breeze caress her cheeks and lift the tendrils of hair that had escaped her ponytail, heard the gurgling of the water as it wandered by and the songs of the birds as they called out to their mates. Her entire body relaxed, totally calm... that is until Zach turned her face into his kiss. In the blink of an eye her world went from serene blue to hot, hot red.

He guided her back onto the blanket, shifting his leg between hers while hovering over her. She flicked his hat aside and circled her hands around his neck, accepting his kiss and asking for more. His hand cupped her breast, his nimble fingers gently caressing and tracing their fullness.

She brought one hand down to tunnel underneath his t-shirt and felt the bulge of his desire against her hip. His hand slipped under the edge of her shirt inching it up over her belly his lips eagerly nipping the newly exposed skin.

They broke apart long enough to shed their clothing and then crashed together to became one – a concept their bodies accepted but their hearts hadn't quite figured out. Zach continued to hold her after they had exploded into a million pieces, letting their pulse rates slowly return to earth. They lay on their sides facing each other. One of Zach's hands lazily traced up and down her arm while the arm under her held her tight to him.

His lips captured her ear lobe then he whispered, "Wish I could stay like this, wrapped around you until I turn old and gray, but if I don't get some of those fence posts in the ground today, my ma will have my hide."

She palmed that firm butt of his and squeezed. "Can't have anyone messing up a work of art so I guess we'd better stop lazing about." She felt his manhood twitch against her leg. "None of that now. All play and no work means... I don't know, but I'm sure something awful."

"But I was planning to work... on you." He smiled seductively against her cheek. She gave him a little push. With a sigh, he rolled onto his back and slung his arm across his eyes.

Ashley propped herself on one elbow and ran one finger down his arm starting at his shoulder. "You are one magnificent man. If Michelangelo had you around, the statue would have been named Zachariah and not David."

He squinted open one eye taking in those luscious curves, silken skin, huge violet eyes, lips that would tempt a saint. He decided he was no saint and pulled her in for another kiss. "Woman, are you trying to kill me? I only have just so much will power." Zach rolled to his feet, grabbed his underwear and jeans and shrugged into them. He sat back down bending his knees to his chest and circling them with his arms.

"No, just working up the energy to move." She pushed herself to a sitting position and looked around for her clothes.

Spying her underwear and bra in a nearby bush, she got up to retrieve them. She could feel Zach's eyes on her as she dressed. Instead of feeling vulnerable, she realized she felt liberated. So *not* the girl her mother wanted her to be.

"The day's not getting any younger," she chided. "We'd better start on those fences."

Zach pulled on his t-shirt, boots and retrieved his hat, then picked up the cooler while Ashley folded the blanket.

"I brought you along to keep me company," he said, "not to help repair fences. Pounding in t-stakes and stringing barbed wire is hard work."

Ashley stopped on the path, hands planted on her hips. "Why Zach Kincaid, I do believe your male chauvinism is showing. Aren't you the one who told me you wanted your woman to be your partner. Are you trying to tell me I can't handle normal ranch chores?"

"Uh, no," he said like he was afraid he had stepped into something he shouldn't track into the house. "I'm pretty sure you could catch on to stringing wire but," that lopsided grin that turned her all mushy inside played around his lips, "sweetheart, pounding in fence posts isn't for half-pints." He side-stepped but the blanket hit him in the chest anyway.

"I'll have you know, buster," she poked him in the chest, "that I've strung barbed wire before. I'm also adept at splicing. I am *not* a helpless female."

"Duly noted. Any fence repair you want to help with, you have my complete and utter backing." He hooked his free arm around her neck and pulled her into him. "Kinda sexy the image of you wielding pliers and crimps. You are too cute. Let's get to work, partner."

The truck bumped across the pasture to the rattling of the tools and metal posts in the truck bed until they reached a section of fence that had seen better days. The majority of the old posts tilted at forty-five-degree angles and some were almost flat on the ground. Wire in some spots was broken and needed to be spliced or replaced but most just needed to be tightened and reattached to the new posts.

Zach walked around to the back of the truck and lowered the tailgate. He pulled out two plastic tool caddies that held the smaller hand tools, leather gloves, wire tighteners, barbed-wire nails, and crimps. Next he lifted out a hi-lift jack to remove the old wooden fence posts, attached the barbed wire spool holder to the trailer hitch so they could easily unwind whatever amount they needed and handed her ten, six-foot long steel T-posts.

"Start here," he motioned to a spot a few feet away, "leave a post about every twelve feet. I'll get started removing the old wooden posts."

Ashley shuffled off carefully balancing the posts and dropping them at the designated intervals. Zach shoved on a pair of leather work gloves, grabbed a pair of pliers and pulled out the old, barbed wire nails freeing the wire from the wooden post. Next he used a chain to attach the hi-lift jack to the base of the old post and cranked the post out of the ground. Ashley leaned against the truck watching Zach, muscles rippling under his cotton t-shirt, as he worked the T-post driver up and down forcing the steel rod into the hard-packed earth. Best entertainment in Texas to her way of thinking. Ashley pushed away from the truck, dug the smallest leather gloves she could find out of the tote along with a tin of wire clips and the fence fork tool used to fasten them to the T-posts.

"I'll just get started attaching the wire." It took her a few tries to get used to working in leather gloves at least two sizes too big, but soon she was smoothly clipping the old wires to the new T-post. Once she had attached all of the strands, she used the wire tightener and clips to tighten any loose wires.

He pulled on one of the strands to test its hold. "You *do* know your stuff. I'm impressed."

She smiled smugly. "Don't you have some more fence posts to pound, cowboy?"

"Yes ma'am, that I do," He sauntered off down the line and got back to work.

Several hours later they had emptied the truck of the replacement posts and were leaning against it chugging water out of canteens. She wrinkled her nose as she pulled the canteen away from her lips.

"Sorry, no fancy bottled water." He used his fingertips to wipe a trickle of sweat from her face. The heat from his touch infused her face with a lovely glow.

"It's the metallic taste. I don't like it but am happy to have the water no matter its taste or its temperature."

"We make a pretty good team," he said. "That's a fair bit of fencing we finished today."

She followed his gaze back to where they had started. "We did do good work. On a spread this size, how often do you need to work on your fencing?"

"We send a crew out at least once a month to one section or another to make repairs – more often if someone notices some fence down. The hands are responsible for most of the maintenance, but whenever

I have time, I go with them. It helps keep my head on straight and reminds me what real ranch work is."

He pushed his hat back on his head and looked into the distance. "Slowly but surely, I'm replacing the old wooden posts with steel posts and someday I'll replace a lot of the barbed wire with electric fencing. I plan to bring the ranch into the twenty-first century."

"Ambitious. So, rodeoing has a limited shelf life?"

"Of course, no one can rodeo forever. I don't know when my last rodeo will be yet but I do know the day will come." He looked over at her. "I had planned to follow Matt's lead and take this next year off, but at Houston another Heeler asked if he could partner with me."

"And are you going to?"

He looked up at the puffy white clouds flitting across the clear Texas sky and took a deep breath. "I don't know. What with taking on more responsibility at the ranch because of dad's health, the roping clinics, sponsorship commitments, and improvements I want to make around here, rodeoing is up in the air right now for next year."

"But rodeo is still your first love." She laid a hand on his arm, "and you shouldn't feel compelled to give it up if you aren't ready."

"Not sure about first love but it is right up there. Still, I'm seriously considering taking next year off to see how it goes." He shifted his weight as though he was trying to move the elephant in the room. "If I weren't rodeoing, do you think you might put me on your list?"

Ashley stepped in front of him and reached up to frame his face in her hands. "You're on my list whether or not you are rodeoing, so don't stop unless *you* want to."

He kissed her long and slow, marking her as his. "On that note, lets head back and check out that foal."

·♥·♥·♥·♥·♥·

"I WISH WE COULD Skype. I miss you and it helps to at least see your face." Ashley could hear the road noise in the background.

"Me too, but on the road, a phone call will have to do. I'll have my computer tonight though." Zach juggled his phone to his other ear as he shoved a French fry in his mouth.

"Where are you and what rodeo are you heading for?" Ashley asked.

"On our way to Athens, Texas for the Stampede Rodeo. Luckily today is dry so the drive is not bad. Not so lucky tomorrow when it's supposed to pour. The arena's covered so we won't be slipping and sliding in the mud but getting back and forth won't be fun."

"As a cowboy, dealing with bad weather must be second nature."

"True enough. Been wet and miserable more than once in my life. If the weather reports are right, you best break out a canoe. I hope you're planning on staying close to home this weekend."

"I don't plan to venture out and may just spend the next few days baking to my heart's content."

"I'll be home for three days next week before hitting the road again. Any chance you could save a crumb or two for me?"

"I imagine you can sweet talk me out of a treat or two. What cha have in mind?" Her voice was low, soft, and sultry.

"If I told you, it'd make Matt blush. I'm sure we can come up with something we both might enjoy."

"I'll hold you to that. You'll be back on Sunday?"

"Late in the afternoon and then we have to get the horses settled. Do you work on Monday?"

"Unfortunately, yes, and it will be a busy week for me. I doubt I'll get a chance to see you until the following week when my parents are in town. Is your dad still going in for angioplasty and stent surgery on that Monday?"

"Yeah, he is. I wish I could take more time off, but nine days is a lifetime in the rodeo world so I'll be there for the surgery and for the first week he's home."

"I'll stop by the hospital Monday morning to be with you before I pick up my parents at the airport."

"I appreciate that. It means a lot to all of us to have you there."

"Are you still planning on joining me and my parents for lunch on Wednesday? I know that's the day your dad will be coming home from the hospital."

"For sure. I want to meet your folks. Josh and Nate are going to help mom get dad home and situated so I'm yours for the day."

"Let me warn you about my mother. Her propriety meter is off the charts and she makes Emily Post look like a slacker. She looks down her lovely, elegant nose at anyone she views as beneath her socially and sadly, that covers a lot of territory."

"Don't worry sweetheart, I will be on my best behavior." His tone the tiniest bit terse. "While it may not seem like it at times, my mama did pound some manners into my thick skull."

"Oh, it's not *your* behavior I'm worried about. I'm more concerned that my mother will hurt your feelings and make you feel uncomfortable."

"Like she does you?"

"Yes, like she does me." She made that little grunt of frustration in the back of her throat he'd come to know when she talked about her family.

His warm, supportive smile came through over the phone. "Don't worry. I've got a pretty thick hide, but thanks for the warning." He paused and his tone turned gruff. "Is Robert getting the same warning?"

She was glad he couldn't see her cringe. "No. His pedigree is perfect. That means my mother will like him and start making wedding plans before dessert arrives. He will never be more to me than a good friend so she will make me feel like the most ungrateful daughter on the planet because, I wouldn't marry him even if he asked."

"I'm sorry you have to go through all this. I wish I could make it better."

"I have a client showing up in a few minutes so I have to go. I hate that it will be over a week before I see you again. Good luck tomorrow and I'll talk to you tonight."

"I'll be counting the minutes."

THE HOSPITAL DOOR SWISHED shut behind Ashley. She was itching to see him again even if it was in a very public place. Zach had said to meet him in the surgery waiting room. She had timed her arrival until after surgery had started, wanting to give the family time to visit with Jack in private. She saw Zach chatting with his brothers. They were a potent trio. Tall, movie star handsome – though not pretty-boy handsome – and sexy as all get out. But something in their demeanor said these men were the salt of the earth and you could count on them no matter what.

Ashley cleared her throat and Zach turned, his smile as big as the state of Texas. In a few long strides he was at her side.

He wrapped her in his arms and breathed in the floral scent of her hair, bending to nuzzle her neck. "You are exactly what my doctor ordered," he murmured in her ear.

"Couldn't have kept me away even if you wanted to." She stepped out of his arms to greet his mom and brothers. Once all the hellos and news was exchanged, Zach led her to a quiet corner and sat down.

"I thought you had the week off?"

"I do." She gave him a puzzled frown.

"But you're dressed like you're heading to the office. Not that I'm complaining." He held up his hands in peace. "You're gorgeous."

She chuckled and stroked her hand down his face. "This is my 'pick up my parents at the airport' attire. My mother would be mortified if I appeared in public in something other than Armani and pearls."

"Oh." Zach's face wrinkled in worry. "Do I need to rent a tux to wear to lunch on Wednesday?"

"As much as I love seeing you in a tux, a morning coat and top hat will suffice." She carefully schooled her face so he wouldn't see the mischief lurking there.

"Huh." His eyes went wide and she couldn't stop her laughter. "Are you sure your middle name's not gullible? You are too cute for words." She leaned closer and patted his chest with the flat of her hand. "You are a cowboy, my dear and I *like* who you are. I expect you to wear your Sunday jeans and the biggest championship belt buckle in your collection."

"You got it, but will I be starting World War Three showing up like that?"

"No, a cold war maybe, so bring a coat. I'm tired of pretending to be someone I'm not in the hopes my mother will be pleased."

"Am I going to be bushwhacked on Wednesday? Do I need to wear my six shooters?"

"No, I just want you to meet them, but I also want you to be prepared for a family dynamic that is very different from your own." She stood up. "Hey all, Zach and I are going to the cafeteria. Who wants us to bring something back?"

After taking orders, they headed down the hall. "I wish I could stay until your dad is out of surgery but I have to meet my parents at the airport. Call me when your dad's in recovery."

·♥·♥·♥·♥·♥·

A FEW HOURS LATER the limo Ashley had rented pulled up to the airport curb. "I'll text you as soon as we're leaving the baggage claim area," she said to the driver. She motioned for the valet she'd hired to follow her. No way would her parents collect their own bags and haul them to the limo.

She waved as her parents entered the baggage area and then air kissed them once she reached them. "Do you have your claim tickets so the valet can collect your bags?"

"They will be brown Louis Vuitton luggage," Ashley's mother said. They were standing off to the side of the baggage claim area to avoid being jostled. Ashley handed the tickets to the valet who strode off in the direction of the carousel.

"How was your flight?"

"It was fine, darling, though honestly, first-class is not what it used to be. Service seems to get worse every year." Her mother smoothed back her perfectly coiffed hair. "You are looking well except your hair hasn't been properly styled in a while. A woman, especially a single woman, mustn't let herself go." Her cultured tones never failed to make Ashley feel like a country bumpkin. Her father was already engrossed in a phone call. So, what else was new?

"I'm so glad you could take a few days to visit. The weather is exceptionally nice this time of year. How are Blaine and Jonathan doing? I don't hear from them often."

"You know how busy they are. They hardly have time to call me and I'm their mother. Did I tell you that Blaine's wife is expecting their second child?" Ashley shook her head. "No? Well they only recently had the pregnancy confirmed. You could pick up the phone and call them."

"That works both ways, Mother. They can call me as well."

"Are you going to be this prickly during our entire visit? I declare, I know I raised you better than that."

"No Mother. I'm looking forward to showing you around San Antonio and introducing you to several of my new friends. Tonight Lauren is joining us for dinner." Ashley glanced toward the rhythmic sound of clicking wheels on concrete. "Ah, here's the valet. Should we head to the limo?" Ashley pulled out her phone and signaled the limo driver to meet them.

Robert stood as Ashley and her parents trailed the waiter to their table. His lips barely brushed Ashley's cheek as he waited for introductions.

"Mother, Father, I would like to introduce you to Robert Prichard III. Robert, I would like you to meet my mother, Susan, and my father, William Drayton." The men shook hands and Susan offered her cheek to Robert for a perfunctory kiss. Once the men helped the ladies get seated, Robert signaled for the waiter.

"May I get you something to drink?" the waiter asked. "We have an exquisite selection of wines."

"May I?" Robert glanced over at William who nodded. Robert opened the wine list. "Please bring us... he rattled off the names of two fine, and very expensive, wines."

"Excellent choices, sir." The waiter collected the wine list and dipped his head in deference before walking away.

"What a lovely setting," cooed Susan. "It's refreshing to see that not all establishments have lowered their standards to today's fast-food mentality. I'm amazed at how few restaurants bother to use linens at lunch anymore. So Robert, tell me about yourself. I understand you live in Dallas and flew in for the afternoon on your private jet."

"I did, although it turns out I am meeting a client for dinner so won't be flying back until late this evening." He shot his cuffs. "I own one of the largest real estate firms in Dallas, but I do come to San Antonio frequently, thanks to our thriving ranch division. Gives me the chance to see Ashley." He reached over and patted her hand.

The waiter and an assistant returned to the table with white and red wine glasses for each person. He placed them precisely on the table then poured one of each bottle and a cleansing glass of water for Robert. He handed the red to Robert who proceeded to sniff and taste the wine. Once both wines were approved the waiter asked each person which wine they preferred, poured it, and then backed away.

"Success suits you," Susan observed.

"If you don't mind my saying, ma'am, success suits everyone who achieves it. We just sometimes wear it in different ways."

"Well said." Susan perused the menu. "Do you have any recommendations?"

"Yes. The beef here is exceptional."

"What is your alma mater," asked William.

"I graduated from Brown University with an MBA."

"Great school."

"My parents would have nothing less than an Ivy League education."

"Tell me more about your parents." Susan tilted her head slightly and fingered the pearls around her neck.

"We're an old Dallas family. My father is a top heart surgeon and mother is involved in charity work."

Ashley listened as the conversation rolled around her and thought how much Robert's story sounded like her family's story. Yikes. Maybe his name wasn't more pretentious than he was. But in her heart she knew he was a decent, caring man. For whatever reason he had turned out more like her brother, Michael, than her other two brothers. She also knew she liked him, she respected him, she enjoyed spending time with him, but he would never be the love of her life.

She felt a touch on her arm, looked up and was greeted by a mischievous twinkle in Robert's grey eyes. "Welcome back. Hope you went someplace fun and exotic."

"Sorry. I think I still feel jet-lagged from tax season and occasionally my mind goes blank."

"Really, darling. When are you going to settle down and quit that vulgar job? I cannot believe that three years out of school, you continue to be a career woman."

"Mother, I did earn a Master's in accounting at Chapel Hill. I'd say that's an indication I wasn't in it for the short haul." She could feel Robert shifting uncomfortably and he busied himself aligning the silverware, but he made no move to defend her.

Susan absently patted Ashley's hand. "We'll discuss this later. Right now I'm sure we can move on to more pleasant topics. Robert, tell us about your mother's charity work."

He glanced apologetically at Ashley. "My mother is on the Board of the Dallas Art Museum..."

Ashley tuned them out. Her jaw clenched tight despite the smile plastered on her face, her shoulder muscles tense, while a gnawing heat built in her core. She let the conversation swirl around her. Trite, vapid, uninteresting, devoid of empathy.

ASHLEY SPOTTED ZACH WAITING for them outside the restaurant, nodding and smiling at the people who either recognized him from the rodeo or spied the big-assed belt buckle at his waist. She supposed it didn't hurt that he was one good looking hunk of humanity. Zach was approachable, a big part of his charm, and people responded to him. It's not that Robert wasn't approachable. He was just less open, like he held a part of himself back.

She sensed her mother's displeasure with the venue choice and the casualness of the popular Riverwalk scene. Ashley loved the charm of the restaurants and shops snugged up against the river and the river boats moored or floating with the current so it figured her mother hated it.

Zach saw them approach and walked forward to meet them, confident, commanding, a man to be reckoned with. Tenderly cradling Ashley's chin in his hand, he bent down and kissed her sweetly on the lips.

Straightening, Zach removed his hat and offered his hand to William. "Hello, sir, I'm Zach Kincaid. Ma'am." He nodded to Susan. "Can't tell you how pleased I am to have met your daughter. She's an amazing woman."

William accepted Zach's hand.

"Zach, I would like to introduce you to my parents, William and Susan Drayton."

"I have a table waiting inside with a nice view of the river." Zach moved to the door and held it open letting everyone pass including a few folks from another group. He smiled good-naturedly and tipped his hat to the ladies.

"How rude to separate a group," Susan huffed. "It's as though civilized behavior has vanished. Poof." Her hand made a graceful circle in the air as she sighed.

"I was already holding the door so I didn't mind letting a few more in." Zach shrugged.

"Zach, it's good to see you again," the head waiter said as he stepped over and warmly shook Zach's hand then clapped him on the shoulder. "We have your table ready." As the group started walking, he said, "It looks like you and Matt are heading for Nationals again."

"Lord willing, but from our season so far, our chances look good." Zach handed his hat to the waiter.

Zach held out a chair for Susan and then Ashley.

"Cozy little place. At least they have cloth napkins," Susan whispered just loud enough for everyone at their table to hear. "The wait staff here is awfully informal. Not as refined as the staff at the restaurant Robert took us to yesterday."

Zach leaned back in his chair, seemingly relaxed. "We're friendly here in Texas, ma'am, and when you are a rodeo champion people in these parts tend to follow your career. I'm honored they care and try real hard to live up to their expectations." He gave her one of his thousand-watt smiles that even made Susan sit up a little straighter. "And while this might not be as fancy as some places in San Antonio, the food is top notch."

"I'm sure it is, dear." She fingered her pearls. "Ashley tells me that in addition to competing in the rodeo," Susan said 'rodeo' like it was something drippy pulled out of the trash, "you own a ranch."

Zach put his hand on Ashley's arm when she started to speak. Susan glanced at her daughter with narrowed eyes.

"Yes, ma'am, my family owns about one hundred thousand acres. It's mostly a cattle operation but my rodeo partner and I also run a clinic for team ropers, sell training videos, and have lucrative endorsement deals so I feel very blessed with my lot in life." His phone dinged and he pulled it out of his jacket pocket to glance at the screen.

"Did your dad get home all right?" Ashley asked squeezing his hand.

"He's grumbling about following orders and being treated like an invalid, but they are all back at the ranch." He slipped the phone back in his pocket.

"What kind of money is in ranching?" William asked while still perusing the emails on his phone.

"Enough to satisfy the needs of me and my family plus put some aside for a rainy day. Is it an easy life? No, but it's one that makes me happy. In the long run, what else can a man ask?"

"If you sold, you'd probably make a lot more money, that invested wisely, would make you a wealthy man." William set down his phone and stared steadily at Zach.

"The land has been in my family for over a hundred years so selling is not on the table. I know it's not a popular notion in a lot of circles, but money isn't everything. Money doesn't translate to a satisfying life. I happen to believe it's more important to do what you love and be surrounded by people you love."

"Really?" William picked up his phone again.

"Are you a happy man, Mr. Drayton?" Zach leaned forward, his forearms resting on the tabletop.

"Happy? I suppose." William put his phone down again and mirrored Zach's pose. "What's your point?"

"My point is that happy people feel good inside and embrace, not just accept, each new day. In my book a big part of that happiness comes from who they are living this life with and for."

"Sounds a little pie in the sky to me," William retorted.

"Maybe." Zach leaned back again regarding Ashley's parents, a fresh understanding entered his sky blue eyes.

The waiter stopped by and took their orders. When he left, Susan refocused the conversation.

"How does your mother fill her days? Is she involved in charity or community work?" Ashley could hear the subtle barb in her mother's question and her fists clenched in her lap.

"Mom does a lot of work through the church. There's always one family or another that needs a hand. In Texas, we take care of our own." His brows pulled together in thought. "As far as keeping busy, on a ranch that's not an issue. My mom and dad are a team. Everyone carries their own weight. When I marry, my wife will be my partner, my equal on the ranch just like my mom is to my dad."

"Please don't put any ideas in Ashley's head. She has enough fanciful notions as it is. She even wanted to run the family plantation." Susan patted Ashley's face and shook her head in resignation. "That is just not a proper occupation for a young woman. The work is so... dirty. Manual labor." Susan shuddered. "Ashley was not raised to do that. We expect her to graciously accept her role in society and help her husband be a leader in the community."

Before Ashley could jump in, Zach said, "I think there is more to Ashley than you give her credit for. Can't quite see the Ashley I know gladly spending her days sitting around sipping tea. My guess is Ashley's path will take a different direction."

"We'll see about that. If any child of mine choses to drag down this family's standing in the community – one we have worked so hard to uphold – by becoming a common laborer... well, that child would be disowned."

Ashley's brows shot up and her eyes went round. She had never heard her mother speak so forcefully.

"But Mother, Michael does landscaping. Do you plan to disown him?"

Susan glared at her daughter. "Michael is a landscape architect, an artist. All the best families vie to have him create a garden masterpiece for them."

"Honestly, Mother. You are such a snob." Ashley gasped and put her hand to her mouth. She couldn't believe she'd said that but had no intention of taking the words back. "I'm not a murderer or a thief. I earn an honest living. I'm not hurting anyone and actually try and make a difference."

"You're wrong. You are hurting your family. That's what comes with associating with people who are beneath you socially."

The waiter arrived with their food interrupting their conversation. Once he retreated, Ashley's pain bubbled over. She could feel Zach's tension but had the feeling he was holding himself in check to give her a chance to have her say.

Ashley looked her mother in the eye. "I wish you could accept me for who I am. Zach is right. I don't want to follow your path. I'm never going to be you. But I think I am making a contribution in my own way. I love working the land. I don't know what errant gene made me this way, but it is who I am. I wish you could respect my choices."

"Respect your choice to degrade yourself." Susan kept her voice low and modulated but fury reverberated through her words. "I'm supposed to be happy that you want to humiliate me, your father, your brothers? If we condone your choice to lower your social standing, I won't be able to hold my head up with my friends."

Zach narrowed his eyes. "Let me get this straight. Your daughter is a kind, honest, decent, law-abiding, hard-working human being and that's not good enough for you?" He sat back. "I'm stunned. I have no words. I don't understand you." He shook his head, dazed.

"I'm not surprised. We come from totally different worlds," Susan replied.

"I can't believe what you just said. I think we've had enough of this meal." Ashley started to rise.

"Sit down," Susan hissed. "We do not flounce out and make scenes. We will continue our meal." She looked over at her husband. "William, change our flight to this afternoon." She looked back at Ashley. "I will expect you to move back to Charleston by the end of the month or consider yourself no longer welcome in our home."

Chapter Thirteen

♥

Ashley slumped over the kitchen counter hands fisted in her hair in a losing battle to hold back the tears. Salty tracks glided down her cheeks leaving rivulets in her makeup and black smudges under her eyes.

Lauren rubbed Ashley's back in slow, soothing circles. "Oh, Ash, I am so sorry. Your mother is a real piece of work."

Sighing, Ashley stood up and swiped at her cheeks then turned and leaned her butt against the lower cabinets. "She makes me feel like I am the same ten-year-old child who sat at her feet clutching at any crumb of affection she happened to drop. Jeez, how can she still tie me up in knots?"

Lauren turned and leaned up against the cabinets next to Ashley. "Because she's your mother. Whether or not they deserve it, most of us love our mothers and expect to be loved back in return. Luckily, even though we all screw up occasionally, in the majority of mother/daughter relationships, the feelings are mutual."

She hooked her arm through Ashley's and leaned sideways so their heads were touching. "If it's any consolation, I do think she loves you as much as she is capable of. I've always thought there was something else at play that makes her react to you the way she does. She hardly reacts to your brothers at all. How is Zach taking all this?"

"Much better than I expected. I thought he'd head for the hills pronto but he didn't." Ashley's smile wobbled a bit. "He met me here after I dropped my parents at the hotel and we talked. He invited me out to Sunday lunch at the ranch before he hits the road again next week."

"Doesn't sound like he's going to scare off easily. I mean, if a meal with your mother doesn't strike fear in his heart, he's solid. What did he say?"

"To paraphrase, '*I am not my mother. Whatever problem she has that causes her to behave the way she does, I am not the cause. He's impressed with the person I've become despite what I've had to deal with.*' He somehow knew the right things to say."

"Zach is one smart man." Lauren pushed off the counter and turned to face Ashley. "Come on. Group hug." The two held each other for a few minutes before Lauren put her hands on Ashley's shoulders and looked into her eyes. "I think it's time I kicked your butt at Super Mario Brothers."

"In your dreams, beeatch. The day you beat me, is the day pigs fly. You're on."

·♥·♥·♥·♥·♥·

"Boy does this feel like déjà vu. You. Me. At the ranch. Two hunky guys waiting for us." Ashley stepped out of Lauren's Honda CRV and walked around to join her friend.

Gloria June bounded down the two steps of the main house's Spanish-style veranda. "I'm so glad you girls could join us. Always puts those boys of mine on their best behavior." She sandwiched herself between them in a bone-crunching hug.

"Thank you for inviting us out. I know between family and ranch hands, you're already feeding a small army," Ashley said hugging Gloria June tightly.

"Oh fiddle sticks. We don't even notice two more," Gloria June scoffed.

"Well, we're grateful anyway. I brought an apple and date salad and fresh rolls and Lauren brought brownies." Ashley held out the picnic basket.

"And flowers for the table," added Lauren retrieving them from the back seat.

"You girls are so sweet. Lauren, why don't you take the food inside and put the flowers in a vase? Nate will show you where."

Lauren took the basket from Ashley and skipped up the steps, calling for Nate as she tugged open the massive, oak door.

"Walk with me," Gloria June instructed Ashley as she began leading her toward the barn, one arm companionably around Ashley's waist. "I hear your visit with your parents wasn't all you had hoped."

"No, but it was what I expected." Ashley's sigh hung in the air as heavy as the summer's most oppressive heat. "I keep hoping it will be different." She shrugged and Gloria June pulled her closer. "I wish I knew what it is about me that sets her off."

"I know I'm not kin, but you and Lauren are exactly what I would have wanted in daughters, so I hope you don't mind me butting in."

Ashley smiled fondly at the no-nonsense woman beside her. "Have at it."

"No offense, 'cause I don't know her, but I believe your mama is, the way your mama is. You didn't make her that way and its high time you let go. Easier said than done, I know. My guess is you'll be a lot better off when you do."

"I know. That's what Zach and Lauren said too." Another deep sigh shuddered through her slight frame. "And I agree with all of you. I've come to see my mother is toxic and that by trying to please her, I hurt me. Moving here and meeting y'all has put a lot of things in perspective."

"It's never easy when your world view takes a wild wobble, but anyone with a few years under their belts has been there. Seeing the situation for what it is, is step one. Talking to your mama and telling her how you feel, is step two."

"Not sure I'm ready for step two yet." Ashley took a shaky breath and swiped at a lone tear threatening to leak out of her eye.

"You will be and when you are, while it's doubtful things will change, at least you'll have cleared the air and gotten that burden off your chest." Gloria June squeezed Ashley's shoulder. "Whatever happens, we're here for you and don't you forget it."

"Thank you." Ashley put her head on Gloria June's shoulder.

They stopped at one of the side paddock fences and a mare and her colt trotted up. Gloria June eased carrot chunks out of a bag in her pocket and handed a few to Ashley.

"Oh, my goodness," exclaimed Ashley. "This can't be Rumor. How did he get so big? It's only been about a month since I last saw him and he was all legs."

"Sure is," chuckled Zach coming up behind Ashley to circle her with his arms and kiss her hair. "They grow up fast."

"I'm going to leave you two now, but don't be late. Lunch is served in twenty minutes, no exceptions." Gloria June turned to go.

"Yes, ma'am," Zach responded.

"I want to apologize again for the way my parents treated you. There was no call for their rudeness." She turned in his arms to look into his eyes.

"No worries. Like I said, I have a thick skin. I'm more upset about the way they treated you. How can they not see how special you are?" Zach laid his lips against her forehead. "It just makes my heart hurt."

Ashley curved her arms around his neck to pull him down for a kiss when she felt a tug at her hair. Laughing she turned out of Zach's arms.

"I guess someone else needs some attention." She held a piece of carrot out to the Bay-colored mare.

"She's needs to get in line. Matt and I will be on the road for the next three weeks and I won't have another chance to see you until June," he said, but pulled a bag of apples from his pocket.

"Are you really going to be gone that long?"

"We might be able to squeeze in a day or two here and there at the ranch, but it's back-to-back rodeos after that."

Do you ever get tired of being on the road so much?"

"Not until recently. Even though dad is mending well after his surgery, he needs to start taking it easy. Sticking around the ranch next year seems like a good decision."

Ashley felt a stab of disappointment. She knew nothing had been decided about what their relationship meant and where it might be going, but she wanted to be one of his reasons for staying close to home.

· ♥ · ♥ · ♥ · ♥ · ♥ ·

"You're not going out there. Period." Zach lifted his Stetson and raked his fingers through his close-cropped hair. "It's too dangerous in these conditions. What with the rain we've already had both horses and cattle are skittish as water on a hot frying pan."

"I've been riding horses since I was in diapers. I can handle myself and my mount. I've even herded cattle on our plantation so I know what I'm doing." Her hands settled on her hips and her booted foot tapped the hardwood floor like the beats of a snare drum.

That precious chin of hers went just a little higher and if she stood on a crate it might almost reach his chin. "Look, I can't be worrying about you and trying to get crazy, wild cattle to go where I want them to go. I didn't take time away from the rodeo on a lark. This is serious. Please," he fanned his hands out in front of him, "be reasonable."

"I am being reasonable you big, dumb cowboy. You need every hand you can get to round up those cattle and get them to higher ground before the next round of storms hits in a few days. Southern women are tough. We don't' need to be coddled and I'm here to help."

"I know you're tough. I know you're smart and capable and brave." He took her face between his palms and kissed her deeply. When he looked up his sigh went clear to the depths of his soul. "All right, but you're riding with me."

The door banged open and Nate stomped in, Lauren hot on his heels.

"Doesn't look like you had any better luck than I did convincing the ladies to stay behind."

"Nope. God didn't make anything more stubborn than a woman who's made her mind up." He looked a little sheepish. "Course it might have helped if some of our female cousins weren't riding."

"Damn straight," Lauren piped in.

"Horses are saddled and loaded in the trailers, hands are assembled so we're ready to go," Nate said.

"I'll meet you around noon with the chuck wagon in the high meadow this side of the river," Gloria June said striding into the room.

Zach turned to Ashley and Lauren. "Are you sure you two wouldn't rather stay here and help my mom with the chuck wagon?"

"Positive." Ashley harrumphed and Lauren nodded. If looks could kill, then someone would be manning a shovel soon. Zach shrugged in defeat.

"Your dad and my sister are going to help me," Gloria June said. "Now get going. The sun's going to be up before you know it."

They all trooped out, moving to their assigned vehicles. Zach's dad and two hands were crowded into the extended cab of Zach's truck. Zack's two ranch dogs hopped in the truck bed, eager to commence the day's work. Four other trucks were similarly packed as were three other trucks not hauling horse trailers. The caravan pulled out each heading to its assigned area. About forty-five minutes later Zach pulled to a stop and everyone clambered out. One of the single trucks dropped off two additional hands and continued down the road. Once the horses were unloaded, Zach's dad climbed back in the truck and with a wave, headed back the way they came.

Noting Ashley's puzzled expression, Zach explained, "The drivers and trailers meet us at the pasture we're moving the cattle to, so at the end of the day, we can truck us and the horses back to the barn."

"I guess because our plantation acreage is so much smaller, it wasn't so complicated."

"We're lucky we can trailer to a staging area. Back in my great-grandfather's day, they would have spent the better part of one day just getting to this point. We can do in one day, granted a very long day, what it took them three or four days to do."

"So, did they get to sleep under the stars?"

"Yup, but it's not as romantic as it sounds. Give me my soft bed and home-cooked meal oversleeping on the hard ground and cooking over a campfire any day." Zach gathered up his reins and swung into the saddle. Ashley and the rest of the party followed suit.

Ashley paused a moment to drink in the pinks and purples of the sunrise's last hurrah, listened to the birds beginning their morning twittering, a gentle breeze whispered through the leaves on the trees. She gazed up into the beginnings of a clear, blue cloudless sky. "Hard to believe a major storm is on the way. After yesterday's rain, everything is so clean and peaceful."

Zach and his cousin, Wayne, exchanged grins. "We'll see if you feel the same in an hour or so when you're covered in mud and cussin' at ornery cattle." He reached over and tugged on her ponytail, grinning when she yawned. "Good thing my mom talked you into spending the night last night so you didn't have to drive out to the ranch this morning."

"It didn't take much convincing once we learned what time we needed to be ready. Besides I like spending time with you and your family." She smiled shyly.

"By the way, I like you without makeup. You're beautiful just the way you are."

"Bite your tongue. Don't tell anyone I've appeared in public without properly applying my face. I'd be drummed out of the Southern ladies corps." Her mouth quirked up. "But thank you."

Wayne cleared his throat and Zach shifted into boss mode. "Jim, Ashley, and I will start at the far fence line. Mike, Bill, and Wayne, start here and move toward the southwest corner. Wait at the stream and we'll meet you there."

Ashley watched him issuing orders, sitting tall and relaxed on his horse. The sight of those broad shoulders stretching his long-sleeved cotton shirt and muscular thighs resting against the horse's flank, reminded her heart it was awake and it was time to do some early morning calisthenics.

They spent the next four hours flushing restive cattle out of gullies and stands of trees, searching rocky outcroppings and basically riding to China and back slowly but surely merging the smaller groups into one herd. Gently they encouraged the cattle to move in the direction they wanted them to go. Jim and the dogs were near the front of the herd while Zach and Ashley were positioned on either side near the rear. He motioned her to fall back and join him so they could chat.

"You've got some serious cattle handling skills. I apologize for doubting you. I guess you did more herding on your plantation than I pictured." Zach swiped his forehead with his bandana.

"A plantation is just a fancy name for a ranch. The work was much the same though not on the same scale and we did have more livestock variety."

"Really? Like what?"

"Some cattle, though mostly breeding stock, and good-sized herds of goats and sheep for milk that we sell to local cheesemakers."

He looked slightly sheepish. "I really thought you'd be whistling and hollering and slapping at the cattle like in the movies, but you know to approach without spooking them by avoiding their blind spot. You understand how to work them so they mostly go where you want."

"I do my best to please." Ashley watched the dogs efficiently round up some cattle that were trying to head back into the brush. "I do hope you're going to feed those dogs steak tonight. They are worth their weight in gold. We would have been on and off our horses a hundred times today flushing cattle out of tight spots without their help."

"Couldn't do this without them." Zach held out an apple and a hunk of cheddar cheese. "Would you like a snack?"

"But aren't we going to each lunch soon? I see the rest of our group waiting for us by the stream."

"We've got about another hour and a half before we reach the chuck wagon. We'll cross this stream, another pasture and then a small river before lunch."

"In that case, thank you." Their hands touched briefly as he handed her the food and she felt the familiar excitement tickle along her fingertips.

Zach trotted off to turn a few cattle who had started to separate from the herd and then joined her again as their herd merged with the one by the stream.

Wayne rode up. "The water is moving swiftly but it's not deep so we should be able to get them across without a problem, even the smaller calves."

"Let's start moving them across." Wayne nodded and rode off.

With gentle pressure from the wranglers on the leaders, the cattle reluctantly stopped grazing and stepped into the water. Bellowing and splashing, the herd made its way to the other side and began following the muddy track through the pasture.

Finally, they saw the wider stream with the chuck wagon waiting for them on the opposite meadow. Ashley and the others stopped and let the cattle graze. Zach waded his horse into the swiftly moving current looking for the best place to cross. Once satisfied he'd found the right spot, he waded back ashore and rejoined the group.

"We'll cross them there." He motioned to a low spot along the bank. "But we'll need to take the smaller calves across first on horseback. Mike, Wayne, stay here with the herd. The rest of you follow me."

The ranch hands each snagged a small calf, threw it over their saddles and forded the stream with the mama cows bawling behind them.

Zach positioned a calf across Ashley's saddle. Follow those guys and then wait for me there."

Once all the smaller calves and their mamas were safely on the far side, the cowboys moved the remaining herd across the stream.

"I do believe we've earned some grub, men, and ladies. Dig in."

The cattle seemed quite happy to stay in one place and graze, but the hands settled in small groups around the perimeter of the herd anyway. The horses were tethered to a temporary line strung between trees and given hay and water.

Ashley found a log to sit on and Lauren joined her. "Good thinking, girlfriend. If I had to get down on the ground, I'm not sure my muscles would let me get back up. Guess it's been a while since I spent an entire day in the saddle." Lauren rubbed her thighs.

"I hear you," Ashley commiserated, then closed her eyes and inhaled deeply of the fragrant stew in her bowl. "I had no idea I was so hungry. No wonder our guys are in such great shape, doing this all the time."

"Our guys. I like the sound of that." Lauren groaned as she grasped the spoon.

"Look at them all manly and protective. Surveying their domain. Too yummy for words." Ashley went all dreamy-eyed. "Maybe I should give Zach a chance. Do you think I would make a good rancher's wife?"

"Uh, Ash. Zach's a great guy, probably great for you and I'm sure you'd make a fine rancher's wife, but maybe you should take this one a little slower than your past relationships. You know, make sure you're really in love." Lauren nudged her friend with her elbow. "Just a thought."

"My comments were purely hypothetical. Taking the idea out for a test drive. See how it tastes on my tongue. I have no intention of making a commitment to anyone in the immediate future. But Zach would make a mighty fine boy toy until I'm sure whether this is true love or simple attraction." Ashley batted her eyes.

"Your Gram would be clapping and dancing if she could hear you say that." Lauren chuckled and shook her head. "That lady had such a zest for life. Sounds like something she would have done back in the day."

"More like something she *did* back in the day." A smile tugged at Ashley's lips as she pictured her maternal grandmother. "Gram was a convention-be-damned kind of soul. How in the world she and my mother are related is beyond me." Ashley shook her head. "I'm positive some genetic god is laughing somewhere."

"You two about ready to go?" Zach bit back a smile at their murderous expressions. "I come in peace. Cookies and milk?" He held out two huge chocolate chip cookies and cartons of milk. "If you're too tired, you can ride back with my mom."

"I am no quitter. I signed on for the duration." Ashley jumped up, wincing at her protesting muscles.

Zach pulled her to him and kissed her until her muscles turned to putty and the pain evaporated like the morning mist softly swirling into the atmosphere.

"That's my girl." He glanced over his shoulder and raised his voice. "Okay everyone. Mount up."

Ashley looked at Lauren then at Nate who stood nearby with his hands in his pockets while Zach kissed Ashley. She raised her brows in question and Lauren shrugged.

When they'd herded the last of the cattle through the last gate and dismounted at the horse trailer, Ashley heaved a sigh of relief. Her inner thighs were feeling the burn, her butt was numb, and her ankles screamed about the abuse of staying in one position for so long.

Zach opened the passenger door of his truck, lifted her onto the seat and then softly kissed her. He held her hands close to his heart and whispered, "You did good today. What's say we relax by the fire after dinner?"

"Sounds like heaven to me. Throw in a beer and you're on, cowboy," Ashley said, trying to stifle a yawn.

Zach climbed in and so did the other passengers. Over his shoulder he said, "By my count, we're only down three head. Not bad and from here it will be easy to give them supplemental feed if need be until we can move them back out to the summer pastures. Hate moving them so much since that will cut down on their weight but can't be helped."

His dad chimed in from the back. "Agreed. I also like the idea of diversifying the herd with some Corriente cattle. I've been doing some research. Let's talk tomorrow."

"Sounds good," Zach replied as he pulled into the barn area.

They all climbed out, unloaded the horses, and began the process of unsaddling and grooming them before turning them loose in the corral.

Zach nestled Ashley's hand in his and kissed the back of it. "You didn't need to do that. You could have gone inside. One of the hands would have taken care of your horse."

"I wanted to. I like to finish what I start. Despite a few muscles that are trying to tell me otherwise, it felt good."

After dinner Ashley and Lauren joined Zach and Nate on the sofa in front of the fire. Zach handed Ashley the promised beer. Even though it's warm outside, starting a fire just felt right." He put his arm around her and she nestled her head on his shoulder melting into him like warm honey.

"I have to leave in the morning since I have a client meeting tomorrow afternoon. What's your schedule?"

"First thing tomorrow, make sure the cattle are settled and then get ready to hit the road again. Matt and I need to be in Houston in two days. From Houston we travel to Kansas, then back to San Saba, Texas. After that we will be home for a few days."

Ashley stifled another yawn. "I'm tired just hearing your schedule. Do you ever wake up and wonder where you are?"

"Well, we do keep a big calendar on the wall in the rig that includes drive times between locations and whether or not we will be passing anywhere near the ranch, but it really doesn't make any difference where we are. The days are pretty much the same. Take care of the horses, practice, run our event, and start all over again in the next location." He stroked her hair, absently staring into the fire.

"As much as I'm enjoying snuggling with you, I'm having trouble keeping my eyes open. I think I'll turn in once I convince my body it can still move."

"I'll walk you to your room." Zach shifted her head off his shoulder and stood up offering his hand to her to pull her to her feet. "Come on, sleepyhead. Let's get you tucked in."

"What's the matter? Afraid I'll get lost? You do realize all I have to do is keep following the interior hallway around the courtyard and I'll eventually find my room." She stabbed a finger into his ribs and scrunched up her face in a grin. "Or did you have something else in mind?" Her voice, meant for his ears only, slid into him like temptation. With arms around each other's waist, they happily bumped and jostled their way to the guest wing of the old hacienda.

At her door, Zach enveloped her in a tight embrace. Lowering his head, lips met, time stopped, and breath mingled. Ashley traced those six-pack abs with her hand, outlining their dips and swells, ran her hand up his broad chest, pausing on his sculpted pectorals before circling his neck. He straightened, lifting her feet off the ground and squishing every lovely, soft bit of her against him from his chest to south of his belt buckle. When he slid her down his hard body so her feet were back on the floor, their breathing was ragged. Color tinged Ashley's neck and cheeks. He kissed her one more time, slowly and gently on the lips.

"Goodnight, darlin'. Best go inside before my mom comes along to make sure you're settled in okay and finds us minus clothing and in a compromising position."

"Do you ever bring women back to your place?"

"Haven't so far, but since meeting you, I'm beginning to reevaluate my options." He nibbled on the tender spot beneath her ear lobe and made her shiver. "These next two and a half weeks cannot go fast enough to suit me," he whispered, causing a flicker of heat to tiptoe up her spine.

Zach backed away, still holding her hand until their fingers slowly slipped apart, leaving a ghostly sensation of loss floating between them. "Sweet dreams."

Ashley opened the door and stepped into her room. She closed the door and leaned against it, softly murmuring, "Fat chance of sweet dreams. I'm thinking hot, heavy, sexy, and wild are more likely."

·♥·♥·♥·♥·♥·

THE FAMILIAR BUBBLY SOUND of a Skype call coming in delivered a bright ray of sunshine into Ashley's otherwise rain-soaked world. She accepted the call and smiled at the cherished face that appeared on her screen.

"Hi," she said softly. "Glad you're not on the road today. I'm beginning to think I should trade in my car for a boat."

"I've never seen rain like this," Zach agreed. "Good thing we moved the cattle when we did. That last stream we had to cross is now a river. Mom and dad drove back to the meadow yesterday morning before the heaviest rain hit to check it out and they said it was tough going getting there. The stream had already overflown its banks by a good ten yards." He rubbed the stubble on his cheek.

"Just wake up, cowboy? Kinda late for you isn't it?" She loved the way he looked, lounging all bare chested on his bed in the fancy living quarters of the horse trailer. He was a sight to behold, tan and sculpted like a Greek god wearing only a pair of sweats.

"With all the rain and wind last night, the horses were restless so Matt and I took turns calming them down. Houston got rain, but nothing like you did." He yawned. "You look like you weathered the storm. Is the power back on?"

"Yes, I'm fine, but I heard on the news that the crazy people who decided they had to be out and about yesterday, it took them hours just to get across town. The power is still out in other parts of town. They said almost ten inches of rain fell at the airport yesterday. People along rivers, especially north of here, have been warned to evacuate."

"I heard about the loss of life and all the rescues when I talked to mom and dad last night. They said it looked like Interstate 35 was going to flood. First time I ever heard of that happening."

"It did flood. I heard it on the news this morning. They had to close it for several hours last night. What a nightmare. So many people have lost their homes. Your ranch is okay?"

"Yes, the ranch compound and high pastures where we moved the cattle are a soggy mess but no flooding."

"I'm glad I got to help. I have a better appreciation for how much work it takes to run a large spread. I don't see how you manage with your rodeo schedule."

"My dad used to do a lot of the day-to-day managing and we are blessed with great ranch hands, but with dad slowing down and wanting to travel more, it's a challenge."

"Changing the subject, what time is your event today?"

"We start at nine this morning so I need to get ready soon. I wish you could be here. They go all out for this rodeo since it honors Navy Seals and raises money for the Navy Seal Foundation – top entertainers, huge sponsors, all the big wigs, some of the best team ropers in the country, and a big prize purse. It's quite a shindig."

"Sounds like fun and I'd much rather be there with you than missing you here. When will you be back?"

"We're thinking about driving home as soon as things wrap up here since tomorrow's weather report doesn't sound promising. We'll have one day at home and then leave for the Midwest Regional finals in Kansas. After that we'll be home the first four days of June before we hit the road again. Will I be able to see you then?" She heard the longing in his voice.

"I'm planning on it. My brother, Michael, will be visiting and I'd like you to meet him."

"Just tell me when and where and I'll be there. Isn't he your favorite brother?"

"That's Michael. My kindred spirit. I adore him." She paused and took a deep breath. "I was hoping I could bring him out to the ranch. He's the landscape architect and would enjoy seeing what your mom has done with the gardens."

"I don't see why not. I'll check with mom and dad and make sure there's not some big project planned while I'm home and will let you know."

They talked for another few minutes before she heard Matt hollering for Zach. Ashley kissed her fingertips and pressed them to her computer screen over Zach's lips. He puckered his lips to kiss her fingers.

"I'll call again this evening. Stay safe."

"You too. I'll see you in a week."

Chapter Fourteen

♥

"MICHAEL!" ASHLEY FLEW INTO the arms of her favorite brother the minute he cleared the security area. At a little under six feet, chiseled face, chestnut brown hair fastened into a man bun, broad shoulders, narrow hips, and steel-blue eyes, he was quite a hunk. He scooped her into a one-armed bear-hugged then held her at arms-length.

"Looking good, little sis. In fact, you look fabulous, glowing, really happy. After mom's and dad's visit, I expected to see nothing but dark clouds hanging over your head."

"I won't lie, it was pretty devastating. Their visit did, however, cement the fact in my poor little brain that I can't let Mother control my life anymore. I'm shaking it off and moving on."

"That's great, but I assume you and I are going to have a nice, long talk about mother's behavior before I leave."

"If we must. Do you have any luggage?"

"Only this." Michael flexed his elbow and wiggled the duffle bag he was carrying.

"I do not understand men. My cosmetics and hair stuff would hardly fit in that thing and yet you're set for five days." She shook her head in disbelief and grinned. "Come on, Lauren's waiting for us at the curb to drive us home.

Lauren pulled into Ashley's driveway fifteen minutes later. Michael hopped out and opened the car door for his sister, then grabbed his bag from the back seat.

"Nice, sis." He nodded appreciatively. "A little creative landscaping would turn this into a real show place." He followed Ashley and Lauren up to the front door.

"It's a rental so I won't be doing much landscaping but would love your input on what to do with the patio."

"Be happy to." He stepped into the living room and looked around. "I like what you've done with the décor. Cozy and feminine. It's very you." He dropped his bag on the floor.

"I had help. You'll meet Robert tomorrow. As luck would have it, you get to meet two special men in my life while you're here, one a very dear friend and one my new honey... at least I think that's where we're headed. Mother thinks the friend is perfect for me and hates the honey." She shrugged. "Figures, right?"

"Don't let her get you down." He rubbed a knuckle against the top of her head. "Come here Lauren." He engulfed her in an embrace. "It's great to see my 'adopted' little sister again." He whispered in her ear. "And thanks for all the support you've given Ashley."

"That's what best friends are for," but a hint of worry flitted at the corners of her eyes.

Michael kissed her on the forehead. "Smile. Big brother is here to make everything better."

"Let's get you settled." Ashley slid her arm around her brother's waist. "Kitchen and breakfast nook, straight ahead. Dining room is through there, and on the other side of the stairs is the laundry room and half bath." Ashley gestured in the general direction of each room as Michael picked up his bag. "The bedrooms and my office are upstairs. Lauren, I have some refreshments ready. Would you set them up in the breakfast nook while I take Michael to his room?"

A few minutes later they gathered at Ashley's round, shabby chic table, seated on the white, ladder-backed chairs with the ruffly, flower-print cushions and munched on cheese and crackers and fresh vegetables and humus. Ashley ran her hand over the distressed pine table top then glanced out the French doors to her patio and the open space beyond.

Michael cleared his throat. "Should we kick the eight-pound gorilla out of the room and talk about Mother first?"

"Might as well so we can just have fun for the rest of your visit." Ashley propped her elbows on the table and rested her chin in her hands, a resigned look on her face. "I want to have lunch along the Riverwalk and then take you over to the Botanical Gardens, so let's get this over with."

"I'm going to say this with all the love I can muster for the woman who gave me birth. Mother is a narcissistic snob who should never have had children. The warm, loving, nurturing gene mothers are supposed to have, skipped her generation and she's done a number on all of us."

"Can't find fault with that description." She looked down and traced a circle on the table with her finger. "While it's been a slow process and," she patted Lauren's knee, "some heavy therapy sessions with my favorite psychologist, I'm not beating myself up anymore..."

Lauren coughed and raised her brows.

"At least not much," Ashley continued, "because Mother disapproves of me."

"Trust me, Mother disapproves of all of us. The only reason she accepts who I am, a gay man who digs in the dirt for a living, is that all her society friends are clamoring for me to work on their gardens. I'm bragging rights for her. Otherwise, I'm sure she would have disowned me." Michael's sadness circled the room and pooled around her feet. "I can't say if she consciously plays each of us against the other to make us feel inferior, but I finally realized that's exactly what she's been doing all our lives."

"I thought it was only me she belittled. She can't wait to tell me how wonderful you boys are, what great things you've accomplished. What can she possibly say to make you feel bad about yourself?" Ashley felt her gut tightening and a mild pounding behind her eyes.

"I'm sure she doesn't know, but I've heard her tell Blaine how impressed she is with something you or I or Jonathan did. Same pattern for each of us, any of the other siblings is superior to the one she's talking to. By inference, we should all be ashamed of ourselves because we don't measure up."

"Are you telling me that Mother has actually said something nice about me to you, to Blaine, to Jonathan? Well strike me dumb. Jeez. How has she gotten away with it all these years?"

"Because we don't talk to each other about what she tells us. Divide and conquer."

"Ash, that's such a typical manipulative, self-centered behavior pattern." Lauren reached over and took Ashley's hand. "Your mother is the poster child for '*Mommy Dearest*.' It's what we've been working through the last few months, but I think there's more to it than that." She hurried on to get it all out. "I think you scare your mother. You are so much like your grandmother, whose flamboyant and unconventional choices constantly embarrassed and upstaged your mother. Given your mother's narcissistic nature that must have made her blood boil. Your effervescent personality and similarity to your Gram, transported your mother right back to her childhood, where her mother controlled the limelight."

Michael slapped his forehead. "You're absolutely right. I'd never thought about it but you're right. Mother needs to be the center of attention. For that to happen, she had to grind us under her feet."

"After our talk about me being so much like Gram, I began to wonder if that was one of the problems Mother had with me. Thanks to you, Lauren, I've started moving forward. Not sure where forward is yet, but the picture is getting clearer."

"And does a certain cowboy happen to be in that picture?" Michael asked in the universal teasing of big brothers everywhere.

Ashley smiled and shrugged. "Maybe. The story is yet to unfold."

"Is this cowboy in question one of the men I'm meeting this week?"

"Yes, and that's all I'm saying on the subject. Now, I suggest we go into town and enjoy the rest of the day."

MICHAEL HAD AN ARM draped across the shoulders of Ashley and Lauren as they strolled into an arbor-covered path at the botanical gardens.

"This is fabulous," he enthused. "The organization did a good job capturing the essence of the region in all its many facets." He steered them to a nearby bench.

"Okay, Michael, what's up? Sitting still is not your style and between the plane trip and lunch you've done more than your fair share of that today." Ashley crossed her arms and eyed her brother like the mongoose does the cobra.

"Can't a guy spend quality time with his two best girls without being accused of ulterior motives?" He tugged on her hand until she reluctantly sat beside him. "You seem happy. Moving here was good for you." He stretched his arms along the back of the bench and shoved his legs out straight.

"It was. Putting distance between my old life, who I was there and for the first time beginning to think about who I am and what is important to me, has changed me."

"You've come a long way in the last six months," Lauren agreed.

"But I'm still a work in progress. Can't believe I thought my *plan* would put me on the road to happiness. Really naïve to think it would be that easy." Ashley chuckled ruefully, "That effort sank faster than the Titanic."

"Hey, we're all a work in progress and your plan wasn't a complete waste. It made you move here and you met some fantastic people. Robert will be a friend for life." Lauren leaned forward and rested her elbows on her knees so she could see Ashley. "Your plan got you moving and taking charge of your life. That was a huge step."

"Speaking of steps, how is your new job going? You haven't talked about it much except to say how busy you are. Still liking the corporate accounting world?" Michael asked.

"For the moment. I do enjoy listening to what the numbers tell me and then helping people make the best use of their resources. I feel like I'm making a difference in people's lives, but I don't know if I want to work for a firm indefinitely. Maybe I'll strike out on my own and give myself the option of limiting my workload when I want to."

Ashley slapped Michael on the knee and stood up. "Enough analyzing Ashley. What's say we head back to the house and put our dancing shoes on? San Antonio has some great night life and I am ready to par-tay."

· ❤ · ❤ · ❤ · ❤ · ❤ ·

ROBERT'S SWING AND FOLLOW through were perfect, as expected. The man needed a flaw or two. Perfect was downright irritating, especially since Ashley's ball was nestled at the edge of the rough. Michael was holding his own. Show off. At least her brother and one of her best friends had golf in common. Ashley caught up with them on the green.

"Why real estate? It's such a cutthroat business. You could have gone a lot of directions with your MBA." Michael said then putted in.

"My family owns a number of rental properties that I managed on the side while I gave the corporate world a whirl my first year out of college. Helped sell one and buy another and I was hooked. Loved the process, loved working with the buyers and sellers. Got my broker's license and never looked back." He putted in. "That's a birdie for you and an eagle for me. Come on, Ash, you can make par."

Ashley stuck her tongue out at Robert who did his best to look contrite. "You are such a comedian and here I picked up a copy of the Downton Abbey Cookbook that I was going to give you. Guess I'll have to give it to someone else." A dramatic sigh followed her statement. Her relief was palpable when her ball made it onto the green and close to the cup.

"And I thought you were a good sport," Robert teased. "Would it help if I agreed to take you shoe shopping next weekend? I'll have my jet pick you up and we'll make a day of pampering – shopping, massage, the works."

"That *would* take the sting out of looking like such a duffer in front of my brother. Okay, deal." She put out her hand so they could shake on it.

Michael watched the friendly banter and could see how much they enjoyed each other's company. He got close friend vibes, but nothing that hinted at a more intimate relationship.

"Anyway," Robert continued, "I discovered I had a knack for seeing the potential in a property. Word got out and here I am today running my own company." He settled his putter in his golf bag. "Next hole is the last one. Do you want to stop for lunch at the club house?"

"I'm ready to eat. How about you, Sis?" Michael asked.

"Definitely. You two might as well tee off first and I'll catch up with you. This hole is longer than I thought. I think I need a driver instead of a two-wood." Ashley walked over to the cart to make the exchange.

Michael stuck his tee in the ground and carefully balanced his ball on top of it then swung. "When are you planning on telling Ashley you're gay?"

"How did you know?" Robert asked his face showing no emotion.

"One gay guy to another. The way you keep looking at me. You did know I was gay, right?"

"I suspected," Robert said, worry lines wrinkled his forehead. "How do you deal with being openly gay? You own your own business. Has it impacted your sales?" He teed up and hit a long drive that landed near Michael's shot.

"Maybe, a little, but for the most part no. People have been fairly accepting. The few that take issue with my sexual orientation, that's their problem." Michael rubbed his jaw as they walked down the fairway. "I suppose it helps that gardens are a big deal in Charleston and I'm the best. People are willing to overlook a lot to say I did their landscaping."

"We're still pretty conservative in these parts. I'm afraid my business would take a hit. It's not like I'm the only realtor around. People do have choices."

"Just remember, you're the best at what you do. Clients come to you for a reason." Michael chipped his ball onto the green and Robert followed suit.

"Hey guys," Ashley hollered. "Fore." The men moved off the fairway and waited while she hit her ball just shy of the green. They motioned for her to hit again.

"Let me ask you something," Michael leaned on his club. "Are you happy having to lie about who you are? If your business did take a hit, do you think it would be big enough to make a difference?"

Robert sucked air in through his teeth and grimaced. "I don't know. A lot of people depend upon my success, but I appreciate your perspective. Something to think about."

"Tell my sister. I know she cares about you. If you're going to be her friend, be honest with her. She *will* understand."

Once they were seated in the elegant Spanish-style dining room, Michael excused himself to go check out the landscaping. "If the waiter comes before I'm back, order for me Sis." He leaned down and kissed the top of her head.

Ashley arched her brows and gave her brother a 'what are you up to' look. "You two were deep in conversation on the course. Anything you want to share?"

Robert cleared his throat and made a show of putting the napkin in his lap. "You know I like you?"

"And I like you too. You're a good friend, one of the best. A terrific shopping companion. An all-around great guy." Ashley stopped speaking and took a breath, trying to quell the sick feeling in the pit of her stomach. She treasured his friendship. Please don't let him say he wanted to be more than friends.

"But I'm gay," Robert finished. "I don't want to lose your friendship."

Ashley bounced out of her chair and threw her arms around Robert's neck. "Yes, I'll be your friend." People turned to watch and Robert blushed.

"Hadn't expected so much enthusiasm to my announcement but I'm glad that you're glad." He put his hands on her waist and steered her back to her seat. "It's not something I've shared with many people, so I'd appreciate it if you'd keep it to yourself for now."

"Of course. I assume Michael had something to do with you opening up to me?"

"Yes and it feels good to tell you. Your brother was right. Friends shouldn't keep secrets."

"So are you and Stephen a couple?"

"Yes." He smiled shyly. "You knew then?"

"Not at first. In fact, I pictured us as a couple, but after a while I wondered. I wanted sparks but there were none and I wondered why?"

"Let me guess. Zach's the one who makes the sparks fly and your heart do double time?"

"He does. I'm not sure yet that he's the one, but he is definitely a contender."

Michael rejoined them as the waiter approached. "You two all set?"

"Yeah, we are." Ashley reached over and clasped each man's hand. "Couldn't be better."

·♥·♥·♥·♥·♥·

ASHLEY SENSED MICHAEL'S EYES on her as Zach strode out of the barn to greet her. It felt marvelous to have Zach's arms around her again, swinging her around for the sheer joy of being able to touch each other after a two-week separation. Once he set her feet on the ground he kissed her senseless with some obvious tongue action and pelvis contact being part of the package. Her blood took on the consistency of melted butter and felt warm and silky flowing through her veins. He ran his hands up and down her arms as though testing to make sure she wasn't a mirage. She cupped his face in her hands, staring into his crystalline blue eyes memorizing the contours of jaw, nose, and lips.

"Are you planning on introducing us to that fine, young man waiting very patiently by your car or are you planning on kissing the living daylights out of my son all day?" Gloria June's good-natured chuckle wrapped around Ashley like a towel fresh out of the dryer.

"Are we voting?" asked Zach. "Then my vote is for kissing the living daylights out of me."

"Mmmm," Ashley purred but moved enough to make the introductions. "Gloria June, Jack, Zach, this is my brother, Michael. Michael, I'd like you to meet the Kincaids. This is Zach's mom and dad and Zach."

Zach kept one arm around Ashley and extended the other to Michael. "Pleasure to meet you. Heard a lot of good things about you. Happy to welcome someone from her family who has her back."

Jack stepped over to shake hands with their guest but Gloria June engulfed Michael in a back-slapping hug. "Ashley tells me you are a landscape architect and might like seeing our place. Don't imagine you have many Spanish Haciendas in Charleston, but I'm happy to show you around. Be fun to talk to someone for a change," she glanced pointedly at her husband and Zach, "who actually cares about plants and design."

"Everything you do looks real nice, Honey," Jack placated.

Gloria June hooked her arm through Michael's and propelled him up the steps onto the veranda. Jack, Ashley and Zach trailed along in her wake.

"Not many Spanish Haciendas but lots of verandas in South Carolina. And we do appreciate a well-turned-out veranda." Michael fingered some plants in one of the many containers lining the wall. "Great idea mixing ginger lilies with gardenias. You must love sitting out here surrounded by all the fragrance."

"I do love sitting out here with the Mourning Doves calling, the horses nickering in the pastures, my chickens clucking, and the breeze rustling in the trees. Paradise, though I don't get to enjoy it as much as I'd like. Ranch keeps us hopping."

As they walked, Michael complemented Gloria June on the artful arrangement of terra cotta pots filled with shade-loving flowers and plants, the colorful blooms lining the low wall along the outside edge of the veranda, the bougainvillea climbing the columns between the arches and the cozy groupings of padded chairs, and occasional tables scattered along the covered walkway. Heads together they exchanged ideas and planting tips.

When they were back where they started, Zach said, "I thought we'd go for a trail ride so Michael can get a feel for the land and our operation before coming back for a late lunch in the courtyard. Sound good?"

"I was hoping we'd get the chance for a ride." Ashley did a 'ta da' move. "We wore our boots and jeans just in case and our hats are in the car."

"Let's go mount up then. The horses are already saddled." Ashley scampered ahead to grab their hats and then darted into the barn.

Michael fell into step beside Zach. "Looking forward to learning more about what it takes to run an operation this size. Ours is pretty small with only about five hundred acres."

"A ranch this size does keep us busy year-round with one chore or another. During rodeo season I'm away a lot or training so depend upon my foreman and ranch hands to keep things in order."

"How many hands do you have?" Michael asked.

"A foreman and his family who live in the house over there," he gestured to his left, "and four full-time hands who stay in the bunkhouse." Zach motioned to a long extension jutting from the Hacienda. "We also hire seasonal hands for the spring calving and fall planting plus the family puts in a lot of time. Dad and I manage the operation, mom handles all the record-keeping and payroll, and my brother, Nate, takes care of our veterinary needs."

"How big is your herd?"

"Given the size of our spread, our herd is pretty small. We run about 2,000 head so usually have around 1,200 calves to fatten and sell each year. We've been focusing on the organic market." Zach handed the reins of a big bay to Michael. Ashley had already mounted her favorite palomino and Zach swung into the saddle of his dun-colored stallion.

They spent the next few hours riding out along the mesquite and oak studded pastures, wading across streams, and admiring the surrounding hills from atop granite outcroppings. They spotted a herd of deer grazing amid the tall brush, their buff coats almost blending into the background. Fields of wildflowers dotted the landscape. They finally stopped to check on the herd of cattle. Ashley rode over to a fading patch of yellow Greenthread and purple Winecup flowers to gather a bouquet.

"The hands will have to move them out to our summer pastures next week. Hate having to move them twice but with the rains we had in April and May it was safer to bring them in off the range rather than risk having them trapped by flooding. We'll likely have to use extra hay to fatten them up when we round them up in the fall for market. That'll eat into the profit."

"Your ranch is spectacular and so diverse." Michael shifted in his saddle, leather creaking, so he could see Zach's face. "So tell me, if you had to choose between rodeoing or full-time ranching, which would it be?"

"No contest. The ranch. Don't get me wrong, I love the rodeo, the adrenalin rush of chasing the steer and the satisfaction of a perfect throw, but this is my heritage." He indicated the scene before them with a sweep of his arm. "When it's time to give up my rodeo career, I have this, and I'll still be a very happy man."

"You're close to your family. You're a lucky man. I wish Ash and I had what you have." Zach's gaze settled on Ashley, surrounded by wildflowers, her horse grazing nearby and felt his heart swell.

He turned his attention back to Michael. "Growing up in this environment, I thought all families were like mine since that's all I'd ever seen." Staring off into the distance, Zach continued, "Nice thing about rodeoing and ranching, people live by a deep-seated code of honor... God, family, country, honesty, hard work..." He looked over at Michael and a touch of sadness crept over his face. "It was an eye-opener to meet your folks and realize the tough road my Ashley had to walk. My life and outlook would have been so different if I'd been in her shoes. She's a strong woman to have become the caring person she is. I admire her."

"So do I and if you tell her I said that, I'll have to kill you." Michael smiled. "Siblings and all, you understand."

"I do. Your secret's safe with me." Zach waved at Ashley to join them and hollered. "Don't want to be late for lunch. I hear Mom's frying up a batch of chicken."

During lunch Ashley could almost see the wheels turning in Michael's head as he gazed around the serene, open-air courtyard, with its lush greenery, spots of colorful flowers and the soothing splash of water in the fountain.

"Wondering how you can get one of these in your Charleston house?" Ashley teased her brother.

"That would be a major remodel, no make that tear down and rebuild project, but this is an amazing space." He sat back with a contented sigh. "Fantastic meal, Mrs. Kincaid."

"Thank you, but it's Gloria June."

"Then, fantastic meal, Gloria June." Michael looked around again. "Wonder what the prospects are for a landscape architect in the San Antonio area?"

Gloria June patted Michael's arm. "While you were out for your ride, I checked your online portfolio. You're an artist and you've worked on some pretty big projects. I got a whole passel of people I could refer to you. Just say the word."

Ashley bounced in her seat and clapped her hands. "Oh Michael, is there a chance you might move out here?"

"I've been looking around for new opportunities, a new challenge. I'm beginning to feel like I'm in a rut. I like what I've seen of the area so far. It has potential, so maybe."

Ashley jumped up and threw her arms around her brother's neck. "I can't tell you how excited I am that you might move here. You can stay at my place until you find your own and we can have gab fests like we used to and..."

Michael pried Ashley's arms loose. "None of that will happen if you strangle me," he said, laughing. "I'm going to give it serious consideration despite the fact that you want to turn me into your man slave."

Zach pulled Ashley onto his lap and rubbed his nose against her back then planted an unhurried kiss on the nape of her neck. "You let us know if you need help with any research on this end."

Ashley fisted her hands in Zach's hair and gave him a quick, hard kiss on the mouth. "I luu... I think you are the best thing since," flustered by the calculating looks around the table. "Well, I just can't think of anything better than you."

Zach returned her kiss but it wasn't quick, just filled with what she thought the word she almost said out loud would feel like.

"Michael, would you like to go out and see our arena before you two have to head back to town?" Zach asked once he'd broken the kiss with Ashley. "Might even give you a few roping pointers, if you like."

"He doesn't know, does he?" Michael asked.

"It never came up in conversation," Ashley shrugged at her brother.

"What?" Zach asked.

"I was the state high school team roping champ in my junior and senior years."

"You set me up with a ringer? Really, Ash?" Zach laughed, pushed her off his lap and swatted her playfully on the butt.

"Hey," she protested. "Debutant remember? Michael's competitions weren't allowed to be a part of my life."

"It's been years, except for a little on the plantation, so my ringer status is questionable, but I think the basics will come back."

Over the next few hours Ashley laughed so hard her ribs hurt. Gloria June, Jack, and a few of the ranch hands joined her on the bleachers. Shouts of dubious encouragement, whistling, and general heckling turned the impromptu session into an event. Zach carried out a practice dummy that they used for a while, then saddled up some horses to chase down the motorized version. Finally, the hands brought out some live steers and loaded them up in the chutes for a real test of their skills.

Zach slapped Michael on the back. "You held your own out there."

"That was fun but I see a long soak in a hot bath with some Epsom salts in my future." Michael shook Zach's hand. "Thanks. This is an amazing set-up."

Michael wandered off to wait in the car. Zach pulled Ashley around the corner of the barn and out of sight. He captured her mouth, curving her soft bits into his hard bits and her back into the barn wall as he molded her to his shape. She felt his heart pounding at the pulse point in his neck. When they came up for air, she felt like she was on fire.

"I haven't left yet and already I miss you." Zach rested his forehead against hers.

"How long this time?" she asked.

"Three weeks with an odd day here and there at the ranch, but I'm home for a week at the end of the month. We can spend time together then." Hope floated through his voice, happy puppy style. Adorable. Endearing. Heart-melting.

"It's a date, cowboy. You're on my dance card," she whispered.

"I'd damn well better be the only cowboy on that dance card," he growled.

"HAND ME THAT TRAY of begonias." Michael knelt by a glazed ceramic pot, trowel in hand. "This is the last one, then I'm ready for that iced tea and cookies."

"Coming right up." Ashley ducked into the kitchen and returned with a tray of the promised refreshments. She placed the tray with the pitcher of tea, glasses, and plate of cookies on the small teak patio table shaded by a red canvas umbrella that Michael had helped her pick out.

Michael stood up, removed his gardening gloves and dusted his hands off. "Not bad," he said glancing around.

"Not bad! Michael, you've transformed the patio from blah to fantastic. Take a load off."

The chair scraped on the concrete as Michael sat down. Ice tinkled against the glass pitcher and plopped into the glasses as Ashley poured the tea.

Michael took a long drink then set the glass down. "He's perfect for you, you know. I feel like I've stepped into one of those television 'made for you' moments when I see you together."

"Who? Zach?"

He gave his sister a 'you're kidding' look. "Do you have someone else waiting in the wings I don't know about?" Sarcasm laced his tone. "Of course, Zach, duffus."

"Don't roll your eyes at me." Ashley landed a glancing blow on her brother's arm and he grinned in response. "I guess there is a little sizzle between us."

"Sizzle? Sis, when you two are together the air feels like it's crackling with blue lightning, the explosive, ground up kind." He leaned on the table, hands encircling his glass and shook his head slowly. "But it's more than that. There's a connection, respect... I'm going out on a limb here and dare I say, love... between you."

Her eyes got big and she grimaced. "Eeeks, the 'L' word. Bite your tongue. You know how much trouble that's caused me the last few years."

"Yeah, I do, but that wasn't real."

"Looking back, I know that now, but how do I know this is any different?"

"I wish I had an answer for that one. I always assumed you'd just know when the right one came along, but so far, I'm batting zero too." Uncertainty filled her brother's eyes. "Guess I'm the wrong one to ask, but when I see you with Zach, the pinball machine goes on full tilt mode, all the bells and whistles and lights go off."

Ashley drew lines in the sweat on her glass. "I want to trust him and I want to trust what I think I'm feeling, that I really know this time. I want to know that all of this is not just a figment of my imagination, but I'm scared."

"I know. I'm here for you, so keep me posted." He stood up. "Now I'd better get ready so you can take me to the airport. Good luck."

Chapter Fifteen

♥

ASHLEY DASHED AROUND THE corner of the barn bearing down on the practice arena and Zach but came to a screeching halt when she spotted him. There he was all rugged and masculine, gently lifting a small child out of a wheelchair and onto a waiting horse. He adjusted the little girl in the saddle, checked her helmet and secured a safety strap around her waist. All the while he kept up a steady stream of conversation that won him the most precious smile. And Ashley had thought Zach couldn't find any new ways to make her heart do flips, gyrations, and tingly contractions than he already had.

Wrong. Wrong. Wrong. He'd obviously found a new way make her all squishy inside. Just when she thought she knew him, he did something totally unexpected. Yes, she knew he was charitably inclined, but she'd never seen this kind, compassionate side in action. If seeing led to believing, then here was proof positive of his innate goodness. A volunteer took the lead rein and Zach walked beside the child around the ring encouraging her to place a plastic ring over a pole and to shift her body to maneuver the horse around some cones. Two other children had a similar team working with them.

They made four circles around the arena, letting the horse move into a trot on the last pass with Zach jogging alongside to ensure that the child felt safe and secure. He noticed Ashley and nodded at her on the final go-round. He motioned for another volunteer to take his place as the riders and mounts were led out of the arena and along a path.

Zach in his long, slow, steady stride made his way to Ashley who was perched on the top rail of the fence. He climbed up and straddled the fence, one of his legs on either side of her, pulling her between his thighs and circling her with his arms. He rested his chin on the top of her head and they sat quietly for several minutes relishing the chance to be together again. Touching, talking, tender. Savoring this precious time. They listened to the murmurings of the waiting children as the final group of three were led into the arena, the swish of the horses' tails, the calm directions of the instructor and volunteers and the process was repeated once more.

"I had no idea you did this. You are full of surprises. Tell me about the program." She stroked her hand down his cheek.

"We've been partnering with a nonprofit out of Austin for about three years now and serve just over seventy children in the San Antonio area. I've donated twelve therapy horses for their use and house them in a separate barn. We let the group use our facility three days a week for three hours each day. These kids are something. I'd like to do more since there is a waiting list. I'm planning to add another two arenas this fall so our roping clinic won't interfere with their work." His voice vibrated against her cheek.

She turned her head and kissed him softly on the lips and felt her heart swell another notch. "Since your roping clinics are part of your livelihood, there aren't many people I know who would be worried about their work interfering with their charitable efforts. It's usually the other way around. You are something special."

"Really? Seeing how much therapeutic riding does for these kids, I can't imagine putting my insignificant wants in front of their needs."

"I don't really know much about how this program benefits children with disabilities. Can you fill me in?"

"Oddly enough the gait of a horse is very similar to the human gait which gives the children the sensation in their hips and pelvic area of walking normally. It gives the ones confined to a wheelchair a freedom of movement they wouldn't otherwise experience. Riding improves their strength, posture, and flexibility. The activities they do while they are riding improve hand-eye coordination and spatial awareness. The joy I see on their faces, there is no way I could ever give up this program."

He scooted back and climbed down off the fence. "Come on." He tugged on her hand. "I want some alone time with my girl." She swung her legs over the top rail and turned to face him, leaning toward him. His hands went around her waist and lifted her like she weighed less than a sparrow.

Hands clasped, they strolled over to a bench under one of the massive old oak trees near the house and eased onto it. Zach lifted his hat and ran his hand over his head, then settled it back into place.

"Did you think any more about staying the night?" he asked, trying so hard not to look eager that she had to bite her lip to keep the giddiness from showing.

"Overnight case is in my trunk. In fact I was hoping the invitation would extend to the entire weekend."

He threw back his head, fisted his hands in the air, and jerked them downward. "Yes! No problem on this end. Stay as long as you like."

"Your parents won't mind?" Nerves tightened her belly just thinking about what her own parents' reaction would be.

"No, I'm a big boy and they know how much I care about you. Besides," he lowered his voice, "I don't think they think I'm a virgin."

Ashley laughed. "Knowing your son is sleeping around and having him do it right under your nose are two different animals."

He pulled her hand up to his mouth and kissed it, then looked her square in the eyes. "I am not sleeping around. I am sleeping with you. Big difference."

Later that evening they sat on his deck, she nestled between his legs, her back against his chest watching the sunset fade into darkness, the stars popping out a few at a time until the night sky bloomed with a million diamonds. Zach trailed a line of kisses along her neck dwelling on each erotic point. His hands cupped her breasts through her shirt, thumbs toying with her nipples that had lightening sparks shooting deep into private places. His ministrations had her wriggling her hips against his growing erection. She felt the wetness and need blossom between her own legs. He scooted her forward, leveraged his legs over the lounge, stood up and led her into the house.

The next morning she knew she should move but her bones seemed to have wandered away from her body. She was limp, relaxed, a little sore in a most delightful place and ambition must have joined her bones in an 'after the most fantastic sex ever' walkabout. They had certainly made up for lost time last night and if the fingers fondling her breast and the bulge pressing into her butt were any indication, breakfast might be delayed a little longer.

Zach turned her toward him. "I need to help with the stock and chores. Ready for a shower? I could use a little help with my back and other hard to reach areas." He waggled his brows suggestively and slipped out of bed as naked as the day he was born. Magnificent!

"Since you are such a feeble soul and I'm so kind-hearted, why not?" She held out her hand, he pulled her up then chased her into the bathroom. Much water, some splashing, a healthy lathering of bodies to create soap-slick skin that felt like silk when they brushed against each other and the fun lasted until the water turned cold.

She fixed breakfast then followed Zach out to start on the chores for the day. She couldn't believe how quickly the day flew by... morning chores, a ride out to check fences, making bread with Gloria June in the afternoon, but most of all, it was a day filled with laughter and a new understanding of what family meant.

Sitting on Zach's deck that evening, he pulled out his guitar and serenaded her in his strong clear tenor. Later as they lay in bed after very satisfying sex, he smoothed her hair away from her face and kissed her eyelids. Contentment filled her top to toes. She could get used to this.

"I'm going to be gone most of July. It's the start of 'Cowboy Christmas' so back-to-back rodeos," he said stroking her hair.

"Cowboy Christmas?" she asked sliding her palm up and down his back.

"That's the nickname given to the month of July when there are so many big pot rodeos, we're talking tens sometimes hundreds of thousands of dollars in payout, and most of us rush from one to the other."

"Oh, so it sounds like I won't see you for a while." She couldn't keep the disappointment out of her voice.

"Heather and the kids are joining Matt for the month so we'll be taking two rigs. I was wondering if there is any chance you could take some time off and travel with me?"

She stroked her fingers across his temple and along his hairline. "Actually, that's a good idea. I'd like to learn more about that part of your life. I'll request vacation time when I go into work tomorrow and will let you know."

· ♥ · ♥ · ♥ · ♥ · ♥ ·

ASHLEY SCROLLED TO HER mother's name in her Skype contact list. She rolled her head trying to work the tension out of her neck and shoulders, then took a fortifying breath before hitting the call button.

"Hello, Mother. How are you? I hear the Garden Society has refurbished the downtown park and turned it into a real showplace." Ashley kept a careful smile on her face.

"Yes, we have and I suppose you had a hand in Michael's crazy scheme to relocate? Everyone was devastated by the news." Her mother's perfectly arched brow announced her displeasure.

No one could deliver a dig like her mother. Cool, elegant, harsh and an unerring sense for hitting the soft spots. "Michael made that decision on his own. I was as surprised as anyone, but I support him. He was restless in Charleston, Mother. He needs a change."

Of course, you support him. Anything to hurt me."

"Mother, I'm not trying to hurt you, but this is not really about Michael, is it?"

"You're not coming back. You're going to stay there with that cowboy?" Her mother didn't even try to hide the sneer on her face.

"I *am* staying here, but as much for me as for finding out if I have a future with Zach. Moving forward, I plan to live my life by my rules, not yours." Fire and determination shone in Ashley's eyes.

"You know he's going to cheat on you, just like the others," Susan said. "He's a player. I could see it in his eyes."

"Right, Mother." Sarcasm laced Ashley's voice. "You hardly looked at him during our lunch. And like *you* were such a good judge of the other men in my life. You encouraged, no make that insisted, I date them. 'They were the right sort,' if I recall your exact words and look how those relationships ended."

"I was wrong. Is that what you want to hear?" Ashley could see her mother's lips thin and that random tick she got in her left eye when she was angry.

"No, what I *want* to hear is that you love me, or at least respect me as a person, but I've given up on that happening any time soon. Maybe someday."

"I believe this conversation is over. You've made your choice, now you will have to live with it." The screen went blank.

Yes, Ashley had made a choice. Now she only hoped her rodeo man was ready to make the same choice. Choose her.

Excitement bubbled inside Ashley like popcorn, pinging and exploding against the bag, hot and happy. Fourteen whole days with Zach. Fourteen days exploring his world. They left the ranch around six in the morning, late for a travel day. Since it was only a four-hour drive to their destination, they had the luxury of avoiding the typical pre-dawn departure time. They also wouldn't have to stop to water and exercise the horses, that chore could wait until they arrived. They would stay two nights at this rodeo and then on to the next one.

It didn't take long to figure out they were going to get to know each other well during the long drives and hours working side-by-side. As the rig ate up the miles, Zach regaled her with stories about Texas... its people and history... his childhood on the ranch and all the mischief young boys could get in when set loose in the wide-open spaces of what Zach cheerfully called 'God's Country'. Ashley reciprocated, only substituting stories of South Carolina for Texas and time spent with Lauren's family for Kincaid family stories.

"No wonder you are so close to Lauren's family. It sounds like you spent more time with them than your own family," Zach observed.

"At least more quality time. They treated me like I was one of their own children and that's probably the only reason I'm not a complete basket case. Speaking of family life, your dad was a rodeo man when you were young, what was that like?"

"Probably as close to perfect as a kid could imagine. We couldn't wait for school to be out so we could join dad on the road. I'm sure we pestered the heck out of the cowboys, but they all seemed to take it in stride. I'm glad there's no video footage to pull out and embarrass us with."

"I'm looking forward to spending time with Heather and her kids. She seems to have made the rodeo lifestyle work for her."

"Have you been giving some thought to maybe spending more time living the cowboy life?"

"Don't look so worried. I'm not trying to hogtie you. Just curious about what it's like for her and the kids."

"I'm not worried and I never said hogtying is a bad thing. Like you, I'm just curious where you might be going with this line of inquiry."

"We'll know when I get there."

Zach flipped on his turn signal and their little caravan pulled into a field jam-packed with vehicles, everything from a pickup with a small, two horse trailer to huge rigs with living quarters and room to haul four to six horses like Zach's and Matt's.

"I had no idea there would be so many people staying here." She leaned forward as far as the seatbelt would allow so she could peer out the windshield. "It's like a small town of horse transport vehicles."

"And these are only the folks who have to haul horses. A lot of the rough stock riders stay in motels or hop on planes right after their event and head on to the next."

Ashley watched Matt's and Heather's boys burst out of the back of their extended cab truck like they'd been shot from a cannon and smiled. She stepped onto the running board and hopped to the ground. "What do we do first?"

"Get the horses unloaded and watered then you and Heather can lead them around to loosen up while Matt and I get the living quarters hooked up." Zach raised his hand in salute at Matt and Matt returned the greeting, then everyone settled into their tasks.

A short while later Ashley and Heather were leading the horses through the crowd to a quieter spot on the perimeter of the field.

"Who are those Daisy Mae wannabes hanging around all over the place?" Ashley asked.

Heather rolled her eyes. "Buckle Bunnies is what they're called and conquest is their game."

Ashley's brows shot up and her mouth formed an 'O' as she studied them more closely. "I guess it is kinda obvious... short shorts, clingy low cut tank tops, and 'I'm available' looks. Don't leave much to the imagination, do they?"

"No, they don't." Heather drew the words out like she'd just pulled a mouse out of a trap and was carrying it by its tail to dispose of it.

Ashley snickered. "Tell me what you really think. So you don't worry about Matt being around these women?"

"No." Heather smiled a Mona Lisa smile. "It's kinda cute actually. He was raised to be a gentleman and treat women with respect, but he also expects women to respect themselves. When one of these she-devils approaches him, he's polite but it is so obvious he's trying to back away and is uncomfortable with the situation."

Heather reached over and squeezed Ashley's arm. "Go on, ask. I know it's going to eat at you till you do."

"Have you ever seen Zach with a Buckle Bunny?"

"Only to sign autographs. Like Matt, he's not interested in one-night stand women." They'd completed the circuit of the field and started back to their trailers.

"What's next on the agenda?"

"The guys will check in, we'll fix lunch, then they'll spend the afternoon practicing, watching film on the steers they drew and getting the horses, and equipment ready for tomorrow. After that we put on our fancy duds and go to whatever hoop-dee-doo is planned, usually a barbeque, so the locals and fans can mingle with the cowboys."

They clipped the tether line to the horses' halters and moved along to Heather's trailer.

"Tomorrow night there will be a dance," Heather continued.

"Will all the rodeos be like this?"

"Pretty much. Some are smaller, some larger, but the formats are similar."

"So what do we do while the guys are busy?"

"Cook, clean, help with the chores, take care of the kids, watch the rodeo... especially their events, visit with the other wives and girlfriends." Heather opened the door and climbed into the trailer.

Ashley stopped, mouth open and looked around. "This is not what I expected." She gazed in wonder at the small kitchen with marble countertops, oven, range, refrigerator, leather banquet seating and sturdy wooden chairs surrounding a small dining table, solid wood cabinets and wood plank flooring. Steps led up to a sleeping loft for the kids. A bathroom was tucked in a corner. Just past the kitchen was a small family area with built-in recliners and large screen television and beyond that the master suite.

"What, no dishwasher?" Ashley brushed her hand up and down the nearest cabinet.

"We did have to make some concessions to being on the road, but it does make a decent home-away-from-home."

"Is Zach's like this?"

"A bit more bachelor pad décor than this, but the layout is about the same. I take it you haven't been inside it yet."

"No, but I can't wait now. Should we get lunch started?"

They ate at a fold up picnic table under a pop-out awning. Ashley held the littlest one on her lap, cutting up his food and listening to his excited chatter. After lunch the men took off, all business now and Ashley had her first chance to witness life behind the rodeo. She was surprised at how many children there were. Little boys and girls perfecting their roping skills on horns mounted to hay bales under the patient tutelage of whichever cowboys happed to be nearby. Moms and dads rode sedately by with babies old enough to sit tucked carefully in front of them in the saddle. Youngsters scampered everywhere often trailing in the wake of one of their cowboy idols. The smell of dust, hay and horses hung in the air. The shouts of children and the chatter of friends and summer neighbors surrounded her. It was a close-knit community, a happy place.

She enjoyed the barbeque and was impressed to see how much respect cowboys and fans had for each other. Sex that night was tender, slow and totally satisfying but the next morning Zach morphed into the calm, confident and mentally tough man who, more often than not, dominated his event.

Those who did well, stayed for the finals, and the rest left, trying to squeeze another rodeo into their schedules. Ashley learned that rodeos have different formats. Some have different competitors on each day and the best times determine the prize winners. This allows the cowboys to enter multiple rodeos in a weekend. Others have qualifying rounds on one day and finals on the next day. These rodeos usually have bigger pots and you get to stay put for the weekend. There are tour rodeos, jackpot rodeos, sanctioned rodeos, non-sanctioned rodeos, circuit rodeos and they all counted differently in the big run toward making the finals in Las Vegas. It was enough to make her head swim.

They planned to leave tomorrow afternoon right after the finals and drive to Oklahoma, then back down to Stephenville Texas for the Team Roping World Series. From there they would send a driver and Zach's rig north to Wyoming and then Matt and Zach would hop a plane to Cheyenne while Heather and Ashley drove Matt's rig home. When all was said and done, between June and the end of September, they would compete in over fifty rodeos. The Saturday night dance was wild and wooly as folks stepped out of the pressure cooker for an evening. Ashley was beginning to understand why they might need to let off steam.

Zach and Matt drew a tough steer the next day in one of their runs and came in second. It was still a respectable showing that continued to add to their earnings standings and put them in good stead to make Las Vegas in December. Ashley wandered down from the stands in search of Zach.

She found him alright with one arm slung around a gorgeous blonde fan. He gave her a friendly squeeze while he held her phone at arms-length to take a selfie. He handed her back her phone, they laughed and chatted for a minute before she wandered off. Jealously, hot and hungry, clawed at her chest, but couldn't break free. It was there but contained.

Zach watched Ashley approach. "Don't give me that look. While we haven't committed to being exclusive, I don't fool around on the woman I'm dating and right now, that's you." He slapped his hat against his thigh. "I would be exclusive. I want to be. I'd give anything to be. It's up to you. You decide. Are you in or are you out?" He put his hat back on his head. "Will I stop smiling at a woman who smiles at me? No, I'm a friendly guy, but I'm also a one-woman man. I don't stray. What's it going to be Ash? Can you trust me?"

Ashley stepped up and ran her hands up Zach's chest, slid them around his neck and pulled him down for a demanding kiss. "I'd like to talk more about that exclusive thing. What exactly does that mean to you?"

"I'd say we turn in early tonight and have ourselves a meeting of the minds."

They had dinner on their own that evening, lingering over coffee and slices of Ashley's dark chocolate cake.

"Describe what an exclusive relationship looks like to you." Ashley twirled her hair around a finger.

"I only date you. You only date me. Not too complicated."

"Is this exclusive relationship meant to lead to something permanent or is it a more 'whenever' arrangement?"

"It can't be permanent until there's trust and a desire to move beyond companions to family. That's a two-way street." He leaned across the table and kissed her, the taste of coffee and chocolate on their lips. "I'm open to taking this up a notch. Be your one and only, but that only happens if you trust it's true."

He stood up and held out his hand to her. "We've got to get up early tomorrow. We drew an early round." His sexy smile told her he wasn't really thinking sleep, at least not right away, which was fine with her. That night she felt his strength, his passion, and the integrity of his character in their lovemaking and her resolve began to slip away.

Zach and Matt joined Ashley, Heather, and the kids after their second run to watch the bronc riding and steer wrestling events. Zach put his arm across Ashley's shoulders and used one hand to turn her face to his for a kiss.

The announcer's voice came over the loudspeaker. "Would Miss Cindy Johnson please come to the announcer's booth?" Several minutes later a confused, young woman was escorted to the center of the arena. A cowboy who had just competed in the Bronc event strode out, dropped to one knee in front of the woman, and held up a small box.

The escort held a microphone in front of the cowboy who said, "Cindy Johnson, I love you with all my heart. Would you make me the happiest man on earth and do me the honor of being my wife?" Her hands flew to her mouth as the stands fell silent waiting for her response. When she whispered, "yes," the crowd erupted and the happy couple kissed. As they stepped apart the escort held their joined hands in the air like the end of a prize fight.

"Aw, isn't that the sweetest thing?" Heather said, patting her chest, unshed tears glistening in her eyes. "Just makes me all gooey inside."

"Sweet? I suppose," Ashley responded, "but it's a little too showy for my taste. A marriage proposal should be a special, private moment between the couple. Somehow this," she fanned her hand toward the arena, "is like... a big dramatic gesture rather than an 'I'm giving my heart to you, will you take it' plea. It just doesn't seem sincere when he puts her on the spot in front of all these people like that."

"So if a man asked you to marry him in front of a bunch of people, you'd turn him down?" Zach asked.

"Are you planning on asking me to marry you?" Ashley blurted out.

Zach only smiled at her and stood up. "We best finish packing up and get on the road. Day's a wasting."

Matt and Heather exchanged 'hmmm' looks.

During the trip back to Texas and the next rodeo, Zach shared more details about his plans for the ranch and expansion of the roping clinic, his hope to work with local high school rodeo teams, and what he could do to increase the size of the therapeutic riding program over the next year.

"Do you really want to take a year off from the rodeo?" Ashley asked. "You do have someone else who wants to team up with you."

"If it weren't for my dad's health, probably not, though it's not as easy as simply finding a new heeler. Like marriage, it has to be the right partner with compatible goals."

"What does the right partner look like?"

He glanced over at her than back at the road. "Are we talking marriage or team roping?"

"You tell me."

"Okay, marriage since it's been on my mind a bit lately, both the good and the bad. I see Matt's happiness with his family and I *do* want that. I see my brother, Josh, being torn apart by divorce, and I *don't* want that."

"What do you want in a woman?"

"She needs to stand on her own two feet, a clinging vine doesn't interest me. She has to enjoy working the ranch with me and for a few more years at least, hopefully enjoy being a rodeo wife. She can have a career if that's what makes her happy. We can figure out how to work with that, but family and faith are important in my life and should be to her too." He grinned at her. "I figure it will take a strong woman to put up with me." Then he turned serious, "I want someone who will help me be the man I want to be once my rodeo days are over... So what are you looking for in a man?"

"He has to love me," she whispered. "Deeply love me. Before all else, love me. Beyond that, someone whose judgement I respect, who cares about others, is an honorable man and will be a good father to the children we'll someday have together." She smiled a sad smile. "I want someone who accepts me warts and all and makes me trust who I am."

She tugged on her seatbelt giving herself breathing room then pushed her head back into the headrest to stare at the roof. "My plan criteria... good job, great benefits, no risk-taking." She made a flipping motion with her hand after each statement. "Out the window. They're not important, except for the no player clause, that still stands."

They settled back into a contemplative silence for the rest of the trip, listening to the radio churn out an endless series of Country music – love, or love gone wrong – songs. Ashley's stomach clenched as she turned over the possibilities in her mind. Was Zach going to propose? Did she want to say yes for the right reasons?

When no proposal came over the next few days, she left for home dejected and deflated.

·♥·♥·♥·♥·♥·

"OH, COME ON ASH, it'll be fun," Lauren cajoled. "You love picnics. You love the ranch. What could be better?"

"Zach could treat me like I'm more than a friend." Hurt feelings kicked her smack in the gut and make her feel like she was going to lose her cookies.

"Hasn't he been calling you every day and as soon as he got back invited you out for a picnic? That's not special?"

"Yes it is special but..."

"But what? He hasn't declared his undying love for you over the phone? Do you really think he would do that?"

"No, but if he really cared, he would have wanted to see me the minute he was back in town, not wait two days. He would have wanted to be alone with me if he felt the same way about me that I feel about him instead of at a big picnic."

"You were working," Lauren reminded her.

"He could have come over in the evening."

"Don't you think you're being a tad bit unreasonable? The man is crazy about you. So he couldn't see you the minute he got back. So what? Look, I'll meet you at the ranch tomorrow and I'm not taking no for an answer."

"Why can't I ride with you and Nate?"

"Because we've got some issues to discuss and need to be alone."

"Oh, Lauren, I'm sorry. Are you two heading into another one of your 'off again' periods?"

"Not if I can help it, but I need you to be there tomorrow just in case I need some moral support. Okay?"

"Fine pair we are. All right, I'll listen to you complain about Nate and you can listen to me complain about Zach."

·♥·♥·♥·♥·♥·

ASHLEY STEPPED OUT OF her car and looked around, wondering where everyone was. Zach had asked her to arrive early so they could have some alone time before the picnic, a good sign in Ashley's book, but she had expected at least a few other early arrivals to help with the food and other preparations.

Gloria June bounced down the steps, grinning like the sun needed help and came over to greet her. Ashley lapped up the hug like a cat after cream. "It's good to see you again. Glad you could make our little shindig. It wouldn't be the same without out. You *are* like family, you know," she said steering her toward the barn.

"Why are we going to the barn? I thought I was going to see Zach."

"You are, but he had to check on some cattle out by his favorite spot and thought that would be a nice place to meet. Do you remember how to get out there?"

"Yes, I do." Ashley's smile went wide. "Your son is a genius. What a great idea. I love that spot." She did a two-step with Gloria June toward the barn.

"Your horse is saddled. Have a good time and we'll see you two later at the swimming hole." Gloria June gave her another hug.

A half hour later Ashley dismounted by Zach's horse and tethered it to the line. She carefully made her way down to the stream, stopping to admire the man she now knew she loved. He was distractedly tossing pebbles into the water.

He turned, melted her heart with his smile and was at her side in seconds, folding her into his arms and searing her with his kiss. She fisted his t-shirt in her hands and leaned into him wondering if it were possible to fuse their bodies together. Her busy fingers worked his shirt free from his jeans and was inching it up his body.

Zach grabbed her wrists and held them against his chest. "We need to talk."

Ashley walked her fingers in place where he held them. "Don't you want to have your wicked way with me? I'm hot and ready. Been thinking about what we're like together all the way out here." She kissed the hollow of his neck then circled it with her tongue.

"You're killing me, woman." His knees started to buckle and he forced them to straighten. "But there's something we need to clear up first."

"We haven't been together in over a week and you want to talk? That doesn't sound promising." She backed over to the log and sat down hard, swiping an errant tear from her eye.

Zach knelt in front of her. "No, no honey, don't cry. Please? I'm doing this all wrong. I'm sorry." He steepled her hands between his then cleared his throat.

"Ashley, ever since you came into my life, you're all I can think about. Your smile lights up my world, your passion for life gives me hope, your quiet strength humbles me, your compassion for others and willingness to help makes me want to do more. You are my joy, my everything."

Ashley sat there stunned but her fingers automatically splayed along his cheek and her thumbs traced his bottom lip.

"Ashley Elizabeth Drayton, I pledge my heart to you and only you until the day I die. I pledge to accept you for the amazing woman you are and will stand with you against anyone who tries to hurt you or make you feel less than you are. I pledge to remind you every day that you are loved and cherished." He pulled a small box from his pocket, opened it and offered the simple diamond solitaire to her. "Please agree to be my wife and share your life with me. I love you with everything

247

that is in me and if giving up the rodeo is what it takes to make you happy, then I am ready to do that. Will you marry me?"

She nodded and he slipped the ring on her finger. Happy tears coursed down her cheeks as she launched herself at him, knocking them both to the ground with Ashley on top. They kissed long and deeply until their breathing grew ragged. He rolled so they were on their sides, facing each other.

"While I'd like to think people would respect the 'no trespassing' rule when I'm in my place so we could spend the rest of the day making love, if we don't show up at the picnic, people will come looking for us." He pushed to a sitting position, rolled to his feet then pulled Ashley to her feet.

"Zach, I want you to know that I'll be happy, no make that proud, to be the wife of a rodeo man. The man you are is the man I fell in love with and part of who you are right now is the rodeo. I will do whatever it takes to make this work. I love you and cannot imagine my life without you in it. I want you to be happy. Kiss me, cowboy."

"My pleasure." Zach wrapped her in his arms and poured every bit of tenderness and love he possessed into the joining of their lips. Finally, he rested his forehead against hers.

"Let's go share the good news with our family and friends. I want to shout from the rooftops that you are mine, now and forever." He snagged her hand, pulling her up the path to their horses.

"Now and forever, has a nice ring to it," she whispered to that solid back she planned to follow wherever it led.

·❤·❤·❤·❤·❤·

If you enjoyed MY RODEO MAN, I invite you to pick up the next book in the series.

You met Nate and Lauren in this book, now it's time to put the spotlight on their story. Can they work past their personal issues and move from fake girlfriend to true love? Are they ready to take a chance and let their hearts lead the way or will the pain of the past hold them back? If you want to find out, pick up a copy – or read in Kindle Unlimited – My Sexy Veterinarian today. For more information read the book description on the next page.

A wonderful, heartwarming storyline with heartaches, romance, real-to-life characters!!! New author for me. Will read more!!! ~ Amazon Review

·♥·♥·♥·♥·♥·

Book Blurb for MY SEXY VETERINARIAN

He's a man broken by love and she's the woman determined to heal him.

Nate Kincaid, wants to get out of debt and get his family off his back over his non-existent relationship status. The first means his fledgling veterinary practice must be successful. Business before anything else. Always. The second means he needs a serious girlfriend, but after the death of his fiancée, he isn't ready. No one knows about his nightmares. The ones that chase him into the dark places of grief. Maybe a pretend relationship would solve his second problem so he can concentrate on the first.

Full-time psychologist and part-time model, Lauren Royall, has the perfect life. As a therapist she helps people. As a model, her free spirit can flourish. When Nate suggests she pose as his girlfriend, she accepts on a lark. Lauren senses his pain and wants to help. She hadn't counted on falling for the guy or having to face painful memories from her past.

Can she convince him to take a second chance on love? That love is worth the risk?

Buy *MY SEXY VETERINARIAN* today and get ready to laugh, cry, and sigh as this delightful cast of characters steals your heart! You can read an excerpt on the next page.

·♥·♥·♥·♥·♥·

Excerpt from MY SEXY VETERINARIAN

Lauren set the basket she'd retrieved from her car on the table and started pulling out containers. She felt Nate's presence behind her. The tightness in her chest eased when he plunked a small pail filled with sunflowers on the table. She hated being out of sorts with people. Made her feel like a piece of jerky inside—tough and without flavor unless you added it. "Your sensitive side?" she asked, a hint of humor in her voice.

He shuffled back a few steps and shoved his hands in his pockets. "Yeah, I guess. Look, I'm sorry I was a jerk. I don't know what gets in to me sometimes."

"Sometimes talking can help us figure out why we react the way we do." He crossed his arms over his chest. Stubborn man. As if asking for help to deal with his issues would suck the life out of him. She closed the lid on her picnic basket and stowed it under the table. Lauren picked up the pail and held it at arm's length. "I love sunflowers. How did you know?"

"You seem like a sunflower person. Cheerful, colorful, carefree." He ducked his head and looked down at his feet like he'd said too much.

"You're a walking contradiction. One of you brings me flowers and the other turns his back on me. One minute I think you like me and the next I feel like a leper." She took a breath and plunged ahead. "Are you playing some kind of game?"

"No, no games. Gun shy, maybe. Getting too close to a woman can open a man up to a world of hurt."

"And you've been there, done that?" His expression closed and she immediately missed the carefree man he'd been before she'd hit whatever nerve had made him flinch. She wanted that relaxed man back.

"Yeah, but I'm not ready to talk about it."

"Fair enough. What *would* you like to talk about? It's a beautiful day. We've enjoyed each other's company. I'd like to keep it that way." She'd find a way to tease out *happy* Nate or die trying.

"Well I do have something on my mind. A problem you might be able to help me solve."

He had the look of a fox approaching the hen house. He wanted what was inside, but wasn't sure what might be lying in wait. She put a smile in her voice to put him at ease. "I'm listening."

"My family's been bugging me about finding a steady girlfriend. They seem to think I'm afraid to get serious about anyone." He picked up one of the containers and lifted the lid.

"*Are* you afraid of getting involved?" She didn't expect him to open up but thought it was worth a shot.

He sniffed the contents of the container and put it back down. "No, just haven't found anyone I want to date on a steady basis."

He swallowed hard and looked away. Nate was lying. What part was the lie—that he hadn't found anyone he wanted to date or that he was afraid to get involved? "What can I do to help you solve your problem?" she asked.

"I was thinking, maybe you and I could date, like we're a couple, so my family would back off."

A spark of annoyance flickered in her chest. He wanted people to think they were a couple but didn't really want to *be a couple*. "Let me see if I understand. We'd date. We'd *pretend* to be serious about each other but it'd really be casual?"

"About sums it up." He ran a hand through his hair. "I like you. I think we have fun together and when my family decides I'm not avoiding having a serious girlfriend, we can still be friends. You interested?"

"We do have fun together and since we're both concentrating on our careers, a serious relationship isn't something either of us needs." She stuck out her hand. "You've got a deal."

"Good." He shook her hand. "What is all this stuff?" He indicated the food.

Silly man thought this was the end of their discussion. She'd let him deflect—for now. "This one is turkey and avocado wraps. I also packed fresh vegetables and humus, fresh fruit kabobs, red potato salad with yogurt dressing, and double chocolate brownies."

"Except for that last thing, it all sounds kinda healthy." She saw the suspicion in his eyes. "I brought my portable grill." He lifted the lid of the basket. "Don't suppose there are any hot dogs or hamburger patties in there?" His expression shifted to hopeful and she had to bite her lip to keep from laughing.

"Only what you see." He looked like he was being sent to the principal's office. She put something from each container on his plate and nudged it toward him. "Who knows, you might learn there's more to eat than steak and potatoes." Getting him to step outside his comfort zone and knock some of the rigid out of his spine would make a good first step in his road to recovery.

"I eat other stuff, but I like what I like," he grumbled.

Parking himself on top of the picnic table, his feet propped on the bench seat, arms resting on his knees, she knew the moment he resigned himself to humor her. His chin dipped, his shoulders sagged, and he picked up a turkey wrap between two of his large fingers like it was a dose of castor oil. He slowly moved the food toward his mouth, opened wide, and bit down. She also knew the moment he discovered he liked it. Yes, another victory. She wanted to fist pump the air, but refrained because nobody liked a showoff.

His eyes closed and a satisfied hum throbbed low in his throat. He swiped a baby carrot through the humus and popped it into his mouth, chewing slowly to savor the flavors. He eased a melon ball off the kabob stick with his teeth. How could a man make the simple art of eating so arousing? Moisture and heat gathered at the apex of her legs.

A predatory grin spread across his face. The man was toying with her. He ran his tongue along a strawberry, slowly capturing it between his teeth before easing it off the skewer and into his mouth. The movement created a slow burn in her center. As he continued eating, the flames licked higher, tinging her cheeks with blush. Her fingers itched to tangle in his hair. Very deliberately, his tongue teased the corners of his lips. He took her hand and pulled her to stand between his legs. His hands smoothed up her arms. How could a simple touch be so magical? He cupped the back of her neck then eased her forward for a kiss.

Firm, full lips slid over hers drawing her into a boiling pool of lust and want. Strong arms pulled her tight—the only thing keeping her tied to earth when she longed to float, to soar, to experience everything that was Nate. His other hand spanned her waist a fistful of her shirt in his grasp. Lauren leaned into his strength. More, more, more ran through her mind. This felt... so... good.

"What the hell," Nate cursed. "Nothing like sixty pounds of demanding dog squirming between us to drag a guy back down to earth." He glared at the unrepentant animal. "Honey, you've got rotten timing." Nate stood, moving Lauren to the side, and took a few steps back, a flush creeping up his neck. If he was embarrassed to be seen with her, why did he want her to be his pretend girlfriend?

He scrubbed his eyes with the heels of his hands. "Maybe I should thank Honey. That kiss was a little too intense for public consumption."

She reached over and stroked a hand down his arm. "It's okay. I get it." His admission added another layer of insight into how his mind worked. The man was uncomfortable getting too lovey-dovey in public. Could this be another tool he used to keep from getting too close?

He joined her on the bench. Leaning to nudge her with his shoulder, he said, "I get carried away when I'm around you. Why is that?"

Her eyebrows furrowed then relaxed. Curious. "You're a closet Casanova and can't always hide your passionate nature?" She shrugged.

He smiled like she knew he would. "You got me." Nate rubbed his jaw. "It would seem I haven't had much adventure in my life." He elbowed her gently in the ribs. "Tell me something wild and crazy you've done."

"I don't know if you can handle it."

"Try me." He picked up her hand and brought it to his lips. The sexually charged banter acted like a spark plug, igniting a longing to have more.

"All I'm going to say right now is, me and Ashley. Sophomore year in college. Spring break. Daytona Beach." She placed a finger under his chin and pushed his mouth closed. "Here have another turkey and avocado wrap."

"You went there? Two women alone?" His voice sounded like they'd done a Thelma and Louise and driven off a cliff.

"Sure did." She propped her chin in her hands. "You never went on spring break in college?"

"No. I usually worked on getting my practical training hours in during spring break or helped my dad at the ranch." His lips quirked in a half smile. "Seems like I've always been dedicated to duty." He bit into one of the brownies. "These are amazing." He studied it before popping it in his mouth and scooping up another. "So where are you off to?"

"I do volunteer work at the children's hospital. I need to get home and change. Today I'm in charge of a puppet show for the kids."

"I'm impressed. Every time I think I have you pegged, you surprise me." He scooped up the picnic basket and slung an arm across her shoulder as they walked to her Honda CRV. She pulled out her car remote and popped the hatch so Nate could put the basket away.

She cupped his face in her hands and kissed him sweetly on the lips. "Call and let me know when you want to start 'operation fool the family'. Just so you know, my schedule is crazy over the holidays. I'll be hosting my family for Thanksgiving week and will be attending a conference right after that. For Christmas I'll be in South Carolina. Maybe we should wait until the new year to get started?"

"I agree. I've got a cousin's out-of-town wedding to attend and I put in more hours at the clinic in November and December so others can take time off." He opened her car door and placed a hand on her shoulder.

Electric sparks tingled all the way down her arm like she'd touched a live wire.

"We should be seen together sometime over the holidays so people start thinking of us as a couple," Nate said scratching his head. "We have a company Christmas party. Maybe that will work."

"Send me the details and I'll be your official 'pretend' date." She still wasn't sure how she felt about this idea. As a psychologist she saw so many ways this could go sideways. Deception was not in Nates wheelhouse. When he looked at his cousins and their young families, it was all over his face how much he envied them. Hopefully spending time with him would give her a chance to delve deeper into his relationship issues.

Buy *MY SEXY VETERINARIAN* today and get ready to laugh, cry, and sigh as this delightful cast of characters steals your heart!

Also By

STAND ALONE BOOKS

Julia's Star

SERIES
The Texas Kincaids

My Sexy Veterinarian: The Texas Kincaids Book 2

My Texas Heart: The Texas Kincaids Book 3

My Army Ranger: The Texas Kincaids Book 4

My Quiet Hero: The Texas Kincaids Book 5

Hearts and Homes

Welcome Home

BONNIE PHELPS

Serenity's Garden

Matchmaking Ghosts

More Than Pretty

About Author

Rumor has it that Bonnie began telling stories at a very early age. Photos exist of the author toddling around the corner of the house covered in mud babbling about magic rabbits leading her through the garden. Her parents were amused only adding fuel to the fire of her passion for writing. From then on, her active imagination continued to churn out plots and character sketches always wondering how different people would behave in similar situations. People are endlessly fascinating and stories are everywhere. She loves exploring, rearranging and weaving her narratives throughout her characters' lives.

When she is not mucking around in her own characters' lives, you will find her perusing her Kindle and reading someone else's story. She also enjoys baking, taking long walks and people watching. Bonnie writes Contemporary Romance and lives in Northern California with her husband.

SIGN UP FOR MY NEWSLETTER Once a month you'll receive the latest news about my books. I also love to share what's happening in my life, what I'm reading, and what's cooking in my kitchen – along with a favorite recipe.

Learn more about Bonnie and her books at her website: Bonnie Phelps Author

Have a question or comment? Send Bonnie an email at: bonnie@bonniephelpsauthor.com

Thank you for reading MY RODEO MAN. I hope you enjoyed Zach's and Ashley's story. If you did, I would greatly appreciate you leaving a review on the review site of your choice. Reviews are crucial for any author and a line or two about your experience can make a huge difference in introducing new readers to this book. To leave a review on Amazon, click here.

Connect with Bonnie:

Facebook

Acknowledgments

Thank you to my Beta Readers, Elsa Bayly and Katherine Couture – and those who prefer to remain anonymous – for helping me fine tune my manuscript and make it better. I take each and every suggestion to heart. Thank you also to my fellow Romance Writers of America friends and colleagues, especially my Yosemite Romance Writer Chapter mates. Your friendship and well-aimed head slaps makes each book I write better – and as writers that's our goal, like fine wine to improve with age!

Made in the USA
Monee, IL
24 January 2024